I0575606

Joseph Banvard

The American Statesman

Or, illustrations of the life and character of Daniel Webster. Designed for American

youth.

Joseph Banvard

The American Statesman
Or, illustrations of the life and character of Daniel Webster. Designed for American youth.

ISBN/EAN: 9783337094034

Printed in Europe, USA, Canada, Australia, Japan

Cover: Foto ©Raphael Reischuk / pixelio.de

More available books at **www.hansebooks.com**

DANIEL WEBSTER, AT THE AGE OF 63.

Frad.

THE

AMERICAN STATESMAN;

OR ILLUSTRATIONS OF

THE LIFE AND CHARACTER

OF

DANIEL WEBSTER.

DESIGNED FOR

AMERICAN YOUTH.

BY

REV. JOSEPH BANVARD,

AUTHOR OF PLYMOUTH AND THE PILGRIMS, NOVELTIES OF THE NEW WORLD
ROMANCE OF AMERICAN HISTORY, ETC.

BOSTON:
PUBLISHED BY D. LOTHROP & CO.
DOVER, N. H.: G. T. DAY & CO.

Entered, according to Act of Congress, in the year 1875,

By D. LOTHROP & CO.,

In the Office of the Librarian of Congress, at Washington.

PREFACE.

THE object of this volume is to present a sketch of the most interesting and important events which occurred in the history of the distinguished statesman who has lately passed away. The author makes no pretensions to the discovery of new facts. He has availed himself chiefly of the published memoirs and reminiscences of Mr. Webster, amongst which were Daniel Webster and his Contemporaries, by Charles W. March; The Private Life of Daniel Webster, by Charles Lanman; Personal Memorials of Daniel Webster; Memoir of the Life of Daniel Webster, by Samuel L. Knapp; Biographical Memoir of the Life of Daniel Webster, by Edward Everett, prefixed to Mr. Webster's Works, and Life and Memorials of Daniel Webster; together with the numerous eulogies,

5

speeches, and sermons occasioned by his decease, selecting such facts and incidents from each as would suit his purpose, and deducing from them such lessons or principles of action as are worthy the contemplation of those for whom the book is specially designed.

That the distinguished subject of this work had his faults, and that there is a difference of opinion as to the wisdom of some of the acts of his political life, no one presumes to deny. But it is of his commendable traits of character that the author here treats. These he would hold up for the admiration and imitation of American youth. He has endeavored to prepare a work which every American patriot would be pleased to have his children read.

CONTENTS.

CHAPTER I.

CHAPTER II.

CHAPTER III.

CHAPTER IV.

CHAPTER V.

CHAPTER VI.

CHAPTER VII.

CHAPTER VIII.

CHAPTER IX.

CHAPTER X.

CHAPTER XI.

CHAPTER XII.

CHAPTER XIII.

CHAPTER XIV.

CHAPTER XV.

CHAPTER XVI.

CHAPTER XVII.

CHAPTER XVIII.

List of Illustrations.

THE AMERICAN STATESMAN.

CHAPTER I.

The two Riders. — A pleasing Proposition. — Accepted. — A
Bite. — A Plunge. — A Trout caught. — Daniel Webster. —
His Birthplace. — Kearsage Mountain. — The toiling Boy. —
The mysterious Well. — Drinking from the moss-covered
Bucket. — Influence of Nature on Style. — Webster's Love for
the Grand in Nature. — Worthy of Imitation. — Pictures ad
mired more than the original Landscapes. — Advice to the
Young. — Influence of the Love of Nature on Character.

ABOUT sixty-five years ago, a man of stalwart
form, broad shoulders, and swarthy complexion,
was riding through Salisbury, in New Hampshire,
on horseback, carrying with him a puny little boy,
with dark features, sparkling black eyes, a round,
projecting forehead, and dressed in coarse, homespun clothes, with two little, shoeless feet projecting
from beneath.   The man had been indulging in
juvenile conversation, adapted to the comprehension
of his young charge, for some time, in which the
little fellow had taken part, with an occasional child-
like remark or question.   As they approached a
brook, whose clear, cool waters flowed, sometimes
murmuringly, at other times silently, through the
woods and fields, marking their course by a vigorous fertility, the gentleman suddenly exclaimed,
"Dan, how would you like to catch a trout!"

The little boy, who perhaps had never used hook
and line before, immediately signified his pleasure
at the proposition.   The horse was checked ; both
riders dismounted, and began to prepare for the
sport.   The tall form and long arms of the gentleman were specially favorable in aiding him to cut
from a neighboring tree a rod.   It would seem as
if he were accustomed to these extemporaneous
fishing excursions, and always went prepared for
them ; for, thrusting his hand into his pocket, he
drew out a string and hook ; then turning over a
stone or two, he found a worm, which he soon adjusted as bait.   After fastening the line to the rod,
he gave it to the little boy, saying, " Now, Dan,
creep carefully upon that rock, and throw the bait
upon the farther side of the pool."   The little fish-
erman did as he was ordered.   His bait was soon
in the water, and his eye intently watching it.   It
was not long before some indiscreet fish, thoughtless
of consequences, darted from his concealment, seized
the bait, and disappeared like a flash of lightning
This was just what the boy wanted.   Being highly
excited with his success, he gave a sudden jerk to
the line ; but, instead of drawing the fish out of the
water, he unfortunately lost his balance, and plunged
headlong into the pool.   The gentleman, seeing that
the boy was more likely, from present appearances,
to die in the water, than the fish was to expire upon

BIRTHPLACE OF DANIEL WEBSTER.

the land, ran to his rescue. He succeeded in reaching him and drawing him ashore, "with a pound trout trailing behind him." This lad was DANIEL WEBSTER, and the person who had him in charge was his own father.

Not far from the place where this rather ludicrous incident occurred, stood, at that time, one of the better class of farm houses; although, at the present period, and in other localities, it might be regarded as a very ordinary building. It was but one story high, with a door in the middle, and a window on each side, and three windows at either end. It contained four rooms on the ground floor, with, probably, chambers in the attic. An addition in the rear answered the purpose of a kitchen. It had only one chimney, and this arose from the centre of the roof, furnishing, probably, three or four fireplaces, in as many different rooms. The framework was of heavy timber, the exterior clapboarded, and the ends pointed, differing in this respect from the gambrel roof. On the green in front of the house arose a large and graceful elm, extending its long and heavy branches over the mansion below, as if, in the exercise of an affectionate interest, it would protect it from harm. Many other trees of the same kind were scattered over the grounds, on which account the place received the appropriate name of "Elms Farm." Near one end of the house was a deep

well, with a long, old-fashioned well sweep, to one
extremity of which was attached a bucket, by means
of which the clear, cool water was drawn up for the
use of the family.   At a short distance, in front of
the house, flowed a beautiful silver stream, over
which was thrown a safe, though rough-looking
bridge.   Farther off was a high hill, crowned with
a church, and beyond all, the lofty Kearsage mountain lifted itself, "head and shoulders" above the
surrounding hills — a beautiful type of him, who,
in intellectual greatness, rose far above his com-
peers.

In this house, on the 18th day of January,
1782, Daniel Webster was born.   Now that he
has departed, after having lived to a good old
age, and after having acquired a world-wide fame,
as a far-reaching statesman, a powerful orator,
and a skilful diplomatist, it is interesting to look
back, and contemplate the circumstances and events
of his early life.   At one time, we see him, a
little, tottling boy, in homespun frock, making
his first essays to balance himself upon his shoeless feet, as he advances from the doorstep to
greet his father, who has just crossed the bridge,
and is approaching, with outstretched hands and
rapid step, to meet him.   Again we see him, amusing himself under the shadow of the friendly elm,
that stands by the door, like a huge grenadier,

guarding the entrance to a fort. A few years later, we behold him tripping over the fields, jumping across the brook, or wandering along its margin, with hook and line, ready to "try his luck" so soon as he shall have reached a place where the water is sufficiently still and deep to give promise of success. Again, wearied with his wanderings, or his labors, is he leaning over the well, gazing at another little boy that he sees far down in the bottom, and who is mysteriously looking up at him. It would not be strange, if at times he imagined it a hole cut through the earth, and that some little fellow, on the other side, was, like himself, indulging his curiosity by looking through. A pebble dropping in disturbs the surface of the water, breaks the mysterious picture into a thousand fragments, and dispels the illusion. Again, in evening twilight, we seem to see him sitting upon the doorsill; and, as the noble Kearsage rises in the distance, with its bold outline clearly defined against the gray-blue sky, he gives reins to his juvenile fancy; and, as the ancient Hebrews "sucked honey from the rock, and oil from the flinty rock," so he drinks in inspiration from the sublimity of the majestic mount before him. Who can tell to how great a degree he was indebted, for the simplicity, the directness, and the majesty of his thoughts, and of his style as an orator, to the noble simplicity and

grandeur of this mountain ?   It was not decorated
with beautiful, terraced, hanging gardens, nor with
graceful, luxuriant vineyards. It arose almost naked
from the plain; as though it spurned ornament — as
though it needed nothing but its own majestic pro-
portions to give it grandeur ; and thus, by its own
silent, powerful, eloquent example, it may have aided to impart those characteristics of thought and
diction which give such a charm and force to the
oratory of Mr. Webster.

From early life Mr. Webster was fond of Nature.
He loved sunlight and shadow, rolling hills, quiet
lawns, turbulent streams, and placid lakes.   Nature, in her milder, her gayer, or her sterner moods,
was to him always pleasing. He was specially
interested in the great things of creation. He delighted to travel through the wildness of mountain
scenery. Its projecting cliffs, its high precipices,
its deep chasms, its lightning-scarred rocks, its thun-
dering cataracts, and its leaning, gigantic trees, with
roots half exposed, threatening every moment to
fall, and ofttimes executing their threatenings, — all
inspired him with pleasing emotions and instructive
thoughts. He loved to wander by the ocean, and
have its huge billows roll up and lay their bubbles
at his feet. Its vast expanse, its ceaseless restless-
ness, its emerald hue, and the music of its roar,
were always grateful to him. He loved to gaze

into the unmeasured spaces above him, and contemplate the stars, as immense globes swinging in their orbits, as if they were the mighty pendulums which controlled the cycles of ages, and regulated the mechanism of the universe.

This love of Nature, Mr. Webster, as we have said, early developed. It strengthened with advancing years, and became a prominent feature in his character. In this respect, his example is worthy of imitation by the young. It seems surprising that, with so many objects of admiration around us, as are presented in the infinite variety of forms, colors, and combinations of natural objects, there are any who derive from their contemplation no enjoyment. Many individuals will gaze upon a picture — a landscape for instance — with the greatest pleasure. Its rough rocks, vine-draped trees, or decaying, misshapen stumps, are pointed out as interesting features, equal almost to the more important combinations of hill and valley, land and water, on which the artist has bestowed his greatest skill. And yet these same persons would ride by the original of that picture, executed with the infinite skill of the Divine Artist, and give it no attention whatever. O, how many magnificent landscapes are every day passed by, without eliciting any praise, or awakening any admiration in the beholder !

Let it not be so with you. On the contrary

cultivate a taste for the beautiful objects of creation
Notice the colors on the petal of a flower, the infinite diversity of forms in the leaves of trees, and
the changing effects of light and shade.   Calmly
contemplate the hues and shapes of the ever-shifting
clouds, the features of the ocean, the lake, or the
river.   Form a habit of observing the peculiarities
of natural objects in your immediate vicinity, and
you will find your heart warming towards them.
The scenery with which you have always been familiar will, to your fancy, put on a new dress, and
invest itself with more pleasing charms.   This is
not all ; for the love of Nature has an elevating
and purifying influence.   It fills the mind with en-
nobling thoughts ; it calms the passions ; it reminds
us of the wisdom, the power, the goodness, and the
omnipresence of the Creator, and makes us more
sensible of our own weakness, and of our entire
dependence upon Him without whom we can do
nothing

CHAPTER II.

THE parents of young Webster appreciated the
value of a good education. His father, knowing
from his own painful experience the disadvantages
of being destitute of so great a boon, was anxious
that his children should escape a similar experience.
He was particularly solicitous with reference to
Daniel, who, in his childhood, was pale, weak, and
sickly. Fearing that he would be unable to perform the heavy work of a farmer, or to obtain his
livelihood from any of the mechanic arts, he was
the more anxious to give him as good an education
as his circumstances would permit. May we not
discover in these facts the development of a wise
Providence ? If Daniel had been a strong muscular boy, or, being weakly, if his parents had not

(23)

set a high value upon education, he would probably have been devoted to an agricultural life, and then the whole current of his history would have flowed in a channel vastly different from that which now marks its course. His noble speeches, his model state papers, his sagacious diplomacy, his legal knowledge, and his clear and comprehensive expositions of the Constitution of the United States, with all the patriotic and conservative influence which has followed them, would have been lost to the world. In what respects the present condition of our country would then have been different from what it is, how far those principles and measures which he opposed would have triumphed, and to how great a degree the adoption of the views and policy which he advocated would have failed, it may not be easy to tell. No one will deny that a great loss would have been experienced to literature, to law, and the science of civil government. This, however, was prevented by the providential sickliness of his youth, and the discretion of his parents. Truly —

> "There's a divinity that shapes our ends,
> Roughhew them how we will."

At the time little Daniel was old enough to commence sitting at the feet of some Gamaliel, it so happened that no "schoolmaster was abroad" in

the vicinity of his home. His mother was his teacher. She gave him the key to all knowledge, by
initiating him into the mysteries of the alphabet.
That she was a suitable person to have the control
of his infantile years, will be made apparent upon
a subsequent page.

As the neighbors, in the vicinity of Elms Farm,
were equally anxious with Mr. Webster to secure
the opportunities of education for their children, a
gentleman by the name of Chase was induced to
open a school near Mr. Webster's house. There
was nothing particularly promising in the enterprise,
nothing imposing in its external demonstrations.
It was not held in a public hall, nor in an edifice
erected for the purpose, which might be dignified
with the name of school house, but in a hired room
in the house of a neighbor, whose name was Sanborn: To this room little Daniel was sent every
day, to learn how to spell and read his mother
tongue. This house has resisted the power of the
elements, and the inroads of modern improvements,
till the present time. It will doubtless be, in future
years, an attractive spot to thousands, who will desire to see the original school room where the giant
intellect of America's greatest statesman received
its first academic instruction. At that early period,
by the law of New Hampshire, each town was
divided into several school districts. Accordingly,

Salisbury, the town in which Mr. Webster resided, contained three school houses, scattered at a distance of several miles from each other. In these, however, school was not kept all the year. A teacher was employed by the town, who taught a third of a year in each of them; so that the opportunity of education was somewhat migratory. These school houses were of a rude, unfinished, log-house character, erected for use, and not for show. By this time they have all passed away, leaving not a trace behind.

When the term arrived for the school house in Mr. Webster's district to be opened, it was easy for Daniel to attend; but when the school was kept in the other districts, the young lad did not stay at home. With basket, or tin pail, containing his dinner, he trudged away, mile after mile, over hill and dale, and through comparatively unfrequented roads, to school, and returned again at night. So highly did his parents value education, that they were willing to subject their children to great inconvenience for its attainment. It is no uncommon thing for both children and parents, in large cities, to indulge in complaints, if the school house happens to be situated a half mile from their residence, although there are good sidewalks all the way. One might infer, from the tone of their remarks, that they considered the sending of their children to school a favor to the teacher or the school committee, instead of a privilege to themselves, and that therefore they were justified in their complaints of its distance. It would be well for such to remember the incon veniences which were endured by their forefathers, in obtaining what at best was only a "little school ing," and contrast their long and dreary walks, over poor roads, in all kinds of weather, their miserable school houses, and ofttimes their equally miserable teaching, with the convenient and well-furnished schools, and the excellent instruction of the present day. The number is not small of those, who, if they were subjected to the embarrassments which the feeble young Webster was obliged to surmount, would be discouraged, and faint by the way.

The next teacher to whom young Webster was sent was James Tappan. This gentleman is still living, and is nearly ninety years of age. He re- sides in Gloucester.* Although there had been a separation between master and pupil for many years, yet they each retained a distinct recollection of each other. That the master should remember the pupil, especially when his subsequent history was radiant with glory, and that he should continue to follow his career with something of paternal pride, is not remarkable; but that the scholar should re- tain a distinct impression of the first instructors of

* See Note on p. 34

his childhood, of their characters and qualifications
for their office, and that that impression should not
be erased during a long series of years, filled up
with ceaseless attention to national cares, and the re-
ception of popular glory, may justly excite surprise.

In 1851, Mr. Tappan, who was in reduced cir
cumstances, took the liberty of addressing a letter
to his old pupil, in which he referred to his recollections of their former relation. This drew from
Mr. Webster the following reply, in which there is
a beautiful blending of the sentiments of friendship
and piety : —

"WASHINGTON, February 26, 1851.

"MASTER TAPPAN : I thank you for your let
ter, and am rejoiced to know that you are among
the living. I remember you perfectly well, as a
teacher of my infant years. I suppose my mother
must have taught me to read very early, as I have
never been able to recollect the time when I could
not read the Bible. I think Master Chase was my
earliest schoolmaster, probably when I was three or
four years old. Then came Master Tappan. You
boarded at our house, and sometimes, I think, in
the family of Mr. Benjamin Sanborn, our neighbor,
the lame man. Most of those whom you knew in
New Salisbury have gone to their graves. Mr. John
Sanborn, the son of Benjamin, is yet living, and is
about your age. Mr. John Colby, who married my

eldest sister, Susannah, is also living. On the
'North Road' is Mr. Benjamin Pettingil. I think
of none else among the living whom you would
probably remember. You have, indeed, lived a
checkered life. I hope you have been able to
bear prosperity with meekness, and adversity with
patience. These things are all ordered for us far
better than we could order them for ourselves. We
may pray for our daily bread; we may pray for the
forgiveness of sins; we may pray to be kept from
temptation, and that the kingdom of God may come
in us, and in all men, and his will every where be
done. Beyond this we hardly know for what good
to supplicate the divine mercy. Our heavenly Father knoweth what we have need of better than we
know ourselves, and we are sure that his eye, and
his loving kindness, are upon us and around us every
moment.

"I thank you again, my good old schoolmaster,
for your kind letter, which has awakened many
sleeping recollections; and, with all good wishes,
I remain your friend and pupil,

"DANIEL WEBSTER.

"MR. JAMES TAPPAN."

The Christian sympathy and consolation which
this letter contained were rendered doubly grateful
to the old gentleman by a fifty dollar bank bill

which it contained ; * for Mr. Webster was not of
the number of those who profess sympathy and
withhold relief, who say, "Depart in peace : be ye
warmed and filled ; notwithstanding they give them
not those things which are needful to the body."
He added to his professions of regard a tangible
seal.

Master Tappan took great delight in talking of
his distinguished pupil. On this, if on no other
subject, he became enthusiastic. A gentleman, who
in 1851 met him on the piazza of the Pavilion,
gives the following account of him : " Master Tappan is now in his eighty-sixth year, somewhat infirm,
but with his intellectual faculties bright and vivid,
especially on the subject of his old pupil, whom he
esteems the foremost man of his times, and in whose
fame he takes a justifiable pride.

" ' Daniel was always the brightest boy in the
school,' said Master Tappan, ' and Ezekiel the next ;
but Daniel was much quicker at his studies than his
brother. He would learn more in five minutes than
any other boy in five hours.'

" It was Master Tappan's practice to hold out occasionally some reward, in order to stimulate his

---

* Hon. Edward Everett states, in a note to his Memoir of Daniel Webster, that a knowledge of this fact was obtained from a
paper,— the Gloucester News,— to which it was probably com
municated by Mr. Tappan.

scholars to their greatest exertion. In the above conversation, he related how his *protégé*, at a certain time, outstripped his competitors, and bore away the prize. 'One Saturday,' said he, 'I remember I held up a handsome, new jackknife to the scholars, and said, the boy who would commit to memory the greatest number of verses in the Bible, by Monday morning, should have it. Many of the boys did well; but when it came to Daniel's turn to recite, I found that he had committed so much that, after hearing him repeat some sixty or seventy verses, I was obliged to give up, he telling me that there were several chapters yet that he had learned. Daniel got that jackknife. Ah! sir, he was remarkable even as a boy; and I told his father he would do God's work injustice if he did not send both Daniel and Ezekiel to college. The old man said he couldn't well afford it; but I told him he must, and he finally did. And didn't they both justify my good opinion? Well, gentlemen, I am an old man, and too much given to talk, perhaps. Well, good by. Beautiful place this! Beautiful sea view; and the air, how soft and refreshing! But I must leave it all soon, gentlemen. I have been suffering from the asthma for fifteen years, and it is now worse than ever. God is calling us all home, some sooner, some later; for me it must

3

needs be soon. But good by. Enjoy yourselves
in this delightful air. Good by!' And the old
gentleman tottered away, after a monologue almost verbatim such as I have recorded. It seems
to be the one sunny spot in his old age, to
talk of his old pupil, and to expatiate on his greatness as a statesman, as an orator, and as a lawyer.
Master Tappan alluded to the news in regard to
the threatened difficulty with Great Britain, on account of the north-eastern fisheries, but confidently
remarked, 'Daniel will settle it all, so that we shall
hold our own, and have no trouble. They couldn't
get along at all at Washington without Daniel. The
country won't get into a scrape while it has the
benefit of his pilotage; be sure of that.' "

This enthusiastic, complimentary language of the
old gentleman, which appeared at the time in the
Boston Evening Transcript, was read to Mr. Webster. Being in this manner reminded of his early
friend again, then experiencing the infirmities of
disease and age, he immediately wrote the following
letter : —

                              "BOSTON, July 20, 1852.

'MASTER TAPPAN: I learn with much pleasure, through the public press, that you continue to
enjoy life, with mental faculties bright and vivid,
although you have arrived at a very advanced age.

and are somewhat infirm. I came to-day from the very spot in which you taught me ; * and to me a most delightful spot it is. The river and the hills are as beautiful as ever, but the graves of my father and mother, and brothers and sisters, and early friends, gave it to me something of the appearance of a city of the dead. But let me not repine. You have lived long, and my life is already not short, and we have both much to be thankful for. Two or three persons are yet living, who, like myself, were brought up *sub tua ferula*. They remember 'Master Tappan.'

"And now, my good old master, receive a renewed tribute of affectionate regard from your grateful pupil, with his wishes and prayers for your happiness in all that remains to you in this life, and more especially for your participation hereafter in the durable riches of righteousness.

"DANIEL WEBSTER."

The "renewed tribute of affectionate regard," alluded to, did not consist so much of the sentiments of the letter, although these were peculiarly grateful to the old gentleman, as of a twenty dollar bill which accompanied them.

The example of Mr. Webster, in giving suustan

* This was Mr. Webster's last visit to his birthplace

tial evidence of his gratitude to an early instructor merits more than a simple statement. It develops an element of character worthy of imitation. Too frequently is it the case that pupils, even when they have attained to manhood, use language with reference to their early instructors, which is expressive of any other than respectful or grateful feelings. This, to use no stronger terms, is unfortunate. The practice of speaking disparagingly of one's early teachers, whose kindness, patience, and skill may all have been exhausted in unwearied efforts for our improvement, with perhaps but little encouragement on our part, deserves severe censure. But we can imagine few things more commendable than a pupil's expression of grateful remembrance of his teacher, by some appropriate tribute, more significant than words, especially when the condition of that teacher is one of infirmity and poverty.*

After our young hero left Master Tappan, he was sent to school to Mr. William Hoyt, the itinerant teacher of the town, who successively occupied each of the school houses a third of the time. When he taught in the one at the greatest distance from the

---

* Since the above was written, we have seen it stated in the newspapers, that this venerable patriarch has died, and that, in a few days after, his wife followed him to the narrow house appointed for all the living. United in life, they were by death not long divided.

Websters, Daniel was usually boarded out in the vicinity of the open school, coming home, however, every Saturday, and returning on Monday, and generally on foot. Hoyt attained to no great distinction in his profession. He could teach what he knew, but that was very little. He excelled in the art of penmanship, but was deficient in every thing else. The most that he could do was to teach spelling, reading, writing, and the elementary rules of arithmetic. Though his advantages at this time were not great, young Webster made the most of them, so that, in the course of a couple of years, he had exhausted his teacher — he could learn no more from him. The character of this man may be learned from the following remarks, which were made by Mr. Webster, after he had attained to high distinction as a statesman and an orator : " William Hoyt was for many years teacher of our county school in Salisbury : I do not call it village school, because there was, at that time, no village, and boys came to school in the winter — the only season in which schools were usually open — from distances of several miles, wading through the snow, or running upon its crust, with their curly hair often whitened with frost from their own breaths. I knew William Hoyt well, and every truant knew him. He was an austere man, but a good teacher of children. He had been a printer in Newburyport, wrote a very fair and excellent hand, was a good reader, and could teach boys, and did teach boys, that which so few masters can or will do — to read well themselves. Beyond this, and, perhaps, a very slight knowledge of grammar, his attainments did not extend. He had brought with him into town a little property, which he took very good care of. He rather loved money — of all the cases of nouns, preferring the possessive; he also kept a little shop for the sale of various commodities, in the house exactly over the way from this."

But little Daniel was not dependent entirely upon his school teachers for instruction. His father was an excellent reader, and was in the habit of reading aloud to his family. Sometimes the book he selected for this purpose was the Bible; at other times, when the mood prompted, it was Shakspeare, or the works of Pope. By hearing his father read, more than from the instruction he received at school, Daniel became a good reader. Having an excellent voice, and a ready perception of the meaning of a writer, with the ability to give the right inflections and emphases to develop that meaning, he was listened to with pleasure. When he was but seven years of age his father kept a public house, at which the teamsters were accustomed to stop for "enter tainment for man and beast" A part of the entertainment which was then and there afforded, consisted of specimens of reading by the young orator. The teamsters were accustomed, as they checked their horses at the door of the inn, to say, "Come, let's go in, and hear a psalm from Dan Webster." The identical house in which this tavern was kept is still standing. Says Mr. Lanman, in his Private Life of Mr. Webster, with reference to this building, " It was only a few months ago when Mr. Webster, bending under the weight of years and a painful illness, sat with the writer upon its little porch, and descanted with streaming eyes upon the various events associated with his boyhood's home."

How interesting the contrast between little Dan Webster reading a psalm in the tavern, for the amusement of his rustic auditors, and the same Webster, more than sixty years after, sitting upon the porch of the same tavern, after astonishing the world with his eloquence, visiting foreign courts — a sovereign among kings ; settling, through the skilfulness of his diplomacy, some of the most difficult questions of international government, and, after attaining to an eminence immeasurably higher than any official distinctions in the gift of the people ! Who, at that early period, under the influence even of the wildest flights of fancy, would have ventured to predict that the little, puny, tavern Bible reader would become the renowned jurist and statesman, and fill the world with his fame ? What a beauti·

ful illustration does this furnish of the influence of
free institutions ? They not only give to genius
room for growth, but assist its development, and
then furnish a large field for its exercise, with the
promise of abundant reward.

The practice adopted by the elder Webster, of
reading aloud from standard authors, has a highly
beneficial effect. A father, who is a good reader,
can do more to make his children such, than any
teacher can, with the time usually devoted to that
branch of education. Children are wonderfully im-
itative. From their observation of others, they
learn how to walk, speak, and act. If they frequently listen to good reading, they become good
readers by mere imitation. They catch the tones,
the cadences, the emphases, and the general manner of him to whom they listen. It was fortunate
for young Webster that his father excelled in this
difficult art.

But this is not the only benefit which results from
such practice. It assists in the cultivation of the
taste of the children. It develops before them the
excellences of whatever is read. It awakens an
attachment to such authors, and, in addition to their
intrinsic merits, it surrounds them with the ever-
pleasing associations of home. It also serves to make
home attractive, and the family circle a sphere of
improvement.

A father surrounded by his children, and reading to them from the Bible, or from some standard author, whilst the mother is engaged with her knitting or sewing, presents a beautiful domestic scene. Such scenes were often witnessed at Elms Farm.

CHAPTER III.

WE have said that Webster had other sources of
instruction besides his teachers. Amongst these
were the books to which he had access in his father's
house, and, after these were exhausted, was the village library. The establishment of these social
libraries had been urged upon the attention of the
people by Dr. Belknap, who, in his History of New
Hampshire, says, the establishment of social libraries "is the easiest, the cheapest, and the most effect-
ual mode of diffusing knowledge among the people.
For the sum of six or eight dollars at once, and a
small annual payment besides, a man may be sup-
plied with the means of literary improvement during
his life, and his children may inherit the blessing."
This hint commended itself to Mr. Webster, and

other gentlemen of Salisbury, among whom were the clergyman and the lawyer of the place, who, at a suitable time, acted upon the suggestion, and established a small library. Here young Webster was able to obtain the means of gratifying his love of reading. Among the books which he perused with interest were the Spectator, Pope's works, and various biographies and travels.

Near the residence of Mr. Webster was a deep, dark dell, covered on either side with lofty trees and overhanging bushes, at the bottom of which flowed a rapid, noisy stream, which was christened with the rather unpoetic name of Punch Brook. In this secluded place the father of Daniel erected a saw-mill. As lumber of different sizes was wanted for building and various other purposes, Mr. Webster's mill was in great demand, and proved to him a source of considerable income. Colonel Webster, as Daniel's father was called, was anxious to form in his children habits of industry. Although he did not prohibit play, he enjoined work. He often took Daniel, when a small boy, to the mill with him. Being quick to learn, and willing to practise what he knew, the little fellow was soon able to render himself quite useful to his father in the capacity of mill boy. He understood how to set the large saw, how to raise the gate, set the machinery in motion, and then, how to attend to the operation until the long log was sawed through its whole length. The sawing of a log once through occupied about fifteen minutes. It then had to be readjusted for the next operation. Whilst the saw was passing through the timber, the little mill boy was not occupied with knife and stick, whittling away his time; neither did he stand in listless indolence, looking on to observe how slowly or how rapidly the saw made progress; but, with book in hand, he was poring over "the best thoughts of the best authors." He was cultivating his taste, and gathering instruction and intellectual stimulus from the pages of such men as Steele, Addison, Pope, Shakspeare, or other valuable writers. "There, in that old saw mill, surrounded by forests, in the midst of great noise, which such a mill makes, and this, too, without materially neglecting his task, he made himself familiar with the most remarkable events recorded by the pen of history, and with the lives and characters of the most celebrated persons who had lived in the tides of time. He has never forgotten what he read there. So tenacious is his memory, that he can recite long passages from the old books which he read there, and has scarcely looked at since. The solitude of the scene, the absence of every thing to divert his attention, the simplicity of his occupation, the taciturn and thoughtful manner of his father, all favored the process of transplanting every idea found in those books to his fresh, fruitful, and vigorous mind. I have not made a visit to any of the scenes of Mr. Webster's boyhood more interesting than to this old mill." *

It will be appropriate to relate, in this connection, another fact, for which we have the authority of Mr. Webster himself. In his conversation respecting his teacher Hoyt, a part of which is given on a preceding page, he said, "Hoyt also kept a little shop, for the sale of various commodities, in the house exactly over the way from this. I do not know how old I was, but I remember having gone into his shop one day, and bought a small, cotton pocket handkerchief, with *the Constitution of the United States printed on its two sides.* From this I first learned either that there was a Constitution or that there were United States. I remember to have read it, and have known more or less of it ever since. William Hoyt and his wife lie buried in the grave-yard under our eye, on my farm, near the graves of my own family. He left no children. I suppose that this little handkerchief was purchased about the time that I was eight years old, as I remember listening to the conversation of my father and Mr. Thompson upon political events which happened in the year 1790." Another account

* Life and Memorial of Daniel Webster

states that he paid for that handkerchief all the
money he had in his pocket, which amounted to
twenty-five cents, and that the evening of that day
was wholly employed in the careful perusal and
study of that novel document, while seated by the
fireside in company with his father and mother.
What an interesting memento that handkerchief
would now be, if it could any where be found!

In the character of the reading which this young
lad selected, we see the direction of his mind; and,
as we review his subsequent career, we may discover
something of the effects which his early reading
produced upon his mental habits and tastes. It
may, perhaps, have been a fortunate circumstance
for him that, at that time, there was no "juvenile
literature." He was therefore obliged, if he read
at all, to peruse works of a higher character, by
means of which his mental powers were tasked and
greatly strengthened. He was one of the very few
who, at an early age, are capable of being interest
ed in the master spirits of literature. Many lads,
if placed in his condition, would have spent their
time in idleness. They have not the mental calibre
for understanding, and perusing with interest, those
works which gave him delight. For such children
juvenile works furnish the appropriate nutriment.
They can endure nothing stronger than intellectual
milk at an age when Webster was digesting strong

meat. Care should be exercised lest they continue the use of such milk too long. So numerous, diversified, and attractive are the juvenile books which are constantly falling from the press, that some individuals make them their exclusive reading, who ought to have advanced far beyond them, and made themselves acquainted with the most eminent authors. Let such be rebuked by the example of the little mill boy of Elms Farm.

Let it not, however, be supposed that Webster, in this early period of his life, was a recluse. Far from it. He loved healthy, out-door sports, as well as other children. In nutting, squirrel hunting, fishing, and, when old enough, in gunning, he took as much pleasure as others.

In his early years, New Hampshire was distinguished for deep snows and long winters. These gave opportunity to Daniel to indulge in sports of another character — skating on the ponds, coasting down hill, or rolling balls, and making snow men and snow houses. Sometimes, so great would be the quantity of snow as to cover up all the rocks and fences, and make a smooth inclined plane from the top of the hill to the shore of the Merrimac, in the vicinity, down which he would coast with the swiftness of the wind, and be carried by his accelerated force nearly across the frozen river. On the , coldest days, our little hero might be seen wading through the deep drifts, and crossing the frozen brooks, dragging after him his sled, that with neighboring boys he might engage in the healthful excitement of this invigorating sport. On one occasion, so interested had he become in this amusement, and so unmindful of the severity of the cold, that he froze the toes of both his feet, and, as a penalty for his indiscretion, was confined to his house several days, until his chilblains were healed.

Like other boys, he would sometimes yield to the temptations of this sport, until it made him late at school, when he was sure to be reprimanded by his father. This led him to say, "there was great fun in sliding down hill, but there was not much fun in hearing his father scold, when he staid out of school to enjoy it." The young should regard it as a settled fact, that there can be no true enjoyment in going contrary to a parent's wishes.

The effect of these out-door, exhilarating exercises was to increase the robustness and strength of the puny boy.

As the parents of Webster were religious people, they taught their children to observe the Sabbath. All toys and sports were laid aside, and the day reverently spent in a manner that harmonized with the object of its appointment. Although the meeting house was four miles from their residence, yet Mr. Webster insisted upon his children's attendance.

To this Daniel demurred, because he was obliged to walk the whole distance. There was on the road a family by the name of True, who lived at an equal distance (of about two miles) from the Websters and the church, and in which there were some boys, playfellows of Daniel, with whom he had many a "good time." When, therefore, Dan complained that he was compelled to walk so far to meeting, his father replied, —

"I see Deacon True's boys there every Sunday regularly, and have never heard of their complaining."

Daniel at once saw that the cases were not parallel, and immediately said, —

"Ah, yes! the deacon's boys live half way there, and of course have only half as far to walk."

"Well," rejoined his father, "you may get up in the morning, dress yourself, and run up to Deacon True's, and go with them; then you will have no farther to walk than they do."

This reply, in which there was a vein of kindness and good humor, was to the lad perfectly satisfactory. It required no self-denial to run up to Deacon True's and meet his playfellows, and with their company, the walk to the church could not be otherwise than pleasant. After this, therefore, on every Sabbath when the weather would permit, Daniel was found in his place at church, notwithstanding

4

the four long miles. His father's **wisdom, in ren**
dering his way **easy,** assisted him **in forming the**
habit of constant attendance upon public worship.
It has been said that "man is a bundle of **habits."**
It cannot be denied that a large part of our conduct is nothing more **than** a repetition of acts previously **performed. By** this repetition habits are
formed. Many individuals regularly absent them-
selves from the house of God, and others as regularly **attend, from mere** habit. **When** either of these
habits is formed, **a** departure **from it is** attended
with difficulty. **We sensitively shrink** from the
violation of our established customs. This is the
reason why individuals, who seldom attend public
worship, find it so irksome to go, and so uninterest-
ing when **there.** This fact furnishes **a** strong in-
ducement **for the** formation of a habit of constant
attendance upon the services of the sanctuary ; for,
when formed, it will become to us a kind of second
nature, which will prevent our absence from public
worship except **from necessity.**

In consequence of **the** constitutional weakness of
young Webster, it appeared impossible for him to
gain a livelihood by **hard labor.** His father, therefore, resolved **to** qualify him **for the** important, but
less arduous, **duty of school teacher.** This had
been suggested to him by Mr. Thompson, a lawyer
who boarded in Mr. Webster's family, and who had

given Daniel some lessons in the Latin Grammar. The ease with which he committed these lessons to memory, and his general quickness of apprehension, induced Mr. Thompson to advise his father to send him to an academy, for the purpose of qualifying him as a schoolmaster. The mother was pleased with the suggestion, and urged its adoption. His brother Joseph, who was then of age, also favored it. He jocosely assigned as a reason. that, "as Dan had not such bright natural talents as his brothers and sisters, a little education would perhaps make up the deficiency." The father consented. He supposed that, according to the customs of the times, his son would teach school in the winter, and work on the farm, if his health allowed, in the summer. As this course had been found profitable by some of the families in town, he inferred that it would result in no loss to his own. He therefore gave consent, little dreaming of the important results which were destined to flow from his decision.

At that time no academical institution stood higher in New England than Phillips Academy, in Exeter. It had been handsomely endowed by John Phillips, LL. D., after whom it was named, whose donations and bequests to it amounted to a hundred and fifty thousand dollars. This large sum made it independent of the income which might be received for tuition from the pupils. To this insti-

tution Colonel Webster determined to send Daniel.
It was a most fortunate circumstance for the rising
republic of the United States, that, immediately after
the war for independence, the attention of the people was directed, in different parts of the country,
with more than usual interest, to educational affairs.
Such was the genius of the new institutions to which
that independence gave rise, and so great was the
controlling power of the people in political affairs,
through the elective franchise, that it was apparent
to all reflecting persons, that general intelligence
among the masses of the people was essential to the
healthful working and the perpetuity of the new
forms of government. Not only, therefore, did state
legislatures. and the municipal officers of the various
towns, give special consideration to educational matters, but wealthy gentlemen, under the influence of
patriotism, contributed freely of their own private
funds for the endowment of schools and colleges.
As, in many respects, the system of government in
the United States was unlike any other that then
existed, or had ever been known to exist, — as it was
an experiment, on a magnificent scale, of the capa-
bilities of a nation for self-government, under peculiar laws, — it was essential for the success of the
experiment that a class of men should be raised up
who would be able to take correct and comprehensive views of all parts of the complicated machinery,

who should understand all the relations and inter
ests of the country as a whole, and of the individual
states of which it was composed, and then be able
clearly to unfold them to others. For this purpose
schools of an elevated character were required, in
order to discover those who possessed the natural
talents for this work, and then, by appropriate cul-
ture, to fit them for the exercise of their talents, in
those departments of influence, whether at the bar,
on the bench, or in halls of legislation, where they
would render the greatest amount of service to their
country. Such an institution was Exeter Academy.
It has had the honor of assisting in the education
of many who have risen to high distinction in the
various professions, and who have wielded a vast influence over the destinies of their country. Dr.
Phillips, by its endowment, rendered essential service to the interests of the new republic. To this
school young Webster was sent.

The 24th of May, 1796, was an important day at
Elms Farm. There had been more than usual bus-
tle in the house; clothes were collected, bundles
tied; children were running to and fro, asking questions and making all kinds of remarks — the reason
of which was, Daniel was getting ready to leave for
the academy. As Mr. Webster had no chaise, or
other light carriage adapted to the journey, it was
to be made on horseback. It so happened that one

of the neighbors was desirous of sending a horse
and side saddle to the very town where the academy
was situated, for some female friend there, to ride
back to Salisbury. It was agreed that this horse
should be used by the young student. When the
time of departure arrived, the two horses were
brought to the door, and Daniel, who was dressed
in a new suit of homespun materials, was lifted upon
the one intended for him. Imagine the scene!
The affectionate mother, who has all along had a
presentiment of Daniel's greatness, stands at the
door, with mingled expressions of solicitude and joy
depicted upon her countenance : she has given abundant good advice, and sealed it with not a few burning kisses. Around are the other children and
members of the family, some holding the horses,
others adjusting the bundles, and all abandoning
their mirthfulness, and becoming more serious as
the moment of departure arrives. The last shake
of the hand and farewell kiss are given, and the
two travellers set out on their journey, — little Dan
being perched upon the lady's side saddle, where he
was destined to become, before night, more fatigued
than he had ever been before. After a romantic,
but tiresome ride, along the banks of rivers, through
valleys, and amid lofty hills and mountains, on the
third day they arrived at Exeter. A boarding place
was obtained for Daniel in the family of Mr. Clif-

WEBSTER LEAVING HOME FOR EXETER ACADEMY. — See p. 52.

ford, with whom his father had some acquaintance. The day after their arrival he was taken to the academy Benjamin Abbott, LL. D., was the principal. He was a gentleman of the old school, and felt it important to maintain great dignity and a regard to form, in the administration of the school. All official duties were performed with pompous ceremony. When Colonel Webster stated the object of his visit to the doctor, who was seated in a large hall connected with the academy, that important personage placed upon his head a cocked hat, in order to make a suitable impression upon the lad, and then said, —

" Well, sir, let the young gentleman be presented for examination."

The slender-looking boy modestly came forward, and, though every thing was new and strange, he submitted to his examination with great self-possession.

" What is your age ? " asked the venerable teacher.

" Fourteen," was the reply.

" Take this Bible, my lad, and read the twenty-second chapter of Luke," at the same time pointing it out to him.

This chapter contains an account of the institution of the Lord's supper, Christ's sufferings in Gethsemane, the betrayal, the seizure, and the examination of Christ. Its different parts required a different style of reading. None but a good reader could do the chapter justice. Daniel took the book and read with so much distinctness of enunciation, correctness of emphasis, and skill in the modulations of his voice, as to bring out the true sense of the passage, — the doctor had no occasion to interrupt him. It was a beautiful specimen of reading. After he had finished the chapter, the doctor, without asking any questions whatever, said, —

" Young man, you are qualified to enter this institution."

The new student remained at this academy nine months. His diligence, and his capacity for acquiring knowledge, secured for him not only the warm commendations of his teachers, but, what was better, a good knowledge of the branches to which he devoted attention, among which, in addition to the usual English branches, was the Latin language.

It is not easy always to predict the man from the indications of youth. With some there appears to be, in early life, a deficiency of the very traits in which they excel in later years. This was true of Webster. Although his fame as an orator is worldwide, yet, when a boy of fourteen, he could not summon sufficient courage to attempt to declaim before the school. His own account of this singular fact is in the following words: " I believe I made

tolerable progress in most branches which I attended
to while in this school ; but there was one thing I
could not do — I could not make a declamation ; I
could not speak before the school. The kind and
excellent Buckminster sought especially to persuade
me to perform the exercise of declamation, like other boys ; but I could not do it. Many a piece did
I commit to memory, and recite and rehearse in my
own room, over and over again ; yet when the day
came, when the school collected to hear the declamation, when my name was called, and I saw all
eyes turned to my seat, I could not raise myself
from it. Sometimes the instructors frowned, sometimes they smiled. Mr. Buckminster always pressed
and entreated most winningly that I would venture
— venture only once ; but I never could command
sufficient resolution."

From any other witness, this would appear almost
incredible. It is difficult to conceive how one who
has been so highly distinguished for self-reliance and
moral courage, as Mr. Webster, should have been
so singularly deficient in these traits when young
It was attributable, probably, in a great degree, to
his physical debility. He subsequently surmounted
it, and, as we shall see, became in college one of
the most popular speakers. What encouragement
does this furnish for the young to set themselves
resolutely to work to surmount any difficulty that

prevents their advancement! By frequent repetition,
by firm resolution, they may overcome embarrassments which would otherwise prove fatal to their
success. Nothing can resist a determined spirit.

When Webster first entered the Phillips Academy,
he was made, in consequence of his unpolished,
country-like appearance, and because he was placed
at the foot of the class, the butt of ridicule by some
of the scholars. This treatment touched his keen
sensibility, and he spoke of it with regret to his
friends where he boarded. They informed him that
the place assigned him in the class was according to
the standing regulations of the school, and that by
diligence he might rise above it. They also advised
him to take no notice of the laughter of the city
boys, for after a while they would become weary of
it, and would cease. The assistant tutor, Mr. Emery, was informed of the treatment which Webster
received. He therefore treated him with special
consideration, told him to care for nothing but his
books, and predicted that all would end well. This
kindness had the desired effect. Webster applied
himself with increased diligence, and with signal
success. He soon met with his reward, which made
those who had laughed at him hang their heads with
shame. At the end of the first quarter the assistant
tutor called up the class in their usual order; he
then walked to the foot of the class, took Webster

by the arm, and marched him, in front of the class, to the head, where, as he placed him, he said, " There, sir, that is your proper place." This practical rebuke made those who had delighted to ridicule the country boy, feel mortified and chagrined. He had outstripped them. This incident greatly stimulated the successful student. He applied himself with his accustomed industry, and looked forward with some degree of solicitude to the end of the second term, to see whether he would be able to retain his relative rank in the class. Weeks slowly passed away; the end of the term arrived, and the class was again summoned to be newly arranged, according to their scholarship and deportment, as evinced during the preceding term. Whilst they were all standing in silence and suspense, Mr. Emery, their teacher, said, fixing his eye at the same time upon the country boy, " Daniel Webster, gather up your books and take down your cap." Not understanding the design of such an order, Daniel complied with troubled feelings. He knew not but that he was about to be expelled from school for his dulness. His teacher perceived the expression of sadness upon his countenance, but soon dispelled it by saying, " Now, sir, you will please pass into another room, and *join a higher class :* and you, young gentlemen," addressing the other scholars, " will take an affectionate leave of your classmate, for *you will never see him again !* " As if he had said, " This rustic lad, whom you have made the butt of ridicule, has already so far outstripped you in his studies, that from your stand-point he is dwarfed in the distance, and will soon be out of sight entirely. He has developed a capacity for study which will prevent you from ever overtaking him. As a classmate you will never see him again."

It would be interesting to know who those city boys were, who made the young rustic an object of sport. What have they come to ? — what have they accomplished ? — who has heard of the fame of their attainments ? Scholars should be careful how they laugh at a classmate because of his unpolished manners or coarse raiment. Under that rough exterior may be concealed talents that will move a nation and dazzle a world, when they in their turn might justly be made a laughing-stock, on account of their inefficiency.

CHAPTER IV.

AFTER leaving Exeter Academy, Webster was placed under the care of Rev. Samuel Woods, D. D., of Boscawen. This change was probably made for economical reasons, as Dr. Woods gave instruction and board to lads for only one dollar per week, which was less than the expenses at Exeter. He was now in his fifteenth year, with a fair knowledge of the English branches, and a considerable acquaintance with the Latin.

On his way to Dr. Woods's, an interesting incident occurred, of which Mr. Webster himself has given the account. It seems that his father, through the kind suggestions of others, who had discovered the innate powers of Daniel, had come to the conclusion to send him to college. But this determination he did not reveal to his son till he was on the way

59

to Dr. Woods's. The announcement deeply affected him.

It was in the depth of winter. The ground was
covered with deep snow. Webster and his father
were travelling in a New England sleigh, common-
ly called a *pung*. As they were ascending a hill, Mr.
Webster told Daniel that he was going to send him
to college. This sudden and unexpected announcement overcame the lad. This was an honor to
which, in his most ambitious moments, he had never
aspired. To be " college learned," in those days,
was a passport to the most intelligent and refined
society. It was regarded as a preparation for any
of the professions. It at once gave an individual a
respectable position in society ; and whilst it developed all the capacities which he possessed, it was
supposed to impart others, of which he was previ
ously destitute. The relative position of a college
graduate, at that time, was far higher in the community than now, when their number is so greatly in
creased.

A lad of fourteen, who had been acquainted with
but very few who had been favored with a collegiate
education, and who regarded them with a veneration
above that which he cherished towards other men,
could not have been otherwise than deeply moved at
such a communication. To use his own language,
" I could not speak. How could my father, with so

large a family, and in such narrow circumstances, think of incurring so great an expense for me? A warm glow ran all over me, and *I laid my head on my father's shoulder, and wept.*" He wept from excess of joy! How different were his feelings from those of many at the present day, who, when the privilege of a collegiate course of education is offered them, regard the proposition as a great affliction, and cry from sorrow! They are unwilling to avail themselves of benefits which others would highly value. They do not appreciate them; the golden opportunity they throw away; and probably, at some future period, when it is too late to repair the disaster, they will deeply regret their folly.

If this book should fall into the hands of any such youth, we would say to them, Look forward to the future. Remember, you will not always be boys. You are in a few years to take your place amongst men, and in order to be qualified to exert much influence over them, you must be educated. You are now placed in an enviable position; by rightly improving your advantages, you will qualify yourselves to occupy important stations; you will be fitted to move, and to feel at home, in the most intelligent circles. Your opinions will be respected; they will have weight with others. Your advice will be sought in important matters. You will be looked

5

to to fill places of trust and responsibility. You
will honor yourselves and your families. And it is
not impossible for you to attain to high distinction in
any of the learned professions, or to reach some of
the most honorable and responsible positions in the
state or national governments. Who would have
supposed that, when that puny lad from the back-
woods of New Hampshire was made an object of
ridicule by the "city boys," that he would ever
reach the exalted stations he did, and after filling the
world with the splendor of his eloquence and states-
manship, would be followed to the grave by the re-
grets of millions ? It is no more unlikely, now, that
you may acquire distinction, than it was in his case,
when he was of your age. But suppose that he had
disliked study ; suppose that, when his father, as
they were ascending that hill in a cold winter's day,
informed him that he might go to college, he had
expressed an unwillingness, and had dissuaded his
father from his purpose ; what would Daniel Webster
have been now ? He might possibly, by the force
of his natural talents, have excelled in any kind of
business to which he would have devoted himself;
but is it probable that he would ever have been a
senator of the United States, or a member of the
president's cabinet ? Indeed, on one occasion, —
as we shall presently relate, — his own father assigns
as a reason why *he* was not elected a member of

Congress, instead of his successful competitor, was because of his *want of education*.

During the time that Webster was with Dr. Woods he always gave satisfactory recitations. But he found it so easy to learn that the preparation of his lessons occupied but a short time; he consequently had much leisure, which he spent in the indulgence of his love of nature, in fishing and gunning. With rod or gun in hand, he spent hour after hour in wandering along the streams, or rambling over the fields. His teacher, who had but little sympathy for these employments, administered to him a rebuke for his wandering habits, tempering it, however, with compliments for his quickness in learning. He was fearful that this fondness for out-door sports might exert an injurious influence upon the other students. Webster felt this rebuke, and determined to retaliate in a way that would tax the doctor's patience. His lesson for the next day was a hundred lines in Virgil. He applied himself diligently, and occupied a good portion of the night, not in simply learning those hundred lines, but in committing to memory many more. At the recitation next morning, he despatched the hundred lines, for which he received the commendation of his teacher. "I can recite some more," said the student. "Go on, then," was the reply. Another hundred lines were repeated. The teacher was equally surprised and gratified.

"But I have not done yet," said Webster ; "I can
give you another hundred lines, and another hundred
beyond that ; *I can give you five hundred* ; *I can recite to the end of the twelfth book.*" The teacher
was amazed ; he had not time to hear so much ;
his breakfast had for some time been waiting for
him, and he was impatient to be at it. This was
what Webster had anticipated, and where he had
intended to tax the old gentleman. He was determined to retain him so long in hearing his recitation
as to make him have a late breakfast ; but the
teacher would not wait : after praising his pupil for
his industry, he asked to be excused from listening to
him any longer, and said, "You may have the whole
day, Dan, for pigeon shooting." Dan rambled to
his heart's content that day, without any compunc-
tions of conscience, or any fear of rebukes from the
doctor.

How much better that mode of retaliation was
than for him to have thrown aside his books in a fit
of passion, and played the, dunce for a few days !
In that case the punishment would have been ex-
exclusively his own.

Prior to the time that Daniel left home, in order
to pursue his studies, he was industrious to the extent of his physical strength. He assisted his father
at the mill ; he worked with the men in the fields
driving the horse in ploughing, pitching hay, or run

ning of errands; but after having been away from home a number of months, these habits of industry were broken up, and when he returned to the old homestead, it was more agreeable for him to play than to work, as the following incident will show.

Whilst he was studying at Boscawen with **Dr.** Woods, his father on one occasion sent for him to come home. Haying season had arrived, and he needed more assistance than usual at Elms Farm. The young lad packed up his clothes, and complied with his father's orders. The day after his arrival, he went into the field to work, the father in the mean time visiting a neighboring town on business. Before the forenoon was expired, Daniel returned to the house, and told his mother that he was greatly fatigued ; and holding up his hands, he showed blisters, which, he said, would prevent him from working any more. His affectionate mother excused him, as he probably anticipated ; but Dan had no idea of losing the whole day ; so, after dinner, he tackled the horse to a wagon, placed into it two of his sisters, and drove off to a well-known berry pasture, where they expected to find an abundance of whortle, or huckleberries. Here he spent the remainder of the afternoon, as boys, under such circumstances, know how.

When his father returned home at night, and ascertained how his son had spent the day, instead of flying into a violent passion, he laughed over the matter, and sent his tender son to bed. After breakfast was over, the next morning, being convinced that he would obtain but little assistance from his son, and not being willing to detain him uselessly from his studies during term time, his father put into his delicate hand his bundle of clothes, and pointed, in a manner too significant to be misunderstood, towards Boscawen. The boy immediately started off. He had not gone far before he saw one of the neighbors, Mr. Thomas W. Thompson, who knew why he had come home.

"Where are you going, Dan ?" he asked.

"Back to school," was the reply.

"I thought it would be so," added Mr. Thompson, with an expressive smile upon his countenance.

And back to the company of Virgil and Cicero did the young student return.

Pronounce not harsh judgment upon this piece of juvenility in Daniel. He seems to have commenced work with hearty good will, but not having been engaged in vigorous, muscular employment for some months, he soon became blistered and tired. Even then he did not throw aside his rake and fork and run off, with the intention of showing his blistered hands to his father in the evening, as his apology. But, as a child in his circumstances should have done, he related the whole case to his mother and obtained her permission to leave the field. And when he found a long afternoon on his hands, instead of strolling off alone, with fishing pole or gun, he tackles the horse, and, like an affectionate brother, takes his two sisters a berrying — an amusement in which children take great delight.

It may be settled as a general fact, that but little physical labor can be expected of students, either during term time or vacations. They leave their studies, not for work, but relaxation, and under these circumstances continuous physical exertion soon becomes irksome to them. It is truly a hardship when students are obliged to work through their whole vacations, in order to defray the expense of their education.

Master Webster pursued his studies with Mr. Wood from February till August, 1797, and fitted himself, imperfectly however, for college. His time of preparation was too limited for him to do it well. "Still, however," says Hon. Edward Everett, in his Biographical Memoir, " when we hear of a youth of fifteen preparing himself for college by a year's study of Greek and Latin, we must recollect that the attainments which may be made in that time, by a young man of distinguished talent, at the period of life when the faculties develop themselves with the greatest energy, studying night and day, summer and winter, under the master influence of

hope, ambition, and necessity, are not to be meas
ured by the tardy progress of the thoughtless or
languid children of prosperity, sent to school from
the time they are able to go alone, and carried along
by routine and discipline from year to year, in the
majority of cases without strong personal motives
to diligence."

This limited degree of preparation for college
studies was to Webster a great disadvantage. It
subjected him to embarrassments during his whole
course, from which his classmates derived advantage.
He often spoke of it, in subsequent years, with
regret.

It is a great mistake in young men to imagine
they have gained a year, when they enter college
poorly fitted, by which means they are able to graduate a year earlier than they otherwise would have
done. They lose in scholarship what they gain in
time.

A young man who commences a college course
poorly qualified meets ofttimes with difficulties which,
though insuperable to him, his classmates easily surmount. This places him in a somewhat false position, especially if such difficulties frequently occur,
for it gives him the appearance of possessing less
intellectual power or acumen than the others, when
such is not the case. It arises simply from the fact
that the subject is comparatively new to him, but,

in consequence of their longer course of preparation, during which the same subject was studied and
reviewed, it is familiar to them. Still the unfortunate student is obliged to go limping after his class,
with a painful feeling of mortification and despond-
ency; and if he succeed in obtaining a diploma, it
is as much as he expects. Any particularly honorable position is out of the question. Yet the same
individual, if he had been well qualified for entrance,
might have led his class in all their studies, and
graduated with the highest honors. We commend
these considerations to the attention of those who
are so impatient to enter college as to shorten their
period of preparation.

When the time arrived for the student of Elms
Farm to visit Dartmouth College, for the purpose
of being matriculated, a neighbor made for him a
new suit of clothes, — coat, vest, and pantaloons, —
all of homespun cloth of the *deepest blue*. He made
his journey on horseback, — not this time, however,
on a side saddle. On his way he was overtaken by
a violent rain storm, which lasted forty-eight hours,
created a freshet, bore away the bridges, and subjected him to the necessity of travelling round the
country twenty extra miles, in order to find a cross-
ing-place over the streams. When he arrived he
was completely soaked with the rain. The new
garments which he wore seem not to have been

made of fast colors, for upon examination **Mr. Web-**
ster found that the indigo hue, after penetrating all
his under clothing, had deeply dyed his skin, so that
instead of being a green country boy, he was de
cidedly *blue*.   After a little attention to his toilet,
he presented himself before the faculty for examination.   After having given an account of the opportunities for study of which he had availed himself,
— the books he had read, the branches he had attended to, and after answering the questions which
they proposed, — he told them of the difficulties he
had experienced in reaching Hanover.   " Thus,"
said he, " you see me as I am " — referring to his
cerulean appearance — "if not entitled to your ap
probation, at least to your sympathy."   He has
since said of himself, when alluding to that interview, that he " was **not** only *black* Dan, but *blue*
Dan."   Very fortunately, **that** change of **color was**
not produced, as in the **case of** some others, **by the**
rejection of the **faculty.**

The object of Daniel's visit to **Hanover was ac-**
complished.   He safely **passed the ordeal which**
students **so generally dread, and was** admitted a
member of the Freshman **class in Dartmouth College**
in August, **1797, at the age of fifteen.**

CHAPTER V.

In consequence of his imperfect preparation for collegiate studies, Webster was obliged to take a low place in his class — it is said, the foot. To a mind constituted like his, that would have been an affliction, provided he had gone over the same preparatory course with the rest of the class. So far was this from being the case, that some of the text books used in college he had never seen, while other members of the class were familiar with them. What to him was the breaking of entirely new ground was to them a mere retracing of old paths, which they had repeatedly traversed before. In the Latin language he was at home. This had always been to him a favorite study. To the Greek he was not particularly partial. For mathematics he had

71

special fondness, though to both these latter branches
he devoted the usual amount of attention, and made
respectable progress. With ancient and modern
geography and history, and with logic, he was highly
delighted. During his course in college he did not
confine himself to the routine of specified studies,
but indulged in a wide range of reading in English
literature and history. He also assisted in conducting a weekly paper, by making selections for its
columns, and occasionally contributing an original
article. It was not long before he reached that
commanding eminence among his fellows, to which,
by his towering talents and great attainments, he
was justly entitled. The faculty, as well as the students, by the respect with which they treated him,
and the deference they paid his opinions, yielded
their willing testimony to his extraordinary abilities.
He thus illustrated the truth, that every person,
however false may be the position in which, by a
combination of unfortunate circumstances, he is at
any time placed, may, by persevering industry, find
his true level.

What his habits were in college we learn from
the following witnesses. Professor Shurtliff, who
was in the same class with him, says, " Mr Webster,
while in college, was remarkable for his *steady habits*, his *intense application to study*, and his punctual
attendance upon all the prescribed exercises. I

know not that he was absent from a recitation, or from morning and evening prayers in the chapel, or from public worship on the Sabbath ; and I doubt if ever a smile was seen upon his face during any religious exercise. He was always in his place, and with decorum suited to it. He had no collision with any one, nor appeared to enter into the concerns of others, but emphatically *minded his own business.* But, as steady as the sun, he pursued with intense application the great object for which he came to college. This I conceive was the secret of his popularity in college, and his success in subsequent life."

What an example is here furnished for undergraduates and all other young students ! If they desire to acquire popularity with their companions, or "success in subsequent life," they must, like the subject of our memoir, be distinguished for " steady habits and intense application to study." They must *mind their own business,* and keep constantly before them the great object for which they are pursuing a course of education. To do all this is no easy task. Temptations to deviate from this straightforward, single-minded course are numerous and strong. They spring out of one's natural indolence ; from the difficulty of acquiring knowledge ; from the enjoyments of social intercourse ; from the enticements of the wine cup ; and from the excitement of the passions. There are circumstances in which

a student may be placed, where, unless he possess
great decision of character and firmness of purpose,
he will certainly be led astray.   He will not be able
to resist the strong current of evil influences which
will bear down upon him.   This, however, will not
be likely to be the case with those who, like Webster, in addition to devoting themselves diligently to
study, are punctual and serious in their attendance
upon morning and evening prayers, and upon the
public services of the Sabbath.   It furnishes an un-
favorable augury to any young man's future prospects, when these religious duties are neglected.

   Another witness, who bears testimony to Mr. Webster's position in college, is Judge Woodward, professor of natural philosophy, who died soon after
Mr. Webster was graduated.   "That man's victory
is certain," said he, " who reaches the heart through
the medium of the understanding.   He [*i. e.*, Mr.
Webster] gained me by combating my opinions,
for I often attacked him, merely to try his strength."
It would be interesting to know what some of those
questions were on which the judge tested the strength
of his pupil, and what line of argument was pursued by the latter.   There can be no doubt, judging
from the effect produced upon the professor's mind,
that, in these intellectual contests, Webster exhibited
great logical power, combined with dignity and courtesy.   He secured the respect of his teacher by his

skill and gentlemanly bearing in debate, and induced him, very early after their first acquaintance, to predict his future greatness. The judge considered it a great privilege to be the instructor of one of so much promise. Says General Lyman, " He took infinite pleasure in assisting to lay the foundation stones of what he felt was to be a magnificent building."

While at college, Mr. Webster devoted special attention to the study of oratory. He made himself familiar with its fundamental principles, and with the speeches of those who had excelled in this delightful art. Having a deep, yet musical voice, a commanding personal appearance, a high, projecting forehead, and dark, piercing eyes, and conducting himself with great dignity of manner, and with courteous deference to his hearers, he was always listened to with pleasure. He became so popular as a speaker, that when only sixteen years of age, he was chosen to deliver an Oration on the Fourth of July, to the members of college and the citizens of Hanover. This, certainly, was a high honor to reach at so early an age, and it was, if possible, increased by the request for the publication of the oration, from those who heard it. It shows that he produced a strong, favorable impression.

As this was the first public address delivered by Mr. Webster, of which any record has been pre served, it is a source of gratification that it was printed, and that one copy, at least, of the original edition has survived to the present time. Of this General Lyman has made copious use in his "Memorials." It is exceedingly interesting to read this oration, and compare the tone of its patriotism, and the style of its composition, with those of his later productions. It will be seen that, though his rhetoric was afterwards greatly modified, his love of country remained unaltered.

We cannot, perhaps, perform a more acceptable service than by presenting several extracts from it, in order to furnish the reader an opportunity of making this comparison for himself. His introduction was as follows : —

"*Countrymen, Brethren, and Fathers :* We are now assembled to celebrate an anniversary ever to be held in dear remembrance by the sons of freedom. Nothing less than the birth of a nation — nothing less than the emancipation of three millions of people from the degrading chains of foreign dominion — is the event we commemorate. Twenty-four years have this day elapsed since these United States first raised the standard of liberty, and echoed the shouts of independence.

"Those of you who were then reaping the iron harvest of the martial field, whose bosoms then palpitated for the honor of America, will at this time

experience a renewal of all that fervent patriotism,
of all those indescribable emotions, which then agi-
tated your breasts. As for us, who were either then
unborn, or not far enough advanced beyond the
threshold of existence to engage in the grand conflict for liberty, we now most cordially unite with
you to greet the return of this joyous anniversary,
to welcome the return of the day that gave us freedom, and to hail the rising glories of our country!

"On occasions like this, you have hitherto been
addressed from the stage, on the nature, the origin,
the expediency, of civil government. The field of
political speculation has here been explored by persons possessing talents to which the speaker of the
day can have no pretensions. Declining, therefore,
a dissertation on the principles of civil polity, you
will indulge me in slightly sketching those events
which have originated, matured, and raised to its
present grandeur this new empire."

After describing the isolated and gloomy condition of the first colonists, he touches upon the
French war, in which he accuses Great Britain of
" presumptuously arrogating to herself the glory of
victories acquired by the bravery of the American
militia," and then adds, —

" But while Great Britain was thus tyrannically
stripping her colonies of their well-earned laurels,
and triumphantly weaving them into the stupendous

6

wreath of her own martial glories, she was unwit
tingly teaching them to value themselves, and effect
ually to resist on a future day her unjust encroach-
ments.

"The pitiful tale of *taxation* now commences :
the unhappy quarrel which resulted in the dismem-
berment of the British empire has here its origin. ·

" England, now triumphant over the united
powers of France and Spain, is determined to reduce to the condition of slaves her American
subjects.

" We might now display the legislatures of the
several states, together with the General Congress,
petitioning, praying, remonstrating, and, like dutiful
subjects, humbly laying their grievances before the
throne.   On the other hand, we could exhibit a
British Parliament · assiduously devising means to
subjugate America, disdaining our petitions, trampling on our rights, and menacingly telling us, in language not to be misunderstood, ' *Ye shall be slaves.*'
We could mention the haughty, tyrannical, perfidious
Gage, at the head of a standing army ; we could
show our brethren attacked and slaughtered at Lexington ! our property plundered and destroyed at
Concord !   Recollections can still pain us with the
spiral flames of burning Charlestown, the agonizing
groans of aged parents, the shrieks of widows, or-
phans, and infants.

"Indelibly impressed on our memories still live the dismal scenes of Bunker's awful mount, the grand theatre of New England bravery; where Slaughter stalked grimly triumphant, where relentless Britain saw her soldiers, the unhappy instruments of despotism, fallen beneath the nervous arm of injured freemen.

"There the great Warren fought, and there, alas! he fell. Valuing life only as it enabled him to serve his country, he freely resigned himself, a willing martyr in the cause of liberty, and now lies encircled in the arms of glory.

"But, haughty Albion, thy reign shall soon be over! Thou shalt triumph no longer; thine empire already reels and totters; thy laurels even now begin to wither, and thy fame to decay. Thou hast at length roused the indignation of an insulted people; thine oppressions they deem no longer tolerable.

"The 4th day of July, 1776, has now arrived, and America, manfully springing from the torturing fangs of the British lion, now rises majestic in the pride of her sovereignty, and bids her eagle elevate his wings!

"The solemn Declaration of Independence is now pronounced, amidst crowds of admiring citizens, by the supreme council of our nation, and received with the unbounded plaudits of a grateful people.

"This was the hour when heroism was proved —
when the souls of men were tried."

At this point Mr. Webster gracefully turned to
the revolutionary soldiers who were present, and
addressing them, said, —

"It was then, ye venerable patriots — it was then
you lifted the indignant arm, and unitedly swore to
be free! Despising such toys as subjugated empires,
you then knew no middle fortune between liberty
and death!

"Firmly relying on the protection of Heaven,
unwarped in the resolution you had taken, you then
undaunted met — engaged — defeated the gigantic
power of Britain, and rose triumphant over the ag-
gressions of your enemies.

"Trenton, Princeton, Bennington, and Saratoga
were the successive theatres of your victories, and
the utmost bounds of creation are the limits of your
fame! The sacred fire of freedom, then enkindled
in your breasts, shall be perpetuated through the
long descent of future ages, and burn with undi-
minished fervor in the bosoms of millions yet unborn.

"Finally, to close the sanguinary conflict, to
grant America the blessings of an honorable peace,
and clothe her heroes with laurels, Cornwallis, at
whose feet the kings and princes of Asia have since

thrown their diadems, was compelled to submit to the sword of Washington.

"The great drama is now completed; our independence is now acknowledged; and the hopes of our enemies are blasted forever. Columbia is now seated in the forum of nations, and the empires of the world are amazed at the bright effulgence of her glory."

After contrasting the peaceful and prosperous condition of this country with the unsettled state of Europe, he refers to those revolutionary heroes who had died, and says, —

"With hearts penetrated by unutterable grief, we are at length constrained to ask, Where is our Washington? Where the hero who led us to victory? Where the man who gave us freedom? Where is he who headed our feeble army, when destruction threatened us, who came upon our enemies like the storms of winter, and scattered them like leaves before the Borean blast? Where, O my country, is thy political savior? — where, O humanity, thy favorite son?

"The solemnity of this assembly, the lamentations of the American people, will answer, 'Alas! he is no more — the mighty is fallen!'

"Yes, Americans, Washington is gone! — he is now consigned to dust, and sleeps in 'dull, cold marble'!

" The man who never felt a wound but when it
pierced his country — who never groaned but when
fair Freedom bled — is now forever silent.

" Wrapped in the shroud of death, the dark do-
minions of the grave long since received him, and
he rests in undisturbed repose. Vain were the attempt to express our loss ; vain the attempt to de-
scribe the feelings of our souls. Though months
have rolled away since his spirit left this terrestrial
orb, and sought the shining worlds on high, yet the
sad event is still remembered with increased sorrow.
The hoary-headed patriot of '76 still tells the mournful story to the listening infant, till the loss of his
country touches his heart, and patriotism fires his
breast. The aged matron still laments the loss of
the man beneath whose banners her husband has
fought, or her son fallen. At the name of Washington the sympathetic tear still glistens in the eye
of every youthful hero ; nor does the tender sigh
yet cease to heave in the fair bosom of Columbia's
daughters."

These extracts are sufficient as specimens of his
production on that occasion. Without indulging in
any elaborate criticism, we cannot refrain from saying, that the Saxon simplicity, and the terseness, for
which Mr. Webster in later years was so remarkable,
must have required on his part a great amount of
persevering labor.

In reading the above passages it must be remembered that we are not perusing the language of Hon. Mr. Webster, member of the Senate of the United States, but of Daniel Webster, an undergraduate of sixteen years of age, and member of the junior class at Dartmouth. As such, it is a credit to its author. To be enabled to appreciate it fully, we need the impassioned tones, the eloquent eye, the manly gesture of the orator; we need to be surrounded with the audience to whom it was delivered, — students, professors, revolutionary heroes, young men and maidens, old men and children, — who listened, smiled, and vociferously applauded the juvenile speaker. We need the soul-inspiring music, and all the excitement of the national anniversary. But without these, it is not difficult to discover gleams of that genius which broke forth with such dazzling splendor in the maturity of his years. It showed that the rich veins of the marble were there, and required only the labor of the sculptor to develop the forms of beauty, and give it the smoothness of surface of which it was capable. It was like a few grains from a mine which had not been worked, but which furnished conclusive evidence that an abundance of pure gold was there. One who remembers the occasion says, that the oration produced a great sensation.

On the 17th of April, 1801, Ephraim Simonds, a

member of the senior class in college, was prema-
turely cut down by death. It was deemed desirable
to make a religious improvement of the event, by
having a eulogy delivered by one of his classmates.
No one being so popular amongst the students as
Mr. Webster, he was chosen for that purpose. The
painful nature of the event, combined with the talents of the orator, drew out a large audience. The
house was completely crowded. After the preliminary services were over, Mr. Webster addressed the
assembled multitude in a dignified and solemn manner. In his exordium he referred to his deceased
fellow-student thus : —

" All of him that was mortal now lies in the char- ·
nels of yonder cemetery. By the grass that nods
over the mounds of Sumner, Merrill, and Cook,
now rests a fourth son of Dartmouth, constituting
another monument of man's mortality. The sun,
as it sinks to the ocean, plays its departing beams
on his tomb, but they reanimate him not. The cold
sod presses on his bosom ; his hands hang down in
weakness. The bird of the evening shouts a melancholy air on the poplar, but her voice is stillness
to his ears. While his pencil was drawing scenes
of future felicity, while his soul fluttered on the gay
breezes of hope, an unseen hand drew the curtain,
and shut him from our view."

The eulogy was listened to with deep emotion.

as was evinced by the tearful eyes of the assembly.

There is something peculiarly affecting in the death of a young man, while pursuing his course of education. The world, with all its posts of honor and usefulness, presents itself before him. He is stimulated by patriotism, philanthropy, and ambition, to qualify himself for some of its many attractive spheres of action. Surrounded by others in a similar condition, he is influenced, also, by a spirit of emulation. He is at the same time the object of deep parental solicitude, and, it may be, of the hopes of a large circle of interested relatives and friends. Whilst pressing on diligently to the goal which he has set before him, he is arrested by disease, and laid low in the grave ! His sun goes down whilst it is yet day. He is like a vessel richly freighted, which, whilst she is getting ready to leave the harbor for the broad ocean before her, strikes upon concealed rocks, and becomes a wreck ; or like a young cadet, who, whilst studying, in a military school, the science of war, and acquiring skill in military tactics, is suddenly cut down without ever seeing an actual engagement. Bright visions of future distinction, which had lured him on, have faded away, and the hopes of parents and friends are blasted forever. As no young man has any guaranty of immunity from a similar catastrophe, it

becomes important that all such make their mortality a prominent principle of action. Whilst preparing themselves to occupy honorable positions in
this life, they should remember the fleeting character of these distinctions, and not pursue them with
an ardor disproportionate to their real value. Much
less should they allow the present to shut out from
their view the distant future. As this life is preparatory to another, *farther on*, the highest wisdom consists in availing ourselves of the transient present,
in such a manner that we shall be well fitted for the
unchangeable future which awaits us. In doing
this, we shall be acting upon a principle similar to
that which governs us in our temporal affairs. The
student at college, the apprentice at a trade, the
merchant, the mariner, the professional man, — are
all acting with reference to the future. By industry, prudence, and economy, they are endeavoring
to acquire a competency, so that at no future period
shall they be reduced to want. They are providing
for the *time to come*. If this be a wise principle of
action with reference to our present existence, can
it be unwise in its application to that period of our
being which lies beyond the grave ? Why provide
for all the future which intervenes between the present moment and the period of our death, and entirely neglect preparation for that which is beyond
death ? Does not consistency require that, if we do

the one, we do the other also ?   In this respect does consistency mark your course, reader ?   With all your learning, see to it that you get that knowledge, the beginning of which is the fear of the Lord, and with all your accumulation fail not to lay up treasures in heaven, on which you may draw when all the riches of the earth shall have passed away.

CHAPTER VI.

DURING the last week in August, 1801, Mr. Webster was graduated. An unusual number of strangers visited Hanover at the time. They commenced coming early in the week, and continued to increase until the important day arrived when the senior students were to bid farewell to the classic shades of Dartmouth College, and scatter for the purpose of seeking their fortunes. At that time college commencement was regarded as an occasion of far greater importance, and it awakened an interest throughout a much wider extent of country than now. Gentlemen and ladies, arrayed in their gayest attire, poured into the town, some on horseback, single, and others on horseback in couples, the lady riding behind the gentleman on a pillion. Some came in a more imposing manner, with horse and

88

carriage, the harness newly cleansed, and the vehicle newly varnished; others felt it a privilege to ride in an open wagon on a temporary rough board seat; whilst, in some instances, groups of the young men and blooming damsels preferred to ride standing up in a large hay cart, which they decorated with evergreens and flowers for the purpose. It was a great gala day, and brought out people in vast numbers.

It was expected by the students that Webster on that occasion, would have had one of the most honorable parts. It is said that in their judgment he deserved the highest. But the faculty decided otherwise, and assigned him a subordinate position. His theme was "The recent Discoveries in Chemistry, especially those of Lavoisier," which were then recently made public.

The assignment of parts at commencement does not depend entirely on scholarship, or studious application. The professors take into consideration the whole deportment of the students, their attainments, their punctuality at prayers, at the recitations and the lectures, and their degree of observance of all the comparatively trivial rules which are laid down for the government of the college, and then graduate their honors according to the degree in which all the requirements of the faculty have been observed.

Mr. Lanman states that the valedictory on this occasion was conferred upon one "whose name has since passed into forgetfulness." If this be true, it shows that the college does not make the man. It is one thing to excel in the quiet retirement of classic cloisters, but quite a different thing to be a victorious champion in the great battle of life. It can seldom be predicted with accuracy from a young man's position in college what he will be when he enters upon the arena of the world. It is not unusual for some to startle their fellow-students with what appears to be the bright scintillations of promising genius, and to take the lead in the recitations of the class. As they pass on their luminous course, predictions of future eminence follow them — predictions which a few years are sufficient to show were uttered by those who had never received the gift of prophecy. After bidding farewell to their *alma mater*, their flame of precocious genius is soon quenched, and they are heard from no more. Whilst others, who exhibited no particular brilliancy during their collegiate course, but were simple, every-day, plodding students, by keeping up their industrious, studious habits in subsequent life, attain to great eminence. They make themselves both heard and widely felt.

There are, however, occasional instances where the boy shadows forth the man, when discreet and experienced observers can foretell, from early indications, approaching greatness, as from the stock and branching of the young tree can be predicted its character at maturity. Such was the case with Mr. Webster. Those who had been observant of his course whilst at Dartmouth looked forward with confidence to his success in future years.

Though he failed of obtaining the principal part at commencement, he secured in another respect the highest honors of the day.

There were at Dartmouth several literary and religious societies, composed of the members of the college, whose anniversaries were held during commencement week. Before each of these societies some member was chosen to deliver the annual address. The largest and most important of these societies was that of "The United Fraternity." To be chosen the orator for this association was, therefore, a higher distinction than to be selected as the speaker for either of the others. At the time he graduated, Mr. Webster was unanimously chosen to perform this honorable service. The public addresses which he had on previous occasions delivered had given him a high reputation. No other student could attract so large an audience. No other could have met the expectations which were awakened by the announcement that he was to be the orator of the day.

When the hour arrived for the commencement of the service, the house was filled. Mr. Webster sustained his previous reputation; he acquitted himself nobly. His subject was "The Influence of Opinion," and was we l adapted to develop the strength and peculiar qualities of his mind. One of the newspapers of the day said that "elegance of composition and propriety of delivery distinguished the performance," and that "a numerous audience manifested a high degree of satisfaction at the genius displayed."

After the honors of the college had been conferred, and Mr. Webster had received his diploma, properly signed and sealed, certifying that he had pursued the usual course of study, he invited a number of his classmates to go with him to a place of some retirement in the rear of the church. When they reached the place, Mr. Webster held up the diploma before them, and said, "My industry may make me a great man, but this miserable parchment cannot." He then deliberately tore it into pieces, and threw it away; then, bidding his fellow-students farewell, he mounted his horse, and set out for Elms Farm.

Although this act was not particularly amiable, it developed certain traits of character which were conspicuous in Mr. Webster's subsequent career. It exhibits the same moral courage, independence, and self-reliance which mark his whole course. It also

WEBSTER'S REPLY TO HAYNE, IN THE U. S. SENATE.

evinces his conviction that a public education is no substitute for future industry ; that to be a successful competitor in the great struggle for positions of influence and usefulness, there must be intense application.

When a young man imagines that the mere possession of a diploma will be a passport to posts of eminence ; that all before him is a smooth sea, over which, with his skiff of papyrus, he may safely float ; that from arduous toil and harassing anxiety he is now forever exempt, — he furnishes conclusive evidence that there are some lessons left for him to learn. Should he attempt to act upon his erroneous convictions, it will not be long before his own experience will convince him of his folly. Before such would we hold up the example of Mr. Webster. Rely not upon past efforts, nor upon present attainments. However great may have been former privileges, regard them only as so many facilities for future efforts, but by no means as a substitute for them. That you have been favored with an education beyond that of many of the community has increased your responsibilities above theirs. Having abilities to render yourself more useful than others, you are under obligation to exercise them. No man has a right to hide his light under a bushel. Unto whom soever much is given, of him is much required. You are stewards in respect of all the knowledge

and the talents which you possess, and it is required
of stewards that a man be found faithful. Industry
in the right direction may make you great and useful; without that your collegiate privileges will not.

After completing his college course, Mr. Webster
commenced the study of law with his father's old
neighbor, Mr. Thompson, who so significantly
laughed when Daniel was sent back to school during haying time, because he had blistered his hands.

Having been so great an expense to his father,
Webster now felt the importance of doing something
for his own support.

It was not long before he had the opportunity.
An academy had been recently founded at Fryeburg, in the State of Maine, and was in want of a
teacher. The trustees, who had received a favora
ble report of Mr. Webster, through Professor John
Smith, extended to him an invitation to become its
principal, with a salary of three hundred and fifty
dollars. This was cheerfully accepted, and the
young student was soon engaged in the perplexing
vocation of a schoolmaster. This new occupation
was advantageous to Mr. Webster in several respects.
Although its pecuniary benefit was not great, being
less than a common, unskilled day laborer now re-
ceives for the lowest kind of employment, it furnished him an opportunity of observing the various
phases of human nature, and studying the principles

of human action. His school was a little world in itself, filled with miniature men, possessing as great a diversity of dispositions as the same number of adults, susceptible of the same passions, and influenced by similar motives. He had, therefore, an opportunity of learning how to *move minds*, and thus of acquiring knowledge which would be of valuable service to him in future life. He taught the children, and the children taught him. It may not be easy to say who were the most benefited. He learned what he never could have acquired in the lecture room or college, nor from books. That school was to him an eminently instructive volume, of which each child was a page, from which might be received some important lesson. It was an intellectual and moral apparatus, by the skilful use of which he might try experiments and arrive at results, respecting the mind and heart, far more important than any conclusions which could be reached in either of the physical sciences.

It also served to develop himself. If there is any one employment that, more than another, will aid a man in learning what manner of spirit he is of, it is school teaching. This brings out the strong and the weak points of character. It calls into exercise innate elements, which, under other circumstances, might have remained dormant for years. Self-knowledge is in some respects the most difficult and the most important of all knowledge. Some advance may be made in it by self-examination. But who indulges in this exercise? — who deals faithfully with himself? — who is willing to drag his "secret sins" before the clear and steady gaze of his own contemplation? — who measures correctly the dimensions of his admitted defects? — who probes deeply the diseased spots? It is too painful — we shrink from it. Yet it is desirable that a person should know the evil tendencies of his character as well as the good — yea, far more so, for these evil tendencies he must specially guard and perseveringly resist, but the others he may let take care of themselves.

The employment of Mr. Webster as a teacher rendered him essential aid in detecting those elements of character in himself which needed restraint, and those which required cultivation. It also gave him an opportunity of reviewing the studies which he pursued in college, and discovering in what branches he was defective, the possession of which was essential to a good teacher.

Those who have ever had a near view of Mr. Webster will not forget his large, lustrous, dark eyes. These constituted a prominent feature in the early part of his life. Persons who were acquainted with him in college refer particularly to them. He was once questioned by Mr. Lanman as to his per sonal appearance, when officiating as principal of Fryeburg Academy. His reply was, " *Long, slender, pale, and all eyes;* indeed, I went by the name of ' *All eyes* ' the country round." The significant appropriateness of this appellation cannot be denied.

When Mr. Webster found that his duties as teacher did not require the whole of his time, he sought additional employment. He had gone to Fryeburg from pecuniary considerations, and was willing to engage in any honorable occupation which promised an addition to his limited resources. Fortunately the office of Assistant Register of Deeds was vacant, and he was invited to perform its duties. This he accepted, which gave him employment for all his leisure hours. His duty was to copy deeds into a large folio volume, for which he received twenty-five cents each. There are at the present time, in the office at Fryeburg, two large, bound volumes of manuscript deeds, in his neat and elegant handwriting. He has been heard to say, that " The *ache* is not yet out of those fingers which so much writing caused them." It, however, brought him in a little income, which he devoted to the *education of his brother.*

The old adage that " Where there's a will there's a way," was illustrated in this part of Mr. Webster's history. He was willing to work. He was not particular about the kind of labor in which he engaged.

provided it was reputable. When the offer of being a copyist of deeds was tendered, he did not decline because of its sedentary character or limited
compensation. If he could not earn much, he was
content with little. He was determined to do something, and something was presented. This was a
much wiser course than though he had lost much
time in waiting for something easier or more profitable to offer. There are some individuals desiring
employment, who, unless they can obtain a berth
which is satisfactory in all respects, prefer to remain
unoccupied. If the time which they lose in looking
for a desirable situation was devoted to such engage-
ments as offer, they might find enough to do — and
of that which would afford them a reasonable compensation   This was Mr. Webster's course, and it
is worthy of imitation.

A short time since, Mr. Webster's son, accompanied by a friend, visited Fryeburg. As might be
expected, they were attracted to the office of the
registry of deeds, that they might see the evidences
of his industry in early life. These evidences were
furnished in the two huge folio volumes to which
we have referred. After examining these with interest, and being astonished that so great an amount
of labor could be performed, in addition to the arduous service of superintending a school, they turned
their attention to the record of the trustees of the

academy, and there discovered satisfactory proof that this extra employment did not interfere with the faithful performance of his duties as teacher. This proof consisted in "a most respectful and affectionate vote of thanks and good will to Mr. Webster, when he took leave of the employment," which they found upon the record. This evinced the high estimation in which he was held by the trustees of the academy.

There was one thing which they did not see, which, if it had been in their power, they would have examined with great gratification — and that was, *the old school house* in which Mr. Webster taught. This had been consumed to ashes many years before. Such is the affectionate reverence in which Mr. Webster is held, that the owner of the land on which the academy stood, Mr. Robert J. Bradley, would never permit any other edifice to be erected upon the spot, and he is determined that none shall be so long as he has control of the lot. This devoted friendship was cherished also by his father, who had probably previously owned the estate. The non-occupation of that site, therefore, is evidence of refined sentiment. The silence of its desolation is eloquently expressive of the ardent attachment of its owner to him who, many years before, commenced his self-support by there keeping school.

Whilst at Fryeburg, Mr. Webster managed, also,

to secure time for the reading of law, and commit
ting to memory important passages from the
speeches of distinguished orators.   Being unable
to buy, he was obliged to borrow Blackstone's' Com-
mentaries, which he then read for the first time.
He also committed to memory the celebrated speech
of Mr. Ames, on the British treaty, which he greatly
admired.

CHAPTER VII.

It is evident from the facts which we have narrated in the preceding pages, that whilst Mr. Webster was at Fryeburg, he must have been "diligent in business;" yet he did not deny himself relaxation. Rural sports were as attractive to him then as at any future period. He was particularly fond of angling, and as there was a delightful sheet of water not far from the village, he availed himself of the opportunity of Waltonizing whenever the mood was upon him. This beautiful gem of a lake was once the scene of a dreadful tragedy, from which it derives its name of Lovewell's Pond, and by which, also, its shores have been consecrated as classic ground.

This tragedy was as follows: In 1725, such frequent barbarous murders were committed by the Indians upon the inhabitants of the exposed frontier,

101

that the General Court of Massachusetts offered a reward of one hundred pounds for every Indian's scalp. This furnished a strong temptation for the brave and the covetous among the whites to engage in a murderous crusade against the lawless aborigines. An Indian chief by the name of Paugus, whose tribe were called the *Pequakets*, resided on territory which is now embraced within the limits of Fryeburg. This chief was terrible to the English, and they were determined, if possible, to extirpate him and his tribe. Captain Lovewell of Dunstable undertook this hazardous service, with thirty four men. He came upon Paugus with eighty warriors, and the battle commenced by the whites' killing one of the Indians, who was returning from hunting. Both parties fought with great fury. "The Indians roaring, and yelling, and howling like wolves, barking like dogs, and making all sorts of hideous noises; the English frequently shouting and huzzaing, as they did after the first round. At one time Captain Wyman is confident they were got to powwowing by their striking on the ground, and other odd motions; but at length Wyman crept up towards them, and firing amongst them, shot the chief powwow, and broke up their meeting.* "

It was a most desperate engagement. Sixty of the Indians and twenty English were slain,† amongst

* Rev. Mr. Symmes.   † Drake's Indians.

whom were both Lovewell and Paugus. The English, however, were conquerors.

Two poems were written, commemorative of the fight, in which all the prominent circumstances were narrated. As many of our readers will be more interested in these poetic descriptions than a mere statement in prose, we insert one below,* of which

* LOVEWELL'S FIGHT.

Of worthy Captain Lovewell I purpose now to sing,
How valiantly he served his country and his king;
He and his valiant soldiers did range the woods full wide,
And hardships they endured to quell the Indian's pride.

'Twas nigh unto Pigwacket, on the eighth day of May,
They spied a rebel Indian, soon after break of day;
He on a bank was walking, upon a neck of land,
Which leads into a pond, as we're made to understand.

Our men resolved to have him, and travelled two miles round,
Until they met the Indian, who boldly stood his ground.
Then speaks up Captain Lovewell, "Take you good heed,'
        says he;
' This rogue is to decoy us, I very plainly see.

" The Indians lie in ambush, in some place nigh at hand,
In order to surround us, upon this neck of land;
Therefore we'll march in order, and each man leave his pack,
That we may briskly fight them when they shall us attack.'

They came unto this Indian, who did them thus defy;
As soon as they came nigh him, two guns he did let fly,
Which wounded Captain Lovewell, and likewise one man more
But when this rogue was running, they laid him in his gore.

Mr. S. G. Drake, of Indian notoriety, says, according to tradition, it was composed the same year of

Then having scalped the Indian, they went back to the spot,
Where they had laid their packs down, but there they found
    them not ;
For the Indians having spied them, when they them down did lay,
Did seize them for their plunder, and carry them away.

These rebels lay in ambush, this very place hard by,
So that an English soldier did one of them espy,
And cried out, " There's an Indian ! " with that they started out,
As fiercely as old lions, and hideously did shout.

With that our valiant English all gave a loud hurrah,
To show the rebel Indians they feared them not a straw ;
So now the fight began, as fiercely as could be ;
The Indians ran up to them, but soon were forced to flee.

Then spake up Captain Lovewell, when first the fight began,
" Fight on my valiant heroes ! you see they fall like rain."
For, as we are informed, the Indians were so thick,
A man could scarcely fire a gun, and not some of them hit.

Then did the rebels try their best our soldiers to surround,
But they could not accomplish it, because there was a pond,
To which our men retreated, and covered all the rear ;
The rogues were forced to flee them, although they skulked for fear.

Two logs there were behind them, that close together lay ;
Without being discovered they could not get away ;
Therefore our valiant English, they travelled in a row,
And at a handsome distance, as they were wont to go.

'Twas ten o'clock in the morning when first the fight begun,
And fiercely did continue till the setting of the sun.

the fight, " and for several years afterward was the
most beloved song in all New England."

Excepting that the Indians, some hours before 'twas night,
Drew off into the bushes, and ceased a while to fight ; —

But soon again returned in fierce and furious mood,
Shouting as in the morning, but yet not half so loud ;
For, as we are informed, so thick and fast they fell,
Scarce twenty of their number at night did get home well.

And that our valiant English till midnight there did stay,
To see whether the rebels would have another fray ;
But they no more returning, they made off towards their home,
And brought away their wounded, as far as they could come.

Of all our valiant English, there were but thirty-four,
And of the rebel Indians, there were about fourscore ;
And sixteen of our English did safely home return ;
The rest were killed and wounded, for which we all must mourn

Our worthy Captain Lovewell among them there did die ;
They killed Lieutenant Robbins, and wounded good young
      Frye,
Who was our English chaplain ; he many Indians slew,
And some of them he scalped, when bullets round him flew.

Young Fullam, too, I'll mention, because he fought so well ;
Endeavoring to save a man, a sacrifice he fell ;
And yet our valiant Englishmen in fight were ne'er dismayed,
But still they kept their motion, and Wyman captain made —

Who shot the old chief Paugus, which did the foe defeat,
Then set his men in order, and brought off the retreat ;
And braving many dangers and hardships in the way,
They safe arrived at Dunstable, the thirteenth day of May.

On this pond, the scene of such dreadful carnage, Mr. Webster was accustomed to sail, and from its clear, cool waters, to draw such unfortunate fish as were too free in their liberties with his bait.

Nature requires relaxation after effort, whether that effort be of a mental or physical character. This principle **Mr. Webster** always recognized. There can be no doubt that an individual who is accustomed to literary pursuits will accomplish more by a judicious alternation of hard study with pleasant recreation than though the latter be entirely neglected. The mind will not endure a constant draught upon its powers. It needs rest for the recovery of its elasticity and vigor; there should be a shutting up of books, a relinquishment of problems, a cessation of mental effort, a throwing open of the door, and an escape of the mind, into unfettered freedom, in order to secure that perfect repose which, after great effort, nature needs. This was Mr. Webster's course; hence his frequent fishing, gunning, and other rural excursions.

In September, 1802, he relinquished his school, and returned home, having made some acquisitions, both of a pecuniary and intellectual character.

Mr. Webster had now passed that important crisis in a young man's life, which, in most cases, gives character to his whole history, namely, the choice of a profession. He had decided in favor of the law.

It may not have been impossible that the proximity of Mr Thompson's office to Webster's residence contributed much towards this decision. It was so easy for him to slip in there, look over the law books, hear conversation upon legal questions, and thus have his taste for such pursuits awakened, that that office, in all probability, assisted 'in turning his mind in this direction. It was, therefore, a providential circumstance that these influences existed, and rendered it so easy for him to enter upon the study of this science. Under another combination of circumstances, he might as easily have been induced to enter upon some other pursuit, and then the world would have lost the benefit of his great talents as a statesman.

After leaving Fryeburg, arrangements were made for Mr. Webster to resume the study of law in the office of Mr. Thompson. This gentleman, though well acquainted with his profession, adopted a mode of instruction with his students which was not popular with them at the time, and which they did not approve in subsequent life. He was accustomed to give them the most difficult books first. On this principle he put into Mr. Webster's hand Coke upon Littleton. It was a hard work for a student to master ; but Mr. Webster, nothing daunted by its difficulties, pored over it six hours daily. Although at first it was like entering a primeval forest, where the

8

traveller has to cut his own way, he believed that, by patient and persevering industry, he would in time see light on the other side ; that by mastering each difficulty as it occurred, as the woodman fells trees singly, he would, before long, successfully cut his way through them all. Still he always regarded that method of introducing a boy to the study of the science as a mistake.. He has expressed himself clearly upon this subject in the following language : —

"A boy of twenty, with no previous knowledge of such subjects, cannot understand Coke. It is folly to set him upon such an author. There are propositions in Coke so abstract, and distinctions so nice, and doctrines embracing so many distinctions and qualifications, that it requires an effort not only of a mature mind, but of a mind both strong and mature, to understand him. Why disgust and discourage a young man by telling him that he must break into his profession through such a wall as this."

He soon got upon other books, which he studied with greater pleasure. Besides the attention which at that period he paid to law, he also found time to read Hume's History of England, Shakspeare's plays, and the Latin classics. Such was the proficiency which he made in his profession, that, during the second year of his studies, he was quite a sound lawyer. General Lyman says, "When clients came for advice, he [Mr. Webster] heard, with Mr. Thomp-

son, a full statement of the facts, and thereupon he
again and again, wrote out opinions, which **Mr**
Thompson, on perusal, adopted, signed, and delivered as his own. He also displayed great tact in
conducting the lawsuits pending, in marshalling the
testimony, and in eliciting from witnesses the facts
to be proved on the trials. Many men, not profound
lawyers, have become eminent in their profession,
and have paved their way to wealth, by their skill in
conducting a cause before it was brought to trial."
It is evident that, as when in college, so when studying law, Mr. Webster *minded his business.* This was
one great secret of his success. Let American
youth remember this. At this period, Mr. Webster
was not a one-idea man ; he did not devote himself
exclusively to the law. He read history and poetry,
and went on excursions of pleasure ; but with all
these other employments, he still *minded his business ;*
he kept his recreations within due limits. The great
difficulty with not a few young men is, that, in order
to find time for amusement, they neglect important
duties ; they have not acquired that discipline, or
formed such habits, that they can, with authority, say
to the attractive pleasures of life, " Thus far shall
ye come, but no farther." Being governed more by
their own passions than by established principle, it
becomes extremely easy for them to throw aside
their books, or abandon their employment, whenever

an opportunity occurs for the enjoyment of some
agreeable amusement. Such may reach mediocrity
but there is little probability of their attaining to a
high degree of excellence, in any profession.

An incident is related which shows that, whilst
Mr. Webster was a student of law, he developed the
same promptness, decision, and energy, which were
such conspicuous traits of character, after he had
entered upon public life.

A Captain Kimball had entered into contract to
open a turnpike. This contract was based upon
subscriptions for the object by gentlemen of wealth,
a number of whom were residents of Portsmouth.
After the work had been in progress for some time,
these gentlemen were called upon to pay their subscriptions : *they refused*. This at once created em
barrassment. It was known from the first that
money would be greatly needed, and their subscriptions had been looked to as the source whence it was
to be obtained. When, therefore, they declined ful-
filling their own obligations, perplexing disappoint-
ment was the result. Captain Kimball regarded
himself as greatly wronged, and applied to Mr.
Thompson for legal advice. Mr. Thompson immediately addressed the delinquent subscribers letters,
earnestly urging them to pay their subscriptions.
The letters were unheeded. He then sent to them
his oldest student, Mr. Noyes, to remonstrate per-

sonally with them, but with no better success When the failure of Mr. Noyes's visit was made known to Mr. Webster, he said, "Let me go to Portsmouth; *I will bring you the money.*" Mr. Thompson concluded to grant his request. Having obtained the necessary authority, he set out; he drove his horse with such speed that when he reached Portsmouth it was covered with foam. Without loss of time he called on some of the subscribers, and sent word to others, that he had come to receive their subscriptions, and the money must be paid. He then despatched a messenger to the sheriff of the county, asking his presence immediately. He next sat down to a table, and very coolly commenced making out writs for the apprehension of every subscriber. When the delinquents understood the bearing of these preparatory measures, they became alarmed. They saw they had a hard customer to deal with, and proposed that they have a conversation upon the subject; it was granted. When the company assembled, Mr. Webster again stated to them the object of his visit, and the grounds on which he made his demands, and then, in a manner in which dignity, courtesy, and authority were blended together, he coolly informed them that he would wait until a certain hour (which he specified) for the money and that if by that time it was not paid, he would put the writs into the hands of tho sheriff, and have *them all immediately arrested.* This produced the desired effect. At that time imprisonment for debt had not been abolished in New Hampshire. The delinquents, therefore, **knew what** they had to expect if they persisted in their refusal. The appointed hour **arrived ; Mr.** Webster's horse **was** ready for him to mount ; the sheriff **was** on hand to receive and execute the writs ; all things **were ready** for the apprehension of the guilty. **They now saw that the** subject could **neither be trifled** with nor postponed ; **the** crisis was reached ; **the money was** paid over to **Mr. Webster** as fast as he could count and receipt for **it.** Having by **his** energy and tact accomplished his object, he returned home and reported his success, to the astonishment **and** great gratification of those immediately concerned.

When any enterprise which will involve a **con**siderable outlay **of** money is projected, **it is a** common practice to receive **subscriptions for that object,** and then commence the **work** *before those subscriptions are paid.* It follows, **as a necessary** consequence, that **if any of those subscriptions are withdrawn,** those persons **who** are practically engaged **in the** enterprise will be subjected to embarrassments to the full extent of **the** amount thus withdrawn, and will either have **to** raise the funds from some other source, or else **create** a debt ; when, if they could have foreseen **this** result, they would have done nothing towards **the** execution of the project until the funds subscribed had been paid in. This is unjust: when a person subscribes towards a railroad, a canal, a church, or any benevolent cause, he is in honor and in justice bound to pay that subscription. He should regard it as sacred as a promissory note ; it has all the elements of such note ; it is a promise to pay a certain specified sum for a certain specified object, and a man has no more right to refuse payment than he has to refuse the payment of any other pecuniary obligation. This obligation is, if possible, strengthened, when, *by virtue of his promise,* the object for which he subscribed is commenced, and debts contracted. He encouraged the enterprise, and he is justly held responsible to the full extent of that encouragement.

These remarks are made because it is sometimes the case, that individuals who have subscribed towards an object afterwards change their minds, and refuse payment. Such instances have occurred in benevolent and religious objects. As there is no danger that the law will be resorted to in order to enforce payment of such subscriptions, they can be repudiated with impunity. But let it be remembered that such conduct is disreputable, and by every man of honor is condemned.

To every young person, whose eye may fall upon this page, would we say, Never subscribe towards an object unless you are convinced of its importance , but *when* *your* *promise* *is* *once* *given*, *sacredly* *redeem* *it*.

After remaining in Mr. Thompson's office two years, Mr. Webster desired a change, where he could acquire a knowledge of other departments of law besides those which were pursued in the office of Mr. T.   For this purpose he removed, in July, 1804, to Boston, and placed himself under the instruction of that distinguished counsellor, Hon. Christopher Gore.   His opportunities for acquiring broader views of his profession were here enjoyed. He had access to an extensive and valuable library, and the privilege of attending the sessions of the Supreme and Circuit Courts, where questions of the gravest importance were discussed by the most learned and eminent lawyers.   He was not idle while attending these sessions; but, with pen in hand, he carefully watched the opinions of the learned judges, and made them matters of record. He continued in Mr. Gore's office nearly a year, where he studied with diligence the principles of the common and municipal law, the laws of nations, and the science of special pleading.   In addition to his laborious professional studies, he managed to secure time for a wide range of general reading.

Being now regarded as qualified for admittance to the bar, his teacher, Hon. Mr. Gore, introduced him to court, and made a motion that he be admitted to practice. It is greatly to the credit of Mr. Webster that he had produced such a favorable impression upon his teacher, that when he made this motion for the admission of his young student to the bar, he accompanied it with some highly commendatory remarks. Mr. Everett says, " He dwelt with emphasis on the remarkable attainments and uncommon promise of his pupil, and closed with a prediction of his future eminence."

It is sometimes the case, that the general estimation in which an individual is held is far higher than that which he enjoys amongst his more intimate associates. In respect to such,

" 'Tis distance lends enchantment to the view ; "

and this enchantment is dispelled in proportion as the distance diminishes. With Mr. Webster it was otherwise. Those who knew him best cherished for him the highest esteem. Admiration for his talents and acquirements increased in proportion to one's familiar acquaintance with him.

By his admission to the bar he was fairly launched upon the world. Where the winds and waves of fickle fortune would carry him, — what shoals and quicksands he would escape, or against what rocks he would dash, — how little did he know ! He doubtless cherished certain aspirations, and probably had a course of life marked out in his own mind, which he expected to pursue. It would be interesting, if we could learn what these expectations were, to see in what respects they were met, and wherein he was disappointed by the events of his subsequent life.

CHAPTER VIII.

Has a Clerkship offered him. — Declines it. — His Father displeased. — Pays his Father's Debts. — His filial Attachment. — Some treat their Parents unkindly. — Mr. Webster's first Plea. — He astonishes every body. — Controlling Witnesses. — The Detection. — The Character of his Arguments. — Webster and Mason. — " Import a young Earthquake."

MR. WEBSTER's stamina of character was severely tested by an incident which occurred about the time that he was admitted to the bar. His father at that period was one of the judges of the County Court in New Hampshire, and though not a man of liberal education, he was highly respected for his strong common sense, his sterling integrity, and his quick perception of the particular points at issue in the various cases of litigation that came before him.

The clerkship of that court, which was then vacant, was tendered to his son. In some respects it was a desirable position. Mr. March, in his spirited account of the affair, says, —

" The office was worth fifteen hundred dollars per annum, which was in those days, and in that neighborhood, a competency — or rather absolute wealth. Mr. Webster himself considered it a great prize, and was eager to accept it. He weighed the ques-

117

tion in his mind. On the one side he saw immediate comfort; on the other, at the best, a doubtful struggle. By its acceptance he made sure his own good condition, and, what was nearer to his heart, that of his family. By its refusal he condemned both himself and them to an uncertain and probably harassing future. Whatever . aspirations he might have cherished of professional distinction, he was willing cheerfully to relinquish, to promote the immediate welfare of those he held most dear.

"But Mr. Gore peremptorily and vehemently interposed his dissent. He urged every argument against the purpose. He exposed its absurdity and its inconsequence. He appealed to the ambition of his pupil — once a clerk, he said, he always would be a clerk — there would be no step upwards. He attacked him, too, on the side of his family affection, telling him that he would be far more able to gratify his friends from his professional labors than in the clerkship. 'Go on,' he said, 'and finish your studies; you are poor enough, but there are greater evils than poverty; live on no man's favor; what bread you do eat, let it be the bread of independence. Pursue your profession; make yourself useful to your friends, and a little formidable to your enemies, and you have nothing to fear.'

"Diverted from his design by arguments like these, it still remained to Mr. Webster to acquaint his father with his determination, and satisfy him of its propriety. He felt this would be no easy task, as his father had set his heart so much upon the office ; but he determined to go home immediately, and give him in full the reasons of his conduct.

"It was midwinter, and he looked round for a country sleigh, — for stage coaches at that time were things unknown in the centre of New Hampshire, — and finding one that had come down to market, he took passage therein, and in two or three days was set down at his father's door. (The same journey is made now in four hours by steam.) It was evening when he arrived. I have heard him tell the story of the interview. His father was sitting before the fire, and received him with manifest joy. He looked feebler than he had ever appeared, but his countenance lighted up on seeing his *clerk* stand before him in good health and spirits. He lost no time in alluding to the great appointment — said how spontaneously it had been made — how kindly the chief justice proposed it — with what unanimity all assented, &c. During this speech it can be well imagined how embarrassed Mr. Webster felt, compelled, as he thought, from a conviction of duty, to disappoint his father's sanguine expectations. Nevertheless he commanded his countenance and voice, so as to reply in a sufficiently assured manner. He spoke gayly about the office ; expressed his great

obligation to their honors, and his intention to write
them a most respectful letter — if he could have
consented to record any body's judgments, he should
have been proud to have recorded their honors', &c.
He proceeded in this strain till his father exhibited
signs of amazement, it having occurred to him,
finally, that his son might all the while be serious.
'Do you intend to decline this office ? ' he said at
length. 'Most certainly,' replied his son ; 'I cannot think of doing otherwise. I mean to use my
tongue in the courts, not my pen — to be an actor,
not a register of other men's actions.'

" For a moment Judge Webster seemed angry.
He rocked his chair slightly, a flash went over his
eye, softened by age, but even then black as jet ;
but it immediately disappeared, and his countenance
regained its usual serenity. Parental love and partiality could not, after all, but have been gratified
with the son's devotion to an honorable and distinguished profession, and seeming confidence of success in it. 'Well, my son,' said Judge Webster,
finally, 'your mother has always said that you would
come to something or nothing — she was not sure
which. I think you are now about settling that
doubt for her.' The judge never afterwards spoke
to his son on the subject."

The account of this interesting event, as given
by General Lyman, in his " Memorials," contains

some additional facts, which ought not to be omitted here. We give them in his own language : —

"The difficulty of satisfying his father that the course he had resolved to pursue was the best, now arose in his mind. To aid Mr. Webster and his brother Ezekiel in obtaining an education, their father had resorted to borrowing money, and there was a mortgage for it to be paid. A debt was a sore encumbrance, more so in those days than at the present time. Ezekiel Webster was doing his best, and was then in Boston, teaching a select school, to earn money towards discharging that mortgage. Edward Everett, since so highly distinguished, was, by the by, one of his pupils. The desire to relieve his excellent father from all pecuniary responsibility on his account, now that he had the power to do it, was of course very great ; but the sacrifice of his future prospects was in the scale weighing against the clerkship and its emoluments. In this dilemma, his friend, Mr. Rufus Green Emery, — be it mentioned to the credit of his fame, — on hearing what the difficulty was, put gold into Mr. Webster's pocket, and sent him home to see his father personally on the subject. I have heard Mr. Webster tell the story, and it is a pity that I should mar it. On arriving at home, he found his father sitting in his easy chair, not knowing one word of what had passed in Boston, or of his intentions as to the clerkship. He received his son

affectionately, and with a manner that seemed to say,
Our anxieties are now ended.' His father lost no
time in telling him how ' readily and how handsomely
his 'request had been complied with. I had not,'
said he to his son, ' more than mentioned it before
it was done.' 'His eyes,' said Mr. Webster, ' were
brimful of the tears of gratitude, as he told it to
me.'

" 'Judge,' said he, ' of my father's disappoint-
ment and manifest vexation, when I told him I must
resign the office. He could not at first believe his
own ears. He of course wanted to know the reason.
I told him I could do better! I laid down the gold
to pay the mortgage, and all the debts on my own
and my brother's account. I wrote a letter thanking
the judges for the honor they had done me, and
most respectfully resigned the office to which they
had appointed me. Thereupon I hastened back to
Boston, where the court was sitting at which I was
licensed to practise. I then for the first time held
up my hand and took the oaths of office.' "

Mr. Gore, for the advice which he then gave, and
Mr. Emery, for his removal of pecuniary embarrassment, merit the thanks of the whole country. That
advice and assistance essentially aided in making
Mr. Webster the great American statesman that he
was. If he had accepted a clerkship in court, he
might have died an incumbent of the office. He

would no doubt have been punctual, faithful, and industrious. He would have been a model clerk, but he probably would never have moved senates, nor negotiated treaties. Here again we may see the intervention of divine Providence. Why did he happen to be a student of Mr. Gore ? Why did that appointment of clerk reach him before he had left his studies and returned home ? Why did Mr. Gore cherish the views and give the advice he did ? Why, too, did Mr. Emery step forward and remove the strongest temptation to acceptance out of the way ? Why this combination of circumstances, except that a kind Providence interfered ? Had Mr. Gore's advice been the opposite of what it was, or had Mr. Emery been indifferent to the subject, who can tell what would have been the results ?

After his admission to the bar, Mr. Webster went to Amherst, in New Hampshire, where his father was holding court, and accompanied him home. It had been his intention to open an office in Portsmouth. That being a large town, and possessing some foreign commerce, it presented a promising field for practice. But filial duty prevented. The infirmities of age were now creeping upon his father His brother Ezekiel was absent, and, it being desirable that one of the sons should be near the homestead, Mr. Webster relinquished the idea of settling down at Portsmouth, and opened an office in Bos-

9

cawen, near the residence of his father, and commenced practice as a country lawyer. This was
not an encouraging field, but the reason of its selection developed a beautiful trait in Mr. Webster's
character. His attachment to his parents was strong
and tender. Although he was now of age, and had
a right to go where he chose to seek his fortune,
yet his filial affection prompted him to forego that
right, and to settle down near the homestead, that
he might cheer the hearts of his parents in their decline of life, and be at hand to render any service
which they might need. No one denies that *young*
children ought to love and reverence their parents ;
but, alas! examples are too numerous of those who
seem to act as if, when they reached their majority,
they outgrew filial obligation — as if from that period their language to their parents was, "It is a
gift by whatsoever thou mightest be profited of
me " — it is a gratuity, a favor, and not the dis
charge of an obligation. Their parents are neglected, their feelings set at nought, their wishes dis-
regarded. They are considered and treated as an
encumbrance; their death approaches too slowly ;
and when it occurs, their *affectionate* children are
relieved of a great burden. With Mr. Webster an
opposite class of feelings predominated. Affectionate attachment to his parents was a prominent trait
of his character. For their comfort he sacrificed

for the time being, whatever emoluments he might
have received in a larger but more distant field of
professional labor. He has said in a letter, " My
opening an office in Boscawen was that I might be
near him," i. e., his father. The sign which he then
hung out, with " D. WEBSTER, Attorney," upon it,
is said to be still in existence. By some of his admirers it would be highly prized, and treasured as a
sacred memento of him whose name it bears.

Down to the time that Mr. Webster commenced
the practice of law, he was a thin and sickly-looking
young man. His appearance in this respect was
very different from what it was in the later periods
of his life. It was not at all adapted to prepossess
his hearers in his favor, if we except his eloquent
eye and expressive countenance. His physical constitution was by no means the appropriate represen-
tation of his mental character. Under his outward
weakness was concealed great intellectual strength,
of which the following incident furnishes a striking
illustration. The first case which he ever plead
before a jury was of a civil character. It was one
of considerable interest to the parties concerned,
and created no small amount of public excitement.
Colonel William Webster, a remote relative of Daniel, was the sheriff of the county. After the trial
was over, the sheriff stated to a friend, that he
thought, " when Mr. Webster rose, that he would

not stand up long; I was ashamed to see so lean and feeble a young man come into court bearing the name of Webster; but he astonished every body with his eloquence, learning, and powers of reasoning."

He exhibited such a familiar acquaintance with the principles of law, such skill in marshalling his facts, such ingenuity in stating them in the most faforable manner for his client, and such power of analysis and argument, that from this time he was never in want of business. Notwithstanding his thin and meagre appearance, he produced a decidedly favorable effect upon those who heard him; his strength was mental, not physical. Under a feeble exterior he concealed the elements of an intellectual giant. This first plea of Mr. Webster was heard by his father, and it was the only one to which he had the pleasure to listen. The old gentleman, who, as we have said, was then one of the judges of New Hampshire, died soon after, but not before he had heard predictions of his son's professional success, and had seen sufficient evidence of his genius to justify their probability.

It was an interesting moment to them both, when the son, after having spent years in his collegiate and legal studies, was, by this first professional essay, to show his father the " first fruits " of his long and laborious training. It was doubtless to Mr. Webster a pleasant recollection all his subsequent life, that his father was favored with the opportunity of hearing him at least once before he died ; and the father must have accounted it no common privilege that he was permitted to witness this early effort of a beloved son in the new and difficult sphere which he had chosen.

This first argument of Mr. Webster before a jury is said to have been founded upon a tavern bill amounting only to about twenty-four dollars. It was an encouraging circumstance that the verdict rendered was in favor of his client, the jury awarding him seventeen dollars.

Another case which he conducted at the same term of court he lost, the jury returning a verdict for an amount somewhat larger than the above against his client. This was in 1805 ; the next year he exhibited in a greater degree his abilities as a counsellor and a pleader. At that time an argument which he delivered made such an impression upon a lad of some ten or twelve years of age, that though nearly fifty years have passed away, he remembers the effect which it produced upon those who heard it, and the strong commendation which it received from them. " I recollect," he writes, " with perfect distinctness, the sensation which the speech produced upon the multitude.* There was a great throng there, and they were loud in his praise As

* B. F. French, Esq.

soon as the adjournment **took** place, the lawyers dropped into my father's office, and there the whole bearing of the young man underwent a discussion. It was agreed on all hands that he had made an **ex-**traordinary effort, when ———— ————, by way of **ac-**counting for it, said, 'Ah, Webster has been **study-**ing in Boston, and has got **a** knack of talk-ing ; **but let him** take it rough and tumble a while here in the bush, and we shall see whether he will do so much better than other folks.' "

After he had fairly entered into practice, **Mr. Web-**ster rose rapidly in his profession.

"It is stated in the Life of Chief Justice Smith, that in 1806, before **Mr.** Webster had been admitted as **a** counsellor in the Superior Court, — and of course before he was entitled to address the jury, — being engaged as attorney in a cause of no great pecuniary importance, but of some interest and some intricacy, he was ' allowed to examine the witnesses, and briefly to state his case, both upon the law and the facts. Having done this, he handed his brief to Mr. Wilson, the senior counsel, for the full argument of the matter. But the chief justice had noticed him, and on leaving the court house said to a member of the bar, that *he* **had** *never before met such a young man as that.*' " *

It is often the case that clients endeavor to con-

* Joel Parker, LL. **D.**

trol the evidence which their witnesses are to give in their case. Sometimes this interference is unduly **excessive, and recoils** with tremendous force upon him who has practised it. Such an instance occurred during the **early** part of Mr. Webster's career. As he occasionally narrated it for the amusement of his friends, **we** will give it **in** his own words : —

"Soon **after** commencing the practice of my profession at Portsmouth, **I was** waited on by an old acquaintance of my father's, resident in an adjacent county, who wished to engage my professional ser-**vices.** Some years previous, he had rented a farm, with the clear understanding that he could purchase **it,** after the expiration of his lease, for one thousand dollars. Finding the said farm productive, he soon determined to **own it ; and, as** he laid aside money for the purchase, **he** was prompted **to** improve what he felt certain he would **possess. But his** landlord, finding the property greatly increased **in** value, cool-**ly** refused to receive the one thousand dollars, when in due time it **was** presented ; and when his extortionate demand of double that sum was refused, he at once brought an action of ejectment. The man had but the one thousand dollars, and an unblemished reputation ; yet I willingly undertook his case.

"**Tho** opening argument of the plaintiff's attorney **left me little ground for** hope. **He** stated that **he** could prove that my client hired the farm, but there was not a word in the lease about the sale, nor was there a word spoken about the sale when the lease was signed, as he should prove by a witness. In short, his was a clear case, and I left the court room at dinner time with feeble hopes of success. By chance, I sat at table next a newly-commissioned militia officer, and a brother lawyer began to joke him about his lack of martial knowledge. 'Indeed,' he jocosely remarked, 'you should write down the orders, and get old W. to beat them into your sconce, as I saw him this morning, with a paper in his hand, teaching something to young M. in the court-house entry.'

"Can it be, I thought, that old W., the plaintiff in the case, was instructing young M., who was his reliable witness?

"After dinner the court was reopened, and M. was put on the stand. He was examined by the plaintiff's counsel, and certainly told a clear, plain story, repudiating all knowledge of any agreement to sell. When he had concluded, the opposite counsel, with a triumphant glance, turned to me, and asked me if I was satisfied. 'Not quite,' I replied.

"I had noticed a piece of paper protruding from M.'s pocket, and hastily approaching him, I seized it before he had the least idea of my intention. 'Now,' I asked, 'tell me if this paper does not detail the story you have so clearly told, and is it not false ? ' The witness hung his head with shame; and when the paper was found to be what I had supposed, and in the very handwriting of old W., he lost his case at once. Nay, there was such a storm of indignation against him, that he soon removed to the west.

"Years afterwards, visiting New Hampshire, I was the guest of my professional brethren at a public dinner; and towards the close of the festivities, I was asked if I would solve a great doubt by answering a question. 'Certainly.' 'Well, then, Mr. Webster, we have often wondered how you knew what was in M.'s pocket.' "

During his practice of the law, Mr. Webster had many cases of great importance committed to him; he very early took a high stand in his profession; he became the acknowledged leader of the bar; he was opposed by the most distinguished lawyers of which the country could boast, yet always maintained an honorable position among them. He was so simple in the statement of his propositions, so forcible in his argument, so clear in his illustrations, there was such an honest, common-sense straightforwardness about him, which prompted him to march, without any circuitousness, directly to his object, that he never failed of producing a deep impression upon the mind of a jury; he addressed them as men capable of understanding an argument, as men not to be borne away by exciting appeals to their passions, but to be moved only by a calm, clear, and logical address to their judgment. Such addresses he gave them. He reasoned to convince, and was successful.

To show how highly his legal abilities and powers of oratory were estimated by his contemporaries, the following anecdotes are given : —

Mr. Webster practised law in Portsmouth nearly nine years, and during that time one of his best friends, and also his most prominent competitor, was the distinguished Jeremiah Mason. On one occasion a gentleman called upon the former for the purpose of securing his services in a lawsuit ; but Mr. Webster was compelled to decline the engagement, but recommended his client to Mr. Mason.

" What do you think of the abilities of Mr. Mason ? " said the gentleman.

" I think him second to no man in the country," replied Mr. Webster.

The gentleman called upon Mr. Mason, and having secured his promise of assistance, he thought he would gratify his curiosity, and therefore questioned him as to his opinion of Mr. Webster. " He's the very devil, in any case whatsoever," replied Mr. Mason ; " and if he's against you, I beg to be excused."

On another occasion, a gentleman of Nantucket

accosted a friend by saying, " I have wished to see you for some days, for I am in trouble, and wish your friendly advice." " What can it be ? " replied the other. " Why, I have a lawsuit, and *Webster* is opposed to me : what shall I do ? " " My advice is," was the answer, " that your only chance of escape is, to send to Smyrna and *import a young earthquake.*"

The extravagant character of these replies was prompted by the high opinion which was entertained of his commanding talents.

CHAPTER IX.

ALTHOUGH it does not fall in with the object of this volume to give an account of the various cases which Mr. Webster conducted through court, yet there was one so peculiar, so exciting, so full of tragic interest, so illustrative of various conflicting moral principles, and which furnished an occasion for one of his most impressive pleas, that we are unwilling to omit its recital here.

In the city of Salem, in the State of Massachusetts, is a house which is pointed out to strangers as a place where an act of thrilling atrocity was a few years since committed. It is in Essex Street, near Newbury Street, with a garden extending in the rear towards Brown Street, this latter street being parallel with Essex Street.*

---

* The facts connected with this murder are derived from Hon Benjamin Merrill's Narrative.

In this house resided a very wealthy, retired merchant of Salem, eighty-two years of age, whose name was Joseph White, Esq. He had neither wife nor children; his family consisted of himself, his housekeeper, Mrs. Beckford, who was also his niece, and two servants, a man and woman.

Early on the morning of the 7th of April, 1830, his servant man discovered that the back window of the east parlor was open, and that a plank was resting against it, as if to furnish assistance in entering the house. His suspicions being excited that robbers had visited them, he immediately went to the parlor, but found all the furniture in its proper place, and no evidence of any person having been there. After informing the maid servant of his discoveries, he visited Mr. White's chamber. As he entered the back door of the old gentleman's chamber, he noticed that the other door, which opened into the front entry, was not closed. He now approached the bed, and there beheld a sight which explained all the previous discoveries. The bedclothes were drenched with blood, and *Mr. White was dead.* The servant was horror stricken; he and the maid servant were the only other persons in the house. Mrs. Beckford was on a visit to her daughter's at Wenham. The alarm was instantly given. A crowd collected; the coroner and physicians were sent for, who, upon examination, found thirteen deep stabs on the body, made by some sharp instrument, and a heavy blow on the left temple ; although the skin was not broken, yet the skull was fractured. Gold coin and silver, to a considerable amount, were in his chamber, yet none of it was taken. With the exception of the bed, the room presented its usual appearance. Nothing was missed from the house, although it contained much silver plate, which might have been stolen, if plunder had been the object of the assassin.

This deliberate, dreadful tragedy, committed, as it was, upon a well-known, respectable citizen, in a densely-settled part of the town, produced a deep and wide-spread excitement. So apparently motive-less was the deed, that all felt exposed to similar danger. Neglected windows and doors were made more secure throughout the town. Watch dogs were obtained, and firearms were bought to increase the safety of the people. No one felt secure. Who was the criminal, or for what purpose the horrid deed had been committed, no one knew. The excitement was the more intense from the impenetrable mystery which enshrouded the whole subject. In addition to large rewards being offered by the heirs of Mr. White, by the town, and by the governor of the state, for the detection of the murderer, the citizens appointed a committee of vigilance, twenty-seven in number, who were to employ every means in their power to discover the perpetrator of this dreadful crime.

During the excitement of the community upon the subject, it was published in the newspapers, that a daring attempt at highway robbery had been made on Joseph J. Knapp, Jr., and John Francis Knapp, in Wenham, on the evening of the 27th of April. They stated before the committee of investigation, that when near Wenham Pond, on their way to Salem in a chaise, three men approached them, one of whom stopped the horse by seizing the bridle ; the others then approached, one on each side, and attempted to seize a trunk which was in the chaise. The Knapps of course resisted. Frank made a thrust at one of them with a sword cane, and Joseph struck the other in the face with the but-end of the whip. This decided resistance compelled them to retreat. After giving a loud whistle, as if it were a signal to their accomplices, they fled, being pursued a short distance, but unsuccessfully, by Frank Knapp. Their size, appearance, and dress were described with considerable minuteness. In the account of this occurrence, as stated in the Salem papers at the time, it was remarked that the gentlemen thus attacked were " well known, and no one questioned their respectability or veracity." This event increased the excitement. It appeared as if there were a gang of robbers

prowling about in the community, ready to plunder
or murder, as opportunity offered. For a number
of weeks not the slightest incident occurred which
served to furnish the faintest hope of discovering
the guilty parties. Finally, the committee of vigilance learned that a prisoner of the name of Hatch,
confined in New Bedford jail, could make disclosures that might be of great service to them. He
was visited, the nature of his disclosures ascertained, and they were regarded as so important, that
when the grand jury met, Hatch was brought in
chains from New Bedford to give his testimony before them. His relation was, that several months
before the murder was perpetrated, he had frequently heard Richard Crowninshield, Jr., of Danvers, say that he intended to destroy the life of Mr.
White. Crowninshield was a young man of bad
character; he is described as " of dark and reserved
deportment, temperate and wicked, daring and wary,
subtle and obdurate, of great adroitness, boldness,
and self-command. He had for several years fre-
quented the haunts of vice in Salem, and though he
was often spoken of as a dangerous man, his person
was known to few, for he never walked the streets
by daylight. Among his few associates he was a
leader and a despot." *

* Hon. Benjamin Merrill.

On the testimony of Hatch, Richard Crownin-shield, Jr., was arrested on the 2d of May, and committed to prison to await his trial. As the evidence of Hatch did not seem sufficient to convict Crown-inshield, the committee of vigilance continued their efforts to discover more convincing proofs. George, the brother of Richard, was also arrested.

On the 15th of May, Captain Joseph J. Knapp, a respectable merchant and shipmaster of Salem, and father of the young men who were said to have been attacked by robbers in Wenham, received, through the mail, the following letter : —

Charles Grant, Jr., to Joseph J. Knapp.

" BELFAST, May 12, 1830.

" DEAR SIR : I have taken the pen at this time to address an utter stranger, and, strange as it may seem to you, it is for the purpose of requesting the loan of three hundred and fifty dollars, for which I can give you no security but my word, and in this case consider this to be sufficient. My call for money at this time is pressing, or I would not trouble you ; but with that sum, I have the prospect of turning it to so much advantage, as to be able to refund it, with interest, in the course of six months. At all events, I think it will be for your interest to comply with my request, and that imme-diately — that is, not put off any longer than you

10

receive this. Then sit down and enclose me the
money with as much despatch as possible, for your
own interest. This, sir, is my advice ; and if you.
do not comply with it, the short period between now
and November will convince you that you have denied a request, the granting of which will never in-
jure you, the refusal of which will ruin you. Are
you surprised at this assertion ? Rest assured that I
make it, reserving to myself the reasons, and a series
of facts which are founded on such a bottom which
will bid defiance to property or quality. It is useless for me to enter into a discussion of facts which
must inevitably harrow up your soul. No, I will
merely tell you that I am acquainted with your
brother Franklin, and also the business that he was
transacting for you on the 2d of April last; and
that I think that you was very extravagant in giving
one thousand dollars to the person that would execute the business for you. But you know best about
that. You see that such things will leak out. To
conclude, sir, I will inform you that there is a gentleman of my acquaintance in Salem, that will observe that you do not leave town before the first of
June, giving you sufficient time between now and
then to comply with my request ; and if I do not
receive a line from you, together with the above
sum, before the 22d of this month, I shall wait upon
you with an assistant. I have said enough to con-

vince you of my knowledge, and merely inform you that you can, when you answer, be as brief as possible. Direct yours to

"CHARLES GRANT, Jr., of Prospect,
"Maine."

This remarkable epistle was entirely unintelligible to Captain Knapp. He was acquainted with no Charles Grant, Jr.; neither did he know a single person in the town of Belfast, Maine. It seemed to be a letter to obtain "hush money" from him, with reference to some crime he had committed, with which the writer was acquainted. As Mr. Knapp had been guilty of no misdemeanor, neither was he willing to have money extorted from him by vague and mysterious threats. As, however, the letter appeared to be serious, and not intended as a joke, Captain Knapp consulted his son, Nathaniel Phippen Knapp, a young lawyer, to see if he could explain it. To him it was as inexplicable as to his father. They then went over to Wenham, and showed the letter to Joseph J. Knapp, Jr., and John Francis Knapp, two other sons of the captain, who were then residing with Mrs. Beckford, to whom we have already referred as the niece and housekeeper of the murdered Mr. White. J. J. Knapp, Jr., read the letter, said it contained a lot of trash, and advised them to hand it to the committee of vigilance.

It will be found in the sequel that this was a very important letter, and J. J. Knapp, Jr., ought to have known this.   It is perfectly amazing that he should have advised their placing it at the disposal of the committee.   Still this was done, and the committee of vigilance obtained possession of the letter.

The next day the committee of vigilance received the following : —

" GENTLEMEN OF THE COMMITTEE OF VIGILANCE : Hearing that you have taken up four young men, on suspicion of being concerned in the murder of Mr. White, I think it time to inform you that Stephen White came to me one night, and told me, if I would *remove* the old gentleman, he would give me five thousand dollars.   He said he was afraid he would alter his will if he lived any longer.   I told him I would do it, but I was afraid to go into the house.   He said he would go in with me ; that he would try to get into the house in the evening, and open the window ; would then go home and go to bed, and meet me again about eleven.   I found him, and we both went into his chamber.   I struck him on his head with a heavy piece of lead, and then stabbed him with a dirk ; he made the finishing strokes with another.   He promised to send me the money next evening, and has not sent it yet, which is the reason I mention this.

" Yours, &c.,   GRANT."

This was directed to the Hon. Gideon Barstow, Salem. At the same time Hon. Stephen White received the following, directed to him through the post office at Salem : —

"LYNN, May 12, 1830.

"Mr. White will send the five thousand dollars, or a part of it, before to-morrow night, or suffer the painful consequences. N. CLAXTON, 4th."

The murdered gentleman was uncle to this Mr. White, and had bequeathed to him the largest part of his property.

Both of these letters were put into the Salem post office on Sunday evening, May 16th.

After mature deliberation, the committee of vigilance came to the conclusion that the letter signed "Charles Grant, Jr.," might, if followed up, result in important disclosures. They therefore sent a judicious messenger to Prospect, in Maine. This messenger visited the postmaster there, confidentially communicated to him his business, and then sent for an officer. All things being ready, he deposited a letter directed to Charles Grant, Jr., in the post office, and then remained there, waiting for Grant to call for it. It was not long before a man came and asked for Grant's letter, when the officer stepped forward and arrested him. Upon examination, it appeared that his real name was Palmer, and that

he resided in the neighboring town of Belfast. Although he was a young man of genteel appearance,
his character was bad. He had served out a term
in the state's prison of Maine. When informed of
the reason of his arrest, and of the suspicious character of his letter to Knapp, he saw that he might
justly be suspected of being accessory to the murder, and therefore, to clear himself, he revealed all
that he knew of the affair. He stated that he had
been a companion of R. Crowninshield, Jr., and
George Crowninshield; that he had spent a portion
of the winter with them in Danvers and Salem, under the assumed name of Carr — part of this time
he had been concealed in their father's house in
Danvers. He further stated that, on the 2d of April,
he saw, from the windows of the house, Frank
Knapp, and a young man named Allen, ride up to
the house; that George and Frank walked away
together, and Richard and Allen together. When
they returned, George told Richard that Frank
wished them to kill Mr. White, and that J. J.
Knapp, Jr., would pay one thousand dollars for the
job. He also said that various methods of executing the murder were proposed, and that they wanted him to be concerned in it, but that he declined.
George said that the housekeeper would be absent
at the time; that the design of J. J. Knapp, Jr., in
projecting the murder, was to destroy Mr. White's

will, because it gave the largest amount of the property to Stephen White; that the will was first to be
destroyed by J. J. Knapp, Jr., and this he could do
by obtaining from the housekeeper the key of an
iron chest in which it was kept. He also stated,
that Frank Knapp called again the same day, in a
chaise, and rode off again with Richard Crowuin-
shield, and that he, Palmer, spent the night, on
which the murder was committed, at the Halfway
House, in Lynn.

The important information communicated by
Palmer was at once transmitted to the committee
of vigilance, and resulted in the apprehension of
Joseph J. Knapp, Jr., and John Francis Knapp,
both of whom were young shipmasters, and of respectable connections. On the third day of their
imprisonment, Joseph J. Knapp, Jr., made a full
confession, and acknowledged that he originated the
plot for the murder. He had married the daughter
of Mrs. Beckford, the housekeeper, and knew that
by his will Mr. White had bequeathed to Mrs. Beckford a legacy of fifteen thousand dollars; but, being
informed that if Mr. White died without leaving a
will, Mrs. B.'s portion would be nearly two hundred
thousand dollars, he projected the plan of destroying Mr. White's will, and then, before he could discover the loss and make another, to put the old
man himself to death. He revealed his plan to his

brother, and Frank agreed to find some one to act the assassin. After this Frank opened the matter to Richard Crowninshield, Jr., who said he would commit the murder for a thousand dollars. Joseph agreed to pay him that amount, and, as he had access to the house at all hours, it was arranged that he should unfasten the back window, so as to give Richard easy entrance to the premises.

He also confessed that, four days before the murder, he stole the will from the iron chest, took it to Wenham in his chaise box, where he had covered it with hay, kept it till after the murder, and then burned it. After he had abstracted the will, he informed Crowninshield that all was ready. On the evening of the same day he met Crowninshield in the centre of Salem Common. Crowninshield had with him a bludgeon and a dagger, with which he intended to commit the deed. Knapp asked him if he intended to do it that night. He replied, he thought not; he did not feel like it. It being ascertained that on Sunday, the 4th of April, Mr. White had gone to take tea with a relative in Chestnut Street, Crowninshield intended to assassinate him with a dirk on his way home, but very fortunately Mr. White returned home before dark. Being disappointed at this time, they next arranged for the tragedy on the 6th of April. Knapp was by some means to induce Mrs. Beckford to spend the night with her daughter at Wenham. This being accomplished, Crowninshield and Frank Knapp met about ten o'clock on the appointed evening, in Brown Street, in the rear of Mr. White's garden, where they could observe the movements in the house, and see at what time Mr. White and his two servants went to bed. Crowninshield requested Frank Knapp to leave him and go home. Frank did so, but shortly after returned to the same spot. In the mean time, however, Crowninshield walked down Brown Street, through Newbury Street, into Essex Street, on which the house fronts, entered a gate, and walked round to the back part of the house. He there found a plank, which he placed against the house; he then climbed to a window, raised it, entered the house, ascended the stairs, noiselessly opened the door of Mr. White's sleeping chamber, cautiously approached the bedside, and saw that the old gentleman was sound asleep. He now raised a heavy bludgeon, which he had carried with him for the purpose, and inflicted a mortal blow. To be certain of accomplishing his fiendish design, he gave the body of the old man many stabs with a sharp dirk or poniard, and then deliberately felt of his pulse, to see that it had ceased to beat! The dreadful deed being accomplished, he retired from the chamber, left the house, hurr'ed back into Brown Street, where he met Frank, who was there waiting to learn the particulars of the deed. Crowninshield ran down Howard Street, concealed the club under the steps of the Orthodox Church, and then went home to Danvers. Joseph also confessed that the story of the attack upon himself and brother, on the 27th of April, in Wenham, was entirely false — it was originated by themselves. He also confessed that he was the author of the two mysterious letters, signed " Grant," and " N. Claxton, 4th."

Not long after the murder, Crowninshield, in company with Frank, went over to Wenham to obtain the one thousand dollars which were to be the wages of his iniquity. He obtained, however, at that time, only one hundred five franc pieces. Crowninshield gave a particular account of all the circumstances connected with his commission of the crime, told where he concealed the bludgeon, and expressed his sorrow that Joseph Knapp had not obtained the right will — that if he had known there was another, he would have gotten it. Joseph sent Frank to find the club, and in some way to destroy it ; but he was unsuccessful in discovering where it was. When Joseph, however, made his confession, he gave particular information of its place of concealment, and there it was found. It was a heavy hickory bludgeon, nearly two feet long, with a large, egg-shaped head. This head had been hollowed out, and then filled with lead. Its surface was smooth, and the handle well adapted for a firm grasp. Crowninshield stated that he turned it in a lathe.

After Crowninshield's arrest and imprisonment, he manifested great indifference — a kind of stoical composure ; but when he was informed of Knapp's arrest, his knees smote together, the sweat stood in large drops upon his brow, and he was so far overcome that he fell back upon his bunk.

When Palmer, alias Charles Grant, Jr., was brought to Salem jail, Crowninshield saw him as he left the carriage and was led by the officers into the prison. Palmer happened to be placed in a cell directly under the one which was occupied by Crowninshield. One day, when several of the members of the committee of vigilance were in Palmer's cell, conversing with him, their attention was arrested by a loud whistle overhead. Presently a voice called, " Palmer ! Palmer ! " Soon a slip of paper and a piece of pencil were seen dangling in the air over their heads, and gradually descending lower and lower. When they came within reach, they were received by the committee. Upon examining the paper, it was found to contain two lines of poetry, in order that, if Palmer was really there, he should signify it by writing two more lines, and make the verse complete. Palmer shrunk away int-the corner of his cell, and was afterwards transferred to another part of the prison. He stood in great fear of Crowninshield.

Upon information received from Palmer, Crowninshield's barn was searched on the 12th of June, and a quantity of stolen goods was found concealed there. Crowninshield, finding that the evidences of his guilt were clustering thickly around him, and being determined, as he had frequently said, not to suffer a public, ignominious punishment, committed suicide by hanging himself with a handkerchief to the bars of his cell.

The trial of the Knapps and of George Crowninshield was commenced in the Supreme Court, at Salem, on the 20th of July, a special term of the court having been held for that purpose. It continued, with a few days' recess, till the 20th of August. John Francis Knapp was indicted as principal, the other two as accessories. Selman and Chase, who had been arrested and retained in prison, on suspicion of being concerned in the murder, were discharged.

John Francis Knapp was tried first. The law required that the principal criminal, in a case of murder, must first be found guilty before any of the accessories could be put upon trial. His counsel were Messrs. Franklin Dexter and William H. Gardiner, gentlemen of distinguished reputation in their profession.

When Joseph J. Knapp, Jr., — who, upon the promise of favor from the government, had made a full confession of the whole plot and of the manner of its execution, — was called upon the stand, he refused to testify. He would make no acknowledgments before the court and jury. The government, therefore, withdrew its pledge of favor; and he was left to the regular course of law, after giving, as he had done by his confession, a clew to sufficient evidence for the conviction of himself and his brother.

The trials proceeded. Both the Knapps were convicted. George Crowninshield proved that he was somewhere else at the time of the murder, and so was cleared.

Mr. Webster had been requested by the officers of government to assist them in conducting the case.

After the evidence was all in, and Mr. Franklin Dexter had pleaded in defence of John F. Knapp, Mr. Webster arose, and addressed the jury in behalf of the government. In the early part of his plea he gave utterance to the following thrilling description of the manner in which the deed was committed. As we read it, we can almost see the assassin engaged in his work of death. His analysis of the operations of conscience is also powerful.

"Gentlemen, it is a most extraordinary case; in some respects it has hardly a precedent any where, certainly none in our New England history. This bloody drama exhibited no suddenly excited, ungovernable rage. The actors in it were not surprised by any lion-like temptation springing upon their virtue, and overcoming it, before resistance could begin. Nor did they do the deed to glut savage vengeance, or satiate long-settled and deadly hate. It was a cool, calculating, money-making murder. It was all 'hire and salary, not revenge.' It was the weighing of money against life; the counting out of so many pieces of silver against so many ounces of blood.

"An aged man, without an enemy in the world, in his own house, in his own bed, is made the victim of a butcherly murder, for mere pay. Truly here is a new lesson for painters and poets. Whoever shall hereafter draw the portrait of murder, if he will show it as it has been exhibited, where such example was last to have been looked for, — in the very bosom of our New England society, — let him not give it the grim visage of Moloch, the brow knitted by revenge, the face black with settled hate, and the blood-shot eye emitting livid fires of malice: let him draw, rather, a decorous, smoothfaced, bloodless demon; a picture in repose, rather than in action; not so much an example of human nature in its depravity, and in its paroxysms of crime, as an infernal being, a fiend, in the ordinary display and development of his character.

" The deed was executed with a degree of self-possession and steadiness equal to the wickedness with which it was planned. The circumstances now clearly in evidence spread out the whole scene before us. Deep sleep had fallen on the destined victim and on all beneath his roof. A healthful old man, to whom sleep was sweet, the first sound slumbers of the night held him in their soft, but strong embrace ; the assassin enters, through the window already prepared, into an unoccupied apartment ; with noiseless foot he paces the lonely hall, half lighted by the moon ; he winds up the ascent of the stairs, and reaches the door of the chamber ; of this he moves the lock, by soft and continued pressure, till it turns on its hinges without noise ; and he enters and beholds his victim before him ; the room is uncommonly open to the admission of light ; the face of the innocent sleeper is turned from the murderer, and the beams of the moon, resting on the gray locks of his aged temple, show him where to strike, the fatal blow is given, and the victim passes, without a struggle or a motion, from.the repose of sleep to the repose of death.

" It is the assassin's purpose to make sure work, and he plies the dagger, though it is obvious that life has been destroyed by the blow of the bludgeon; he even raises the aged arm, that he may not fail in his aim at the heart, and replaces it again over the wounds of the poniard. To finish the picture, he explores the wrist for the pulse; he feels for it, and ascertains that it beats no longer: it is accomplished; the deed is done; he retreats, retraces his steps to the window, passes out through it as he came in, and escapes. He has done the murder; no eye has seen him, no ear has heard him; the secret is his own, and it is safe.

"Ah, gentlemen, that was a dreadful mistake; such a secret can be safe nowhere. The whole creation of God has neither nook nor corner where the guilty can bestow it, and say it is safe. Not to speak of that eye which pierces through all disguises, and beholds every thing as in the splendor of noon, such secrets of guilt are never safe from detection, even by men.

"True it is, generally speaking, that 'murder will out;' true it is, that Providence hath so ordained, and doth so govern things, that those who break the great law of Heaven by shedding man's blood seldom succeed in avoiding discovery; especially in a case exciting so much attention as this, discovery must come, and will come, sooner or later. A thousand eyes turn at once to explore every man, every thing, every circumstance, connected with the time and place ; a thousand ears catch every whisper ; a thousand excited minds intensely dwell on the scene, shedding all their light, and ready to kindle the slightest circumstance into a blaze of discovery. Meantime, the guilty soul cannot keep its own secret ; it is false to itself ; or, rather, it feels an irresistible impulse of conscience to be true to itself ; it labors under its guilty possession, and knows not what to do with it. The human heart was not made for the residence of such an inhabitant ; it finds itself preyed on by a torment which it dares not to acknowledge to God or man. A vulture is devouring it, and it can ask no sympathy or assistance either from heaven or earth. The secret which the murderer possesses soon comes to possess him ; and like the evil spirits of which we read, it overcomes him, and leads him whithersoever it will ; he feels it beating at his heart, rising to his throat, and demanding disclosure ; he thinks the whole world sees it in his face, reads it in his eyes, and almost hears its workings in the very silence of his thoughts ; it has become his master ; it betrays his discretion, it breaks down his courage, it conquers his prudence. When suspicions from without begin to embarrass him, and the net of circumstances to entangle him, the fatal secret struggles with still greater violence to burst forth ; it must be confessed, it will be confessed ; there is no refuge

11

from confession but suicide, and suicide is confes
sion."

As a specimen of Mr. Webster's directness, clearness, and logical power, when arguing a case to a
jury, we give the following extract from the same
plea.   The counsel for the defendant had spoken of
the evidence against the prisoner as "circumstantial
stuff."   Of this phrase Mr. Webster makes effective
use ; it was a powerful weapon furnished him by his
adversary.

"And now, gentlemen, in examining this evidence,
let us begin at the beginning, and see first what we
know independent of the disputed testimony.   This
is a case of circumstantial evidence ; and these circumstances, we think, are full and satisfactory.
The case mainly depends upon them, and it is common that offences of this kind must be proved in
this way.   Midnight assassins take no witnesses ;
the evidence of the facts relied on has been somewhat sneeringly denominated by the learned counsel
'circumstantial stuff ;' but it is not such stuff as
dreams are made of.   Why does he not rend this
stuff?   Why does he not scatter it to the winds ?
He dismisses it a little too summarily.   It shall
be my business to examine this stuff, and try its
cohesion.

"The letter from Palmer, at Belfast — is that no
more than flimsy stuff ?

" The fabricated letters from Knapp to the committee, and to Mr. White — are they nothing but stuff ?

" The circumstance, that the housekeeper was away at the time the murder was committed, as it was agreed she should be — is that, too, a useless piece of the same stuff?

" The facts that the key of the chamber door was taken out and secreted ; that the window was unbarred and unbolted — are these to be so slightly and so easily disposed of ?

" It is necessary, gentlemen, to settle now, at the commencement, the great question of a conspiracy. If there was none, or the defendant was not a party, then there is no evidence here to convict him. If there was a conspiracy, and he is proved to have been a party, then these two facts have a strong bearing on others, and all the great points of inquiry.

" The defendant's counsel take no distinct ground, as I have already said, on this point, either to admit or to deny. They choose to confine themselves to a hypothetical mode of speech. They say, supposing there was a conspiracy, *non sequitur* that the prisoner is guilty as principal. Be it so. But still, if there was a conspiracy, and if he was a conspirator, and helped to plan the murder, this may shed much light on the evidence which goes to charge him with the execution of that plan.

"We mean to make out the conspiracy, and that the defendant was a party to it, and then to draw all just inferences from these facts.

"Let me ask your attention, then, in the first place, to those appearances, on the morning after the murder, which have a tendency to show that it was done in pursuance of a preconcerted plan of operation. What are they? A man was found murdered in his bed; no stranger had done the deed — no one unacquainted with the house had done it; it was apparent that somebody within had opened, and that somebody without had entered; there had obviously and certainly been concert and coöperation; the inmates of the house were not alarmed when the murder was perpetrated; the assassin had entered without any riot or any violence; he had found the way prepared before him. The house had been previously opened: the window was unbarred from within, and its fastening unscrewed; there was a lock on the door of the chamber in which Mr. White slept, but the key was gone; it had been taken away and secreted; the footsteps of the murderer were visible, out doors, tending towards the window; the plank by which he entered the window still remained; the road he pursued had been thus prepared for him. The victim was slain, and the murderer had escaped; every thing indicated that somebody within had coöperated with somebody without. Every thing proclaimed that some of the inmates, or somebody having access to the house, had had a hand in the murder. On the face of the circumstances, it was apparent, therefore, that this was a premeditated, concerted murder ; that there had been a conspiracy to commit it. Who, then, were the conspirators ? If not found out, we are still groping in the dark, and the whole tragedy is still a mystery.

"If the Knapps and the Crowninshields were not the conspirators in this murder, then there is a whole set of conspirators not yet discovered. Because, independent of the testimony of Palmer and Leighton, independent of all disputed evidence, we know, from uncontroverted facts, that this murder was, and must have been, the result of concert and coöperation between two or more. We know it was not done without plan and deliberation ; we see that whoever entered the house to strike the blow was favored and aided by some one who had been previously in the house, without suspicion, and who had prepared the way. This is concert, this is coöperation, this is conspiracy. If the Knapps and the Crowninshields, then, were not the conspirators, who were ? Joseph Knapp had a motive to desire the death of Mr. White, and that motive has been shown. He was connected by marriage with the family of Mr. White ; his wife was the daughter of Mrs. Beckford, who was the only child of a sister of the deceased. The deceased was more than eighty years old, and had no children; his only heirs were nephews and nieces. He was supposed to be possessed of a very large fortune, which would have descended, by law, to his several nephews and nieces in equal shares; or, if there was a will, then according to the will. But as he had but two branches of heirs, the children of his brother, Henry White, and of Mrs. Beckford, each of these branches, according to the common idea, would have shared one half of his property. This popular idea is not legally correct; but it is common, and very probably entertained by the parties. According to this idea, Mrs. Beckford, on Mr. White's death without a will, would have been entitled to one half of his ample fortune; and Joseph Knapp had married one of her three children. There was a will, and this will gave the bulk of the property to others; and we learn from Palmer that one part of the design was to destroy the will before the murder was committed. There had been a previous will, and that previous will was known or believed to have been more favorable than the other to the Beckford family, so that by destroying the last will, and destroying the life of the testator at the same time, either the first and more favorable will would be set up, or the deceased would have no will, which would be, as was supposed, still more favorable; but the conspirators not having succeeded in obtaining and destroying the last will, though they accomplished the murder, —that will being found in existence, and safe, and that will bequeathing the mass of property to others, — it seemed at the time impossible for Joseph Knapp, as for any one else, indeed, but the principal devisee, to have any motive which should lead to the murder. The key which unlocks the whole mystery is the knowledge of the intention of the conspirators to steal the will. This is derived from Palmer, and it explains all; it solves the whole marvel; it shows the motive which actuated those against whom there is much evidence, but who, without the knowledge of this intention, were not seen to have had a motive. This intention is proved, as I have said, by Palmer; and it is so congruous with all the rest of the case, it agrees so well with all facts and circumstances, that no man could well withhold his belief, though the facts were stated by a still less credible witness. If one desirous of opening a lock turns over and tries a bunch of keys till he finds one that will open it, he naturally supposes he has found *the* key of *that* lock. So, in explaining circumstances of evidence which are apparently irreconcilable or unaccountable, if a fact be suggested, which at once accounts for all, and reconciles all, by whomsoever it may be stated, it is still difficult not to believe that such fact is the true fact belonging to the case. In this respect Palmer's testimony is singularly confirmed. If it were false, his ingenuity could not furnish us such clear exposition of strange-appearing circumstances. Some truth not before known can alone do that."

"The acts of the parties themselves furnish strong presumption of their guilt. What was done on the receipt of the letter from Maine? This letter was signed by Charles Grant, Jr., a person not known to either of the Knapps, nor was it known to them that any other person beside the Crowninshields knew of the conspiracy. This letter, by the accidental omission of the word *Jr.*, fell into the hands of the father, when intended for the son; the father carried it to Wenham, where both the sons were. They both read it. Fix your eye steadily on this part of the *circumstantial stuff*, which is in the case, and see what can be made of it. This was shown to the two brothers on Saturday, the 15th of May; neither of them knew Palmer, and if they had known him, they could not know him to have been the writer of this letter. It was mysterious to them how any one at Belfast could have had knowledge of this affair. Their conscious guilt prevented due circumspection. They did not see the bearing of its publication. They advised their father to carry it to the committee of vigilance, and it was so carried. On the Sunday following, Joseph began to think there might be something in it. Perhaps in the mean time, he had seen one of the Crownin shields. He was apprehensive that they might be sus pected ; he was anxious to turn attention from their family. What course did he adopt to effect this ? He addressed one letter, with a false name, to Mr. White, and another to the committee, and to complete the climax of his folly, he signed the letter addressed to the committee " Grant," the same name as that which was signed to the letter received from Belfast. It was in the knowledge of the committee that no person but the Knapps had seen this letter from Belfast, and that no other person knew its signature ; it must have been, therefore, irresistibly plain to them that one of the Knapps was the writer of the letter received by the committee, charging the murder on Mr. White. Add to this the fact of its having been dated at Lynn, and mailed at Salem four days after it was dated, and who could doubt respecting it ? Have you ever read or known of folly equal to this ? Can you conceive of crime more odious and abominable ? Merely to explain the apparent mysteries of the letter from Palmer, they excite the basest suspicions against a man, whom, if they were innocent, they had no reason to believe guilty, and whom, if they were guilty, they most certainly knew to be innocent. Could they have adopted a more direct method of exposing their own infamy ? The letter to the committee has intrinsic marks of a knowledge of this transaction. It tells the *time*. and the *manner* in which the murder was committed.

Every line speaks the writer's condemnation.   In
attempting to divert attention from his family, and
to charge the guilt upon another, he indelibly fixes
it upon himself.

"Joseph Knapp requested Allen to put these letters
into the post office, because, said he, "I wish to nip
this silly affair in the bud." If this were not the
order of an overruling Providence, I should say
that it was the silliest piece of folly that was ever
practised.   Mark the destiny of crime!   It is ever
obliged to resort to such subterfuges; it trembles in
the broad light; it betrays itself in seeking concealment.   He alone walks safely that walks uprightly.
Who for a moment can read these letters and doubt
of Joseph Knapp's guilt?   The constitution of nature is made to inform against him.   There is no
corner dark enough to conceal him.   There is no
turnpike road broad enough or smooth enough for
a man so guilty to walk in without stumbling.   Every
step proclaims his secret to every passenger.   His
own acts come out to fix his guilt.   In attempting to
charge another with his own crime, he writes his
own confession.   To do away the effect of Palmer's
letter, signed 'Grant,' he writes a letter himself, and
affixes to it the name of Grant.   He writes in a
disguised hand.   But how could it happen that the
same Grant should be in Salem that was at Belfast?
This has brought the whole thing out.   Evidently

he did it, because he has adopted the same style. Evidently he did it, because he speaks of the price of blood, and of other circumstances connected with the murder, that no one but a conspirator could have known."

These specimens are sufficient to show that the plea of Mr. Webster, on that occasion, was one of great power. It produced a thrilling effect. The prisoners were convicted, and it cannot be doubted that Mr. Webster's argument contributed in no small degree to secure that result. The excitement on the occasion was intense. The court house was crowded, yet the stillness of the tomb reigned there during the delivery of this plea; for it was believed that life or death was depending upon the words which were being uttered.

Before leaving this trial, in which Mr. Webster occupied so important a part, it will be proper to call special attention to a few of the more extraordinary features of the astounding deed, for the commission of which the defendants were convicted and executed.

It was remarkable that the evidence which first directed public attention to the guilty parties should have grown out of casual remarks which dropped from one of the criminals some months before the murder was committed, which remarks were revealed to the committee of vigilance by Hatch, who was

himself an imprisoned convict, in a distant part of
the state, at the time of the perpetration of the
bloody deed, and who, therefore, must have been
ignorant of all the circumstances connected with it.

Little did Crowninshield imagine, when he expressed, in the hearing of Hatch, his determination
to put Mr. White to death, that he was furnishing
evidence which would lead to his own apprehension
for the murder. Yet so it was. And herein are
we furnished with an illustration of the truth, that
the wicked are insnared by the words of their
mouth, and that, in the providence of God, a criminal is allowed to weave a net for his own entangle-
ment, in which, after the commission of his crime,
he is effectually caught.

It was very extraordinary that the letter signed
"Charles Grant, Jr.," from Belfast, Maine, should
have reached J. J. Knapp, the father, instead of J.
J. Knapp, Jr., the son, for whom it was intended.
Still more extraordinary was it, that when this letter
was shown to J. J. Knapp, Jr., instead of perceiving
how strongly it would bear against him, he pretend-
ed that it contained merely "trash," and advised
his father to hand it to the committee of vigilance,
thereby unwittingly furnishing them with evidence
which resulted in directing their attention to him,
and ultimately in revealing the whole conspiracy.

It was strange that, after the apprehension of the

Knapps, Joseph should make a confession of the whole matter, upon the pledge of favor from the government, and then, after furnishing the government with a solution of all the labyrinth of circumstances connected with the tragedy, should withdraw that confession, refuse to testify upon the stand, and be willing himself to go to trial. It is believed that if he had adhered to his confession, his brother Frank would not have been convicted, because his confession stated that, on the night of the murder, Crowninshield told Frank, in Brown Street, to go home; that he went home, went to bed, and then got up and returned to Brown Street, to learn the circumstances of the deed. If this was believed, then Frank would not have been convicted as a principal, because it would have appeared that he was not there to " aid and abet " in the murder, according to the legal signification of those terms. Whilst Joseph, being state's evidence, would not have been tried at all.

It was extraordinary that the murder was projected under the influence of two errors — one of law and the other of fact. The error *of law* was, that if Mr. White died without a will, Mrs. Beckford would inherit one half of his estate, whereas Joseph Knapp knew that, by his will, he had left her a great deal less than one half.

The error *in fact* was, that when the will, as was

supposed, was taken from Mr. White's iron chest, it proved to be the *wrong* will.   Mr. White had made one of later date.   So that the specific object of the murder was effectually defeated.

It was also a remarkable development of the hardening nature of human depravity, that, on the night following the tragedy, Knapp should have watched with the body of the murdered old man, and at the funeral should have officiated as one of the chief mourners, even following him to the grave in that capacity, without, by the slightest word or act, creating the least suspicion of his own guilt.

Let the young be admonished, by the dreadful fate of these offenders, (one of whom committed suicide in prison, and the two others being executed,) to avoid evil associates.   They cannot mingle with the wicked without being contaminated by them.   In view of this thrilling tragedy, how significant is the language of Solomon ! —

"My son, if sinners entice thee, consent thou not. If they say, Come with us; let us lay wait for blood; let us lurk privily for the innocent without cause ; let us swallow them up alive, as the grave, and whole, as those that go down into the pit.   We shall find all precious substance ; we shall fill our houses with spoil.   Cast in thy lot among us; let us all have one purse.   My son, walk not thou in the way with them ; refrain thy foot *from* their path.

For their feet run to evil, and make haste to shed blood. Surely in vain the net is spread in the sight of any bird. And they lay wait for their own blood; they lurk privily for their own lives. So are the ways of every one that is greedy of gain ; which taketh away the life of the owners thereof."

Mr. Webster has been repeatedly heard to say that he was indebted in no small degree to Mr. Jeremiah Mason for his attainments in legal science, and his skill in argument. Mr. Mason was a most powerful competitor in any cause ; hence, when Webster was opposed to him, as was often the case, he was compelled to make a careful and elaborate preparation to meet his opponent.

Joel Parker, LL. D., Royall professor in the University of Cambridge, in his interesting address before the students in the Law School, on the character of Daniel Webster as a jurist, says, —

" Some half dozen years since, in a company of gentlemen, Mr. Webster was applied to for his opinion of Mr. Mason's ability as a lawyer. Speaking deliberately, and in a manner denoting his intention to give emphasis to what he uttered, he replied that he had known, as a young man knows his superiors in age, the bar of a former generation, — all the leading men in it, — and he was intimately acquainted with all the leading lawyers of the present bar of the United States ; but for himself, he had rather

meet, if it could be combined, all the talent and
learning of the past and present bar of the United
States, than Jeremiah Mason, single-handed and
alone. The man who had Jeremiah Mason for his
counsel was sure of having his case tried as well as
it was possible for human ingenuity and learning to
try it." *

In a beautiful tribute to the character of Mr.
Mason, at a bar meeting upon the occasion of his
death, Mr. Webster said, " I am bound to say, that
of my own professional discipline and attainments,
whatever they may be, I owe much to that close
attention to the discharge of my duties which I was
compelled to pay for nine successive years, from day
to day, by Mr. Mason's efforts and arguments at the
same bar. *Fas est ab hoste doceri ;* and I must have
been unintelligent indeed not to have learned something from the constant displays of that power which
I had so much occasion to see and to feel."

It would appear, however, that there were
" blows to take, as well as blows to give," from the
time of the earliest meeting of Mr. Mason and Mr.
Webster as opposing counsel. In another note to
the Life of Chief Justice Smith, it is stated, apparently on the authority of Mr. Mason himself, that
the first time they met was in a criminal trial. The

* P. Harvey, Esq.

defendant was indicted for counterfeiting. Mr. Mason was in the defence, and Mr. Webster, in the absence of the attorney general, was applied to by the solicitor for the county to act in behalf of the state. Mr. Mason, it is said, had heard of him as a "young man of remarkable promise;" but he had heard such things of young men before, and prepared himself as he would have done to meet the attorney general. But he soon found that he had quite a different person to deal with. The young man came down upon him "like a thunder shower," and Mr. Mason's client got off, as he thought, more on account of the political feelings of the jury, than from the arguments of the counsel. Mr. Mason was particularly struck with the high, open, and manly ground taken by Mr. Webster, who, instead of availing himself of any technical advantage, or pushing the prisoner hard, confined himself to the main points of law and fact. Mr. Mason did not know how much allowance ought to be made for his being taken so by surprise, but it seemed to him that he had never since known Mr. Webster to show greater legal ability in an argument.*

It may be added, that the defendant in that case had been a member of the legislature — one of the creators of law. This led Mr. Webster, in

* Life of Judge Smith, p. 263.

12·

his argument to the jury, to say, in connection with the sentiment that no position in society could place a man above the reach of law, that "the majesty and impartiality of the law were such, that it would bring even its guilty creator to its feet " — a passage which has been much admired for its felicity and power.

In his own, and in other states, Mr. Webster was engaged in some of the most important cases ever tried in the country. In all of them he developed the same great talents, and extensive information upon the points of law involved; the same clearness, terseness, directness, and logical power, whether pleading to the court or to the jury. These cases embraced almost every principle which is made the subject of litigation in our courts, and in all of them Mr. Webster proved himself to be at home. Those who wish to know the character of his pleas on those great occasions are referred to his works, as edited by the Hon. Edward Everett. They cannot be too strongly recommended to the young men of our land.

CHAPTER X.

No individual possessed of Mr. Webster's abilities could remain long in the quiet practice of any
profession. His country needed his talents, and demanded that all should be laid as an offering upon
the altar of patriotism. Great genius and great
modesty are ofttimes inseparable companions. This
was seen in the case of Mr. Webster. He was not
anxious to enter into the troubled whirlpool of politics. He was satisfied with his profession, and was
not desirous to relinquish it for the honors or emoluments of public office. Yet, at the call of his
fellow-citizens, he consented to enter upon the un-
tried labors and responsibilities of congressional
life.

At the early age of thirty he was chosen to a seat
in the national House of Representatives, where he

was immediately brought into contact with a galaxy
of the most distinguished men of the country.   He
was at once appointed on the most important committee in the house — that of foreign relations.
The United States were then at war with Great
Britain, and consequently an unusual amount of responsibility and labor devolved upon this committee.

Although he was now introduced upon a stage
where every thing was novel to him, — where the
characters, the scenes, the machinery, and the cast
and strength of the company, were all to be learned,
— yet he soon proved himself to be an apt scholar.
Yea, before long he became a teacher there.   Not
satisfied with being like a spectator at a theatre, —
an inactive beholder of other men's performances, —
he preferred to take part in the important drama
himself.   Accordingly, in the early part of the session, he presented a series of resolutions of inquiry,
concerning the repeal of the Berlin and Milan de-
crees, and on the 10th of June, 1813, he made his
first speech in Congress in their support.   As no
report of the speech has been preserved, we have
no other means of knowing its character, and the
impression which it produced, than from tradition,
and the remarks of those who were favored with the
privilege of hearing it.   Mr. Everett says that it
was a calm and statesmanlike exposition of the object of the resolutions he had introduced, and was

marked by all the characteristics of **Mr. W.**'s maturest parliamentary efforts — " moderation of tone, precision of statement, force of reasoning, absence of ambitious rhetoric and highflown language, occasional bursts of true eloquence, and, pervading the whole, a genuine and fervid patriotism."

Mr. March says of it, " The opening of his speech was simple, unaffected, without pretension, gradually gaining the confidence of his audience by its transparent sincerity and freedom from aught resembling display. As the orator continued and grew animated his words became more fluent and his language more nervous; a crowd of thoughts seemed rushing upon him, all eager for utterance. He held them, however, under the command of his mind, as greyhounds with a leash, till he neared the close of his speech, when, warmed by the previous restraint, he poured them all forth, one after another, in glowing language.

" The speech took the house by surprise, not so much from its eloquence as from the vast amount of historical knowledge and illustrative ability displayed in it. How a person untrained to forensic contests, and unused to public affairs, could exhibit so much parliamentary tact, such nice appreciation of the difficulties of a difficult question, and such quiet facility in surmounting them, puzzled the mind. The age and inexperience of the speaker had prepared the house for no such display, and astonishment for a time subdued the expression of its admiration."

"No member before," says a person then in the house, "ever riveted the attention of the house so closely, in his first speech. Members left their seats where they could not see the speaker face to face, and sat down, or stood on the floor, fronting him. All listened attentively and silently during the whole speech; and when it was over, many went up and warmly congratulated the orator; among whom were some, not the most niggard of their compliments, who most dissented from the views he had expressed."

Chief Justice Marshall, writing to Judge Story some time after this speech, says, "At the time when this speech was delivered, I did not know Mr. Webster; but I was so much struck with it, that I did not hesitate then to state that Mr. Webster was a very able man, and would become one of the first statesmen in America, and perhaps the very first."

"Such praise, from such a man," says Judge Story, "ought to be very gratifying. Consider that he is now seventy-five years old, and that he speaks of his recollections of some eighteen years ago with a freshness which shows how deeply your reasoning impressed itself upon his mind. Keep this *in memoriam rei*." *

The speech immediately raised its author to the

* Story to Webster.

first consideration in the house, and gained him great reputation throughout the country.

Not only was this maiden speech commended in the strongest terms by those who heard it, but, more than this, it accomplished the object for which it was delivered, viz., the adoption of the resolution, in reply to which, Mr. Monroe, the secretary of state, presented an elaborate and full report, furnishing all the information that was called for.

It will not be possible, in the limits which we have assigned for this volume, to give at any length the history of Mr. Webster's congressional career, which extended through a series of forty years; neither is it necessary for those for whom we write. It must suffice to say, that during this long period he was a member of the national Congress, either as a member of the House of Representatives or of the Senate. He was not a frequent speaker; he reserved his strength for great occasions. An important motto with him was, "Some questions will improve by keeping." Whilst, therefore, others dashed impatiently into debate upon the first opportunity, he calmly waited. By listening to the discussions of others, he not only understood what was said, but saw clearly what was left unsaid. He not only perceived on what points light was shed, but also what was left in darkness. He also learned the objections which were cherished to any views which he intended to

advocate; and consequently, when he arose, he was
better prepared to meet the issues of the case than
those who took the initiative in the debate.   He was
prepared to shed light upon those points which were
left in shadow, and unravel the difficulties which
others had in vain tried to solve, or which, in conscious weakness, they had wisely left untouched.
He was therefore always listened to with interest
and profit.   He always contributed something new,
either in fact or argument.

As a debater he was unsurpassed : with deep, so-
norous, bass tones of voice, susceptible of a great
variety of modulation ; with deep-set, dark, bril
liant eyes, overshadowed by a high projecting forehead, yet susceptible of great expression ; with a tall,
well-developed, manly form, — he possessed all the
physical elements of a great orator.   When to these
it is added, that he always possessed an accurate
and extensive knowledge of every question on which
he intended to speak, and of its various relations to
collateral themes, that he exhibited a marked simplicity in the statement of his propositions, a wonderful power of condensation in his use of language,
great care in his narrative of facts, a lucid arrangement in the divisions of his subject, close logical
consecutiveness in his reasoning, and a delivery at
first calm and deliberate, but as he advanced in his
argument, impassioned and earnest, it need awaken

no surprise that he was listened to with equal pleasure by highly-cultivated scholars, and by plain, unlettered men.

An amusing evidence of Mr. Webster's simplicity of expression is furnished in the following anecdote: On the arrival of that singular genius, David Crockett, at Washington, he had an opportunity of hearing Mr. Webster. A short time afterwards he met him, and abruptly accosted him as follows : " Is this Mr. Webster ? " " Yes, sir." " The great Mr. Webster, of Massachusetts ? " continued he, with a significant tone. " I am Mr. Webster, of Massachusetts," was the calm reply. " Well, sir," continued the eccentric Crockett, ' I had heard that you were a great man, but I don't think so; I heard your speech, and *understood every word you said.*" Mr. Webster was always understood ; he possessed the rare ability of presenting the most difficult and abstruse themes in language so simple, yet appropriate and beautiful, that any individual of even ordinary capacity could comprehend them.

After, by a few forensic efforts, he had established his reputation as an orator, a report that he was to speak upon any subject was sure to fill the Senate chamber to its utmost capacity. One of his most remarkable displays of eloquence was given in his great debate with Colonel Hayne, of South Carolina.

This latter gentleman had made in the Senate

what was regarded as a most unjustifiable and violent attack upon Mr. Webster and the institutions
of New England. The speech produced a profound
sensation. If its false statements and erroneous principles were not corrected, there was danger of its
doing much mischief.

Mr. Webster felt called upon to reply. At the
same time he regarded himself as placed in a critical
position ; and the more so as he was aware that some
of his political friends might not agree with the views
he was about to present in answer to Colonel
Hayne. It appeared to him that the constitution
and the peace of the country were in danger. He
earnestly desired to give utterance to his sentiments,
and yet he did not wish to assume a position adverse
to any of his friends. On the morning of the day
on which he made his reply, he invited Hon. Mr.
Bell, of New Hampshire, into the robing room of
the Senate, and revealed to him his embarrassment.
"You know, Mr. Bell, my constitutional opinions ;
there are among my friends in the Senate some who
may not concur in them. What is expedient to be
done ?" " I advise you," said Mr. Bell, in a very
emphatic manner, "to speak out boldly and fully
your thoughts upon the subject. It is a critical mo
ment," he added, " and it is time, it is high time,
that the people of this country should know what
this constitution *is*."

"Then," replied Mr. Webster, in a calm, but determined manner, "by the blessing of Heaven, they shall learn this day, before the sun goes down, what I understand it to be."

Thanks to Mr. Bell for his word of encouragement at that trying moment; it had its influence.

No one has given a more lifelike and vivid account of that great occasion than Mr. March, and we are persuaded that we cannot render a better service to our readers than by transferring a part of his description to our pages.

"It was on Tuesday, January the 26th, 1830, — a day to be hereafter forever memorable in senatorial annals, — that the Senate resumed the consideration of Foot's resolution. There never was before, in the city, an occasion of so much excitement. To witness this great intellectual contest, multitudes of strangers had for two or three days previous been rushing into the city, and the hotels overflowed. As early as nine o'clock of this morning, crowds poured into the Capitol, in hot haste; at twelve o'clock, the hour of meeting, the Senate chamber — its galleries, floor, and even lobbies — was filled to its utmost capacity. The very stairways were dark with men, who hung on to one another like bees in a swarm.

"The House of Representatives was early deserted. An adjournment would have hardly made it emptier. The speaker, it is true, retained his chair,

but no business of moment was, or could be attend
ed to.   Members all rushed in to hear Mr. Webster,
and no call of the house or other parliamentary
proceedings could compel them back.   The floor
of the Senate was so densely crowded, that persons
once in could not get out, nor change their position ;
in the rear of the vice-presidential chair, the crowd
was particularly intense.   Dixon H. Lewis, then a
representative from Alabama, became wedged in
here.   From his enormous size, it was impossible
for him to move without displacing a vast portion of
the multitude.   Unfortunately, too, for him, he was
jammed in directly behind the chair of the vice
president, where he could not see, and hardly hear,
the speaker.   By slow and laborious effort — pausing occasionally to breathe — he gained one of the
windows, which, constructed of painted glass, flank
the chair of the vice president on either side.
Here he paused, unable to make more headway ;
but determined to see Mr. Webster as he spoke, with
his knife he made a large hole in one of the panes
of the glass ; which is still visible as he made it.
Many were so placed as not to be able to see the
speaker at all.

   " The courtesy of senators accorded to the fairer
sex room on the floor — the most gallant of them
their own seats.   The gay bonnets and brilliant

dresses threw a varied and picturesque beauty over the scene, softening and embellishing it.

"Seldom, if ever, has a speaker in this or any other country had more powerful incentives to exertion — a subject, the determination of which involved the most important interests, and even duration, of the republic ; competitors unequalled in reputation, ability, or position ; a name to make still more glorious, or lose forever ; and an audience comprising not only persons of this country most eminent in intellectual greatness, but representatives of other nations, where the art of eloquence had flourished for ages. All the soldier seeks in opportunity was here.

"Mr. Webster perceived, and felt equal to, the destinies of the moment. The very greatness of the hazard exhilarated him. His spirits rose with the occasion. He awaited the time of onset with a stern and impatient joy. He felt like the war horse of the Scriptures, who 'paweth in the valley, and rejoiceth in his strength ; who goeth on to meet the armed men ; who sayeth among the trumpets, Ha, ha! and who smelleth the battle afar off, the thunder of the captains and the shouting.'

"A confidence in his own resources, springing from no vain estimate of his power, but the legitimate offspring of previous severe mental discipline, sustained and excited him. He had gauged his op ponents, his subject, and *himself*.

"He was, too, at this period, in the very prime
of manhood. He had reached middle age — an
era in the life of man when the faculties, physical
or intellectual, may be supposed to attain their fullest
organization and most perfect development. Whatever there was in him of intellectual energy and
vitality, the occasion, his full life and high ambition,
might well bring forth.

"He never rose on an ordinary occasion to address an ordinary audience more self-possessed.
There was no tremulousness in his voice or manner; nothing hurried, nothing simulated. The calmness of superior strength was visible every where —
in countenance, voice, and bearing. A deep-seated
conviction of the extraordinary character of the
emergency, and of his ability to control it, seemed
to possess him wholly. If an observer, more than
ordinarily keen-sighted, detected at times something
like exultation in his eye, he presumed it sprang from
the excitement of the moment, and the anticipation
of victory.

"The anxiety to hear the speech was so intense,
irrepressible, and universal, that no sooner had the
vice president assumed the chair, than a motion was
made, and unanimously carried, to postpone the ordinary preliminaries of senatorial action, and to
take up immediately the consideration of the resolution.

" Mr. Webster rose and addressed the Senate. His exordium is known by heart every where : ' Mr. President, when the mariner has been tossed, for many days, in thick weather, and on an unknown sea, he naturally avails himself of the first pause in the storm, the earliest glance of the sun, to take his latitude, and ascertain how far the elements have driven him from his true course. Let us imitate this prudence, and, before we float further on the waves of this debate, refer to the point from which we departed, that we may, at least, be able to form some conjecture where we now are. I ask for the reading of the resolution.'

" There wanted no more to enchain the attention. There was a spontaneous, though silent, expression of eager approbation, as the orator concluded these opening remarks; and, while the clerk read the resolution, many attempted the impossibility of getting nearer the speaker. Every head was inclined closer towards him, every ear turned in the direction of his voice, and that deep, sudden, mysterious silence followed, which always attends fulness of emotion. From the sea of upturned faces before him, the orator beheld his thoughts reflected as from a mirror. The varying countenance, the suffused eye, the earnest smile, and ever-attentive look, assured him of his audience's entire sympathy. If among his hearers there were those who affected at
13

first an indifference to his glowing thoughts and fervent periods, the difficult mask was soon laid aside,
and profound, undisguised, devoted attention followed.   In the earlier part of his speech, one of his
principal opponents seemed deeply engrossed in the
careful perusal of a newspaper he held before his
face ; but this, on nearer approach, proved to be
upside down.   In truth, all, sooner or later, voluntarily, or in spite of themselves, were wholly carried
away by the eloquence of the orator.

   " Those who had doubted Mr. Webster's ability
to cope with and overcome his opponents were
fully satisfied of their error before he had proceeded
far in his speech.   Their fears soon took another
direction.   When they heard his sentences of powerful thought, towering, in accumulative grandeur,
one above the other, as if the orator strove, Titan-
like, to reach the very heavens themselves, they
were giddy with an apprehension that he would
break down in his flight.   They dared not believe
that genius, learning, any intellectual endowment,
however uncommon, that was simply mortal, could
sustain itself long in a career seemingly so perilous.
They feared an Icarian fall.

   " Ah, who can ever forget, that was present to
hear the tremendous, the *awful* burst of eloquence,
with which the orator spoke of the *Old Bay State !*
or the tones of deep pathos in which the words were
pronounced ? —

" 'Mr. President, I shall enter on no encomium upon Massachusetts. There she is — behold her, and judge for yourselves. There is her history — the world knows it by heart! The past, at least, is secure. There is Boston, and Concord, and Lexington, and Bunker Hill — and there they will remain forever. The bones of her sons, falling in the great struggle for independence, now lie mingled with the soil of every state, from New England to Georgia — and there they will lie forever. And, sir, where American Liberty raised its first voice, and where its youth was nurtured and sustained, there it still lives, in the strength of its manhood, and full of its original spirit. If discord and disunion shall wound it — if party strife and blind ambition shall hawk at and tear it — if folly and madness, if uneasiness under salutary and necessary restraint, shall succeed to separate it from that Union, by which alone its existence is made sure, it will stand, in the end, by the side of that cradle in which its infancy was rocked; it will stretch forth its arm, with whatever of vigor it may still retain, over the friends who gather round it; and it will fall at last, if fall it must, amidst the proudest monuments of its own glory, and on the very spot of its origin.'

" What New England heart was there but throbbed with vehement, tumultuous, irrepressible emotion, as

he dwelt upon New England sufferings, New England struggles, and New England triumphs, during
the war of the revolution ?   There was scarcely a
dry eye in the Senate; all hearts were overcome ;
grave judges, and men grown old in dignified life,
turned aside their heads to conceal the evidences of
their emotion.

"In one corner of the gallery was clustered a
group of Massachusetts men.   They had hung from
the first moment upon the words of the speaker, with
feelings variously but always warmly excited, deepen
ing in intensity as he proceeded.   At first, while the
orator was going through his exordium, they held
their breath and hid their faces, mindful of the savage attack upon him and New England, and the
fearful odds against him, her champion ; as he went
deeper into his speech, they felt easier; when he
turned Hayne's flank, on Banquo's ghost, they
breathed freer and deeper.   But now, as he alluded
to Massachusetts, their feelings were strained to the
highest tension ; and when the orator, concluding
his encomium upon the land of their birth, turned,
intentionally or otherwise, his burning eye full upon
them, *they shed tears like girls!*

"No one who was not present can understand
the excitement of the scene.   No one who was can
give an adequate description of it.   No word-paint
ing can convey the deep, intense enthusiasm, the

reverential attention, of that vast assembly, nor limner transfer to canvas their earnest, eager, awe-struck countenances. Though language were as subtile and flexible as thought, it still would be impossible to represent the full idea of the scene. There is something intangible in an emotion, which cannot be transferred. The nicer shades of feeling elude pursuit. Every description, therefore, of the occasion, seems to the narrator himself most tame, spiritless, unjust.

"Much of the instantaneous effect of the speech arose, of course, from the orator's delivery — the tones of his voice, his countenance, and manner. These die mostly with the occasion that calls them forth; the impression is lost in the attempt at transmission from one mind to another. They can only be described in general terms. ' Of the effectiveness of Mr. Webster's manner, in many parts,' says Mr. Everett, ' it would be in vain to attempt to give any one not present the faintest idea. It has been my fortune to hear some of the ablest speeches of the greatest living orators on both sides of the water ; but I must confess, I never heard any thing which so completely realized my conception of what Demosthenes was when he delivered the oration for the crown.' "

Another gentleman who was present on that deeply interesting occasion, in describing the effect pro-

duced upon his own mind by this speech of Mr
Webster, said, —

"He was a totally different thing from any public
speaker I ever heard.   I sometimes felt as if I were
looking at a mammoth treading, at an equable and
stately pace, his native canebrake, and, without
apparent consciousness, crushing obstacles which nature had never designed as impediments to him."

On the evening of the day on which this great
speech was delivered, the president held a levee in
the White House. as his mansion is called.   A large
and brilliant company were assembled.   The famous
east room was crowded.   There were representatives, senators, judges, naval officers, gentlemen of
distinction from abroad, private citizens, and ladies,
all attired in elegant costume befitting the occasion.
At one end of this spacious apartment was Colonel
Hayne, surrounded by his friends; at the other end
was Daniel Webster, in the centre of a group of his
admirers.   During the evening Mr. Hayne made
his way to the opposite end of the room, for the
purpose of expressing his congratulations to his
distinguished opponent.   Mr. Webster saw him approaching, and when he had arrived sufficiently near,
he advanced with his hand extended, and in his accustomed familiar manner said, "How are you,
Colonel Hayne!" to which the colonel immediately
replied, "*None the better for you, sir.*"   A frank
acknowledgment of a painful truth.

Mr. Webster's reply in the Senate to Mr. Hayne was soon widely circulated. It was printed in the papers of all the states of the Union ; it was read and commented on by thousands ; it assisted to dissipate the dark clouds which were gathering over our country ; it arrested nullification ; it neutralized the effect of wrong views respecting state rights, and the relation of the several states to the national government, by presenting those which were correct ; it rendered important assistance in saving the country from a civil war, and perhaps from a dissolution of the Union. The crisis was one of great responsibility, and nobly was it met. This single speech, viewed in connection with the circumstances under which it was delivered, and the important effects which followed it, was enough to have given him great and permanent renown, though he had performed no other public act during his life ; but when we remember that this was only one of a long series of important acts, scattered over a period of forty years, in which Mr. Webster proved himself equal to every occasion, and competent to suggest remedies, in accordance with his views of the constitution, for every difficulty, however great or intricate, in which the nation was involved, our admiration of his transcendent abilities is greatly increased.

Another speech which was delivered by Mr Webster in the Senate of the United States, and which produced a profound sensation throughout the country, was given on the 7th of March, 1850, and is in his printed works entitled the Constitution and the Union; it is more generally known as his speech in support of the fugitive slave bill. As this was one of the most important speeches of Mr. Webster during his long congressional career, it is proper that we allude to it in this connection.

It should be remembered that when the union of the states was formed, a number of the states at the north, as well as those at the south, sanctioned slavery. It was no uncommon thing for the slaves — apprentices and servants — to escape from one state and flee into another; it was, therefore, deemed important that, in the constitution of the United States, provision should be made for the reclaiming of these fugitives. The south was unwilling to form a union with the north without such provision. The north consented; it was accordingly inserted in the constitution, that persons held to service in one state, who should escape and flee into another state, might be reclaimed by those who held them as servants. With this the Southern States were satisfied, and believing that in this matter the north was acting in good faith, they cheerfully came into the Union.

In the course of years, great difficulty was expe rienced in executing this provision of the constitu tion. The men who framed that important document passed away; other generations arose and took their places; amongst these were many who regretted the existence of this provision, and who were unwilling to comply with it. The legislatures of some of the states passed laws adverse to it, and designed to impede its execution. Associations were formed at the north to aid the flight of slaves into Canada, which were instrumental in bringing many out of bondage into the enjoyment of personal liberty. The south became irritated, accused the Northern States of violating the constitution, and threatened to withdraw from the Union. The excitement occasioned by this state of things was widespread and intense. It was believed by some that the Union was in danger.

Under these circumstances, Mr. Webster felt it to be his duty to exert himself to the full extent of his ability to allay the universal agitation. For this purpose he delivered, on the 7th of March, 1850, his great speech for the Constitution and the Union, in which he favored the passage of a law for reclaiming fugitive slaves.

This speech awakened widely different feelings throughout the country.

There were those who regarded it as evidence of treason to freedom — as an act which sullied what would otherwise have been his spotless fame. Many

of his own political friends deeply regretted the position which he then assumed.   The pulpit and the
press poured out upon him their burning anathemas.
No language was too strong in which to give expression to the animadversions which were indulged.
But others took a directly opposite view.   They regarded it as preëminently judicious and timely, as a
neutralizing element, thrown into the caldron of
public opinion, where the elements of disunion were
in violent effervescence.   It appeared to them as the
greatest and most valuable offering Mr. Webster
ever made for his country's good — as the crowning glory of his life.

The following extracts are presented as specimens of these opposite views.   The first is from
an article on Mr. Webster in one of our leading
Quarterlies.

"We were in Boston when the telegraph brought
a few brief lines, indicating the positions of that 7th
of March speech.   Almost every body seemed filled
with amazement, and suggested that the Washington
telegraphist must be a mischievous wag, or that the
lightning had falsified the message with whose delivery it had been charged.   The wisest editors confessed themselves puzzled, and besought the public
to suspend their judgment till the facts could be
learned.

"The speech itself came in due time, and then

there was doubt no longer. The whole north seemed indignant, and Massachusetts hung her head in mortification. Even in her legislative halls, men who had never been suspected of radical tendencies shook their heads meaningly, and muttered of treachery and Benedict Arnold. The Bay State felt that her honest pride had been heartlessly humbled, and her confidence abused. But Daniel Webster was a great man, having great influence; and the question was mooted, at first privately, whether we could afford to lose him. The tone of the press was changed; the legislature laid the proposition to request him to resign his seat under the table; political commentators wrote parodies on the speech; the merchants apologized for its seeming severity on northern heresies; the pulpit pleaded for moderation; a thousand men of standing and property wrote him a letter of thanks; he himself came on, and rode through the streets of Boston, telling her, as he went, that he was on the road of political safety; and then we knew that the battle of freedom was to be fought, not only without his assistance, but with his giant form towering up in the van of the hosts of despotism, making a mock of our faith and our feebleness."

The next is from a Eulogy of Daniel Webster, by a distinguished divine.

" At a later period, and nearer to our own times,

the prevalence at the north of hostility to southern
institutions gave birth to projects by which the
Union and the constitution were again endangered
— the Union by fostering a spirit of desperate sec-
tional animosity, the constitution by trampling
on the guaranties established by it for the protection of the rights of the slaveholding states.
Through the excitement consequent upon these
projects, the public business was brought to a stand,
and the public mind dismayed with the apprehension
of coming evils. In this crisis, the veteran senator
from Massachusetts was seen again at his post, looking somewhat older, but showing no abatement
either in the power of his mind or the fire of his
patriotism. He stood where he always had stood,
and where he had promised he should always be
found — for the constitution and the Union. The
assailants came from the opposite point of the
compass, and so he had faced about ; but he had
not changed sides. It was no longer the gay and
prancing chivalry of the south which he had to en-
counter ; but a sturdy and multitudinous northern
constituency, and foremost among them his old
friends from Massachusetts, with whom and for
whom he had stood so long, now advancing under
new leaders, and impelled to constantly new en-
croachments by the aggressive force of moral and
religious convictions. The impending contest im

posed upon him the severest trial of his life. It
required his parting with old friends, for whom he
cherished profound esteem, and whose animating
convictions on the great question at issue were
deeply shared by him, in every thing but in their
threatening aspect to the Union and the constitution.
But so long as he believed these to be in danger, it
concerned him little who were friends or foes. In
the similar crisis just referred to, he had united in
the defence of the constitution with an administration to the general policy of which he was strongly
opposed, and against which he had always acted ;
and he was prepared now, in a case equally involv-
ing the stability of the government, to separate from
those whose general policy he approved and had always supported. He foresaw the storm he was
raising ; but it did not move him from his purpose.
He was willing now, as before, to take his chance
among those upon whom blows might fall first and
fall thickest. And accordingly on the 7th of March
his voice was again heard, in tones as earnest as ever
came from his lips, speaking, not as a Massachusetts
man, nor as a northern man, but as an American,
and as a member of the Senate of the United
States. ʻHe felt,' he said, ʻthat he had a duty to
perform, a part to act, not for his own security, for
he was looking out for no fragment upon which to
float away from the wreck, if wreck there must be,

but for the good of the whole, for the preservation of the Union.' It has turned out here, as before, that the post of danger, assumed voluntarily in the spirit of self-sacrifice, became the post of honor. By a singular felicity of fortune, Mr. Webster became, the second time, the principal instrument of a deliverance as signal as any which has occurred in the history of the nation. By common consent he is entitled to the principal credit of this great settlement, in which the north and the south have once more embraced each other with fraternal affection, and under which the country has resumed its wonted career of peace and prosperity."

The above quotations are sufficient to convey an idea of the conflicting opinions which were cherished of Mr. Webster's course on that trying occasion by different portions of the community.

This diversity of sentiment will long exist, and will doubtless have — whether justly or unjustly — great influence upon the opinions of men, not only respecting his policy and conduct in that particular instance, but also as to his general character.

CHAPTER XI.

WITH all his greatness, Mr. Webster was a man of tender sensibility. His domestic attachments were strong. His exalted honors did not dry up the fountains of deep feeling. Several incidents, illustrative of these traits of character, we propose to group together in the present chapter.

While Mr. Webster was pursuing his course of studies at college, his brother Ezekiel was at home, assisting his father in carrying on the farm. He was a strong young man, both physically and intellectually. Daniel appreciated his talents, and believed that, with suitable cultivation, he might attain to distinction in professional life. He was unwilling to enjoy the benefits of a public education alone. He earnestly desired that the same boon might be conferred upon his brother, and he resolved that it should be, if any influence of his could effect it. He determined to make the effort by introducing

the matter first to Ezekiel and then to his father.
When spending the vacations at home, he and his
brother were accustomed to sleep together. One
night, after they had retired to rest, Daniel opened
the matter to his brother, and they conversed freely
upon it. "Daniel utterly refused to enjoy the fruit
of his brother's labor any longer. They were united
in sympathy and affection, and they must be united
in their pursuits. But how could they leave their
beloved parents, in age and solitude, with no protector? They talked and wept, and wept and
talked, till dawn of day. They dared not broach
the matter to their father. Finally Daniel resolved
to be the orator upon the occasion. Judge Webster
was then somewhat burdened with debts. He was
advanced in age, and had set his heart upon having Ezekiel as his helper. The very thought of
separation from both his sons was painful to him.
When the proposition was made, he felt as did the
patriarch of old, when he exclaimed, 'Joseph is not,
. . . and will ye also take Benjamin away?'
A family council was called. The mother's opinion
was asked. She was a strong-minded woman. She
was not blind to the superior endowments of her
sons. With all a mother's partiality, however, she
did not over-estimate their powers. She decided the
matter at once. Her reply was, 'I have lived long
in the world, and have been happy in my children.

If Daniel and Ezekiel will promise to take care of me in my old age, *I will consent to the sale of all our property at once, and they may enjoy the benefit of that which remains after our debts are paid.*' This was a moment of intense interest to all the parties. Parents and children all mingled their tears together, and sobbed aloud, at the thought of separation. The father yielded to the entreaties of the sons and the advice of his wife. Daniel returned to college, and Ezekiel took his little bundle in his hand, and sought on foot the scene of his preparatory studies. In one year he joined his younger brother in college." *

All honor to that self-denying, noble mother, who, for the intellectual improvement of her children, would have consented to the sale of all the property, and who " decided the matter at once." Let her character ever be held in grateful remembrance. With such mothers, our country will never want for able statesmen. How affecting, too, is the scene of that night's interview between those two brothers, talking and weeping about their difficulties and prospects till the dawn of day — the younger laboring to persuade the elder to relinquish the tilling of the land, in order to cultivate his own mind, and the elder dwelling upon the obstructions in the way, only, however, to hear a method suggested by Daniel, by which those impediments might be removed!

* Lyman's Memorial.

14

This attachment between these two brothers continued through life. Ezekiel being the elder, the
other was accustomed to cherish great respect for
his opinions. Daniel seems to have regarded the
approbation of Ezekiel as a higher commendation
than the praises of the multitude. After his splendid
reply to Hayne, in the United States Senate, and
when no language was strong enough to give full
expression to the admiration which it had awakened
throughout the land, he was heard to say, " How I
wish that my poor brother had lived till after this
speech, that I might know if he would have been
gratified ! " He, on whose lips a vast multitude had
hung with delight, — who had astonished the greatest
minds in the nation by his wonderful versatility of
talent, in which satire, pathos, logical power, keen
analysis, and beauty of rhetoric, were all combined,
and by means of which an ingenious and graceful
competitor was effectually overthrown, in one of the
most powerful intellectual contests that this or any
other country has ever witnessed, and whilst the
victor's enthusiastic praises were on every tongue, —
his heart was modestly going forth towards his
brother, as if his satisfaction could not be complete without that brother's commendation !

And where, in the history of political literature
is there a more affecting tribute of fraternal love
than in the following dedication of the first volume
of his speeches · —

" *To my Nieces, Mrs. Alice Bridge Whipple, and Mrs. Mary Ann Sanborn.*

" Many of the speeches contained in this volume were delivered and printed in the lifetime of your father, whose fraternal affection led him to speak of them with approbation.

" His death, which happened when he had only just passed the middle period of life, left you without a father, and me without a brother.

" I dedicate this volume to you, not only for the love I have for yourselves, but also as a tribute of affection to his memory, and from a desire that the name of my brother, Ezekiel Webster, may be associated with mine, so long as any thing written or spoken by me shall be regarded or read.

"DANL. WEBSTER."

As in early life he resolved that his brother should share the benefits of education with him, so in the zenith of his glory he desired to make him a participant of his honors, by indissolubly associating their names together.

The following characteristic letter of Mr. Webster, written May 3, 1846, at Franklin, New Hampshire, contains some allusion, not only to his brother, but to other members of his family, which are beautifully illustrative of his affectionate domestic attachments : —

" Sunday, 1 o'clock.

" MY DEAR SIR:

. . . .

' I have made satisfactory arrangements respecting the house, the best of which is, that I find I can leave it where it is, (that is, the main house,) and yet be comfortable, notwithstanding the railroad. This saves a great deal of expense.

. . . .

" This house faces due north. Its front windows look towards the River Merrimack. But then the river soon turns to the south, so that the eastern windows look towards the river also. But the river has so deepened its channel in this stretch of it, in the last fifty years, that we cannot see its water without approaching it, or going back to the higher lands behind us. The history of this change is of considerable importance in the philosophy of streams. I have observed it practically, and know something of the theory of the phenomenon; but I doubt whether the world will ever be benefited either by my learning or my observation in this respect. Looking out at the east windows, at this moment, (2 P. M.,) with a beautiful sun just breaking out, my eye sweeps a rich and level field of one hundred acres. At the end of it, a third of a mile off, I see plain marble gravestones, designating the places where repose my father, my mother, my brother

Joseph, and my sisters Mehetabel, Abigail, and Sarah, good and Scripture names, inherited from their Puritan ancestors.

"My father, Ebenezer Webster, born at Kingston, in the lower part of the state, in 1739, was the handsomest man I ever saw, except my brother Ezekiel, who appeared to me — and so does he now seem to me — the very finest human form that ever I laid eyes on. I saw him in his coffin — a white forehead, a tinged cheek, a complexion as clear as heavenly light. But where am I straying? The grave has closed upon him, as it has on all my brothers and sisters. We shall soon be all together. But this is melancholy, and I leave it. Dear, dear kindred blood, how I love you all!

" This fair field is before me. I could see a lamb on any part of it. I have ploughed it, and raked it, and hoed it; but I never mowed it. Somehow, I could never learn to hang a scythe. I had not wit enough. My brother Joe used to say that my father sent me to college in order to make me equal to the rest of the children!

"Of a hot day in July — it must have been in one of the last years of Washington's administration — I was making hay, with my father, just where I now see a remaining elm tree. About the middle of the afternoon, the Honorable Abiel Foster, M. C., who lived in Canterbury, six miles off, called at the

house, and came into the field to see my father
He was a worthy man, college learned, and had
been a minister, but was not a person of any considerable natural power. My father was his friend
and supporter. He talked a while in the field, and
went on his way. When he was gone, my father
called me to him, and we sat down beneath the elm,
on a haycock. He said, ' My son, that is a worthy
man. He is a member of Congress. He goes to
Philadelphia, and gets six dollars a day, while I toil
here. It is because he had an education, which I
never had. If I had had his early education, I
should have been in Philadelphia in his place.
I came near it as it was. But I missed it, and now
I must work here.' ' My dear father,' said I, ' you
shall not work. Brother and I will work for you,
and wear our hands out, and you shall rest.' And I
remember to have cried, and I cry now at the recollection. ' My child,' said he, ' it is of no importance
to me ; I now live but for my children. I could not
give your elder brother the advantages of knowledge, but I can do something for you. Exert yourself ; improve your opportunities ; *learn, learn* .
and when I am gone, you will not need to go
through the hardships which I have undergone, and
which have made me an old man before my time.'

" The next May he took me to Exeter, to the
Phillips Exeter Academy, placed me under the

tuition of its excellent preceptor, Dr. Benjamin Abbott, still living, and from that time .   .   .

"My father died in April, 1806. I neither left him nor forsook him. My opening an office at Boscawen was that I might be near him. I closed his eyes in this very house. He died at sixty-seven years of age, after a life of exertion, toil, and exposure — a private soldier, an officer, a legislator, a judge, every thing that a man could be to whom Learning never had disclosed her 'ample page.' My first speech at the bar was made when he was on the bench. He never heard me a second time. He had in him what I collect to have been the character of some of the old Puritans. He was deeply religious, but not sour; on the contrary, good humored, facetious; sharing, even in his age, with a contagious laugh; teeth all as white as alabaster; gentle, soft, playful; and yet having a heart in him that he seemed to have borrowed from a lion. He could frown, — a frown it was, — but cheerfulness, good humor, and smiles composed his most usual aspect

'Ever truly yours, &c.,.

"DANIEL WEBSTER."

How touching is the allusion to Ezekiel! "a white forehead, a tinged cheek, a complexion clear as heaven's light. The grave has closed upon him as it has upon all my brothers and sisters. We shall soon all be together. *Dear, dear kindred blood, how I loved you all!* "

And then his reference to his father : " My father died. I neither left him nor forsook him. *I closed his eyes.*"

During the presidential campaign of 1840, the opponents of General Harrison sneered at him because he was born in a log cabin. This gave occasion for the following outburst of moving eloquence from Mr. Webster, in which there are other affecting allusions to his father.

" Gentlemen, it did not happen to me to be born in a log cabin; but my elder brothers and sisters were born in a log cabin, raised amid the snowdrifts of New Hampshire, at a period so early as that, when the smoke first rose from its rude chimney, and curled over the frozen hills, there was no similar evidence of a white man's habitation between it and the settlements on the rivers of Canada. Its remains still exist. I make to it an annual visit. I carry my children to it, to teach them the hardships endured by the generations which have gone before them. I love to dwell on the tender recollections, the kindred ties, the early affections, and the touching narrations and incidents, which mingle with all I know of this primitive family abode. I weep to think that none of those who inhabited it are now among the living; and if ever I am ashamed of it, or if I ever fail in affectionate veneration for HIM who raised it and defended it against savage violence and destruction, cherished all the domestic virtues be neath its roof, and through the fire and blood of a seven years' revolutionary war, shrunk from no dan-ger, no toil, no sacrifice to serve his country, and to raise his children to a condition better than his own, may my name, and the name of my posterity, be blotted forever from the memory of mankind."

The same delicate sensibility was evinced by Mr. Webster in the dedications of the last five volumes of his works. It is appropriate, therefore, that they be inserted here as illustrative of an interesting fea ture of his character.

Second Volume.

" To Isaac P. Davis, Esq.

" My dear Sir: A warm private friendship has subsisted between us for half our lives, interrupted by no untoward occurrence, and never for a moment cooling into indifference. Of this friendship, the source of so much happiness to me, I wish to leave, if not an enduring memorial, at least an affectionate and grateful acknowledgment. I inscribe this volume to you.

" Daniel Webster."

Third Volume.

" T) Mrs. Caroline Le Roy Webster.

" My dearly-beloved Wife : I cannot allow these volumes to go to the press without containing a tribute of my affection, and some acknowledgment of the deep interest that you have felt in the productions which they contain. You have witnessed the origin of most of them, not with less concern, certainly, than has been felt by their author ; and the degree of favor with which they may now be received by the public will be as earnestly regarded, I am sure, by you as by myself. The opportunity seems also a fit one for expressing the high and warm regard which I ever entertained for your honored father, now deceased, and the respect and esteem which I cherish towards the members of that amiable and excellent family to which you belong.

" Daniel Webster."

Fourth Volume.

"To Fletcher Webster, Esq.

" My dear Sir : I dedicate one of the volumes of these speeches to the memory of your deceased brother and sister, and I am devoutly thankful that I am able to inscribe another volume to you, my only surviving child, and the object of my affection and hopes. You have been of an age, at the appearance of most of these speeches and writings,

at which you were able to read and understand
them ; and in the preparation of some of them you
have taken no unimportant part. Among the diplomatic papers, there are several written by yourself
wholly or mainly, at the time when official and con-
fidential connections subsisted between us in the department of state. The principles and opinions
expressed in these productions are such as I believe
to be essential to the preservation of the Union, the
maintenance of the Constitution, and the advancement of the country to still higher stages of prosperity and renown. These objects have constituted
my polestar during the whole of my political life,
which has now extended through more than half the
period of the existence of the government. And I
know, my dear son, that neither parental authority
nor parental example is necessary to induce you, in
whatever capacity, public or private, you may be
called to act, to devote yourself to the accomplish-
ment of the same ends.

"Your affectionate Father." ·

Fifth Volume.

"To J. W. Paige, Esq.

"My dear Sir : The friendship which has subsisted
so long between us, springs not more from our close
family connections than from similarity of opinions
and sentiments. I count it among the advantages

and pleasures of my life, and pray you to allow me
as a slight, but grateful token of my estimate of it,
to dedicate to you this volume of my speeches.

"DANIEL WEBSTER."

Sixth Volume.

"With the warmest parental affection, mingled with
afflicted feelings, I dedicate this the last volume of
my works to the memory of my deceased children,
Julia Webster Appleton, beloved in all the relations
of daughter, wife, mother, sister, and friend; and
Major Edward Webster, who died in Mexico, in the
military service of the United States, with unblemished honor and reputation, and who entered the
service solely from a desire to be useful to his country, and do honor to the state in which he was born.

> " ' Go, gentle spirits, to your destined rest ;
> While I — reversed our nature's kindlier doom,
> Pour forth a father's sorrow on your tomb.'

"DANIEL WEBSTER."

Over Mr. Webster's farm at Marshfield are scattered numerous trees, many of which have a history
that associates them directly with the owner of the
estate; among these are two small elms, which
stand immediately in front of the mansion. They
were planted there for a special purpose, under the
following circumstances: one day, after Mr. Webster had been absent from the house for some

time, he was seen returning with two small trees, and the shovel with which he had removed them. Calling for his son, Fletcher, he conducted him to the front of the house, and, after digging the holes and planting the trees without assistance, he turned to his son, and said, in a subdued tone of voice, " *My son, protect these trees after I am gone; let them ever remind you of Julia and Edward.*" In the presence of his only surviving child he planted those trees, as living monuments to the memory of the two who had departed.

Step, now, into the house, and, amongst the many objects of interest which will there be seen is a small profile cut in black, elegantly framed, with a single line in Mr. Webster's own writing : —

"MY EXCELLENT MOTHER.

"D. W."

We venture the prediction that that modest profile will awaken in the breasts of the Marshfield visitors far deeper and tenderer emotions than many of the more costly and showy articles which may there be seen.

In one of his letters to that "true man," John Taylor, who had charge of Elms Farm, he gave him a strict charge to take care of his mother's garden, though it required the labor of one man.

Mr. Webster provided, n Marshfield, and not far

from his residence, a family cemetery. It is upon
the summit of a hill, from which may be seen, on
one side, a wide extent of country, embracing,
amongst other interesting objects, the site of the
old church, — the first ever erected in the town, —
and the ocean, rolling its blue waves in ceaseless
sublimity to the shore.

On one of his last visits to this sacred spot, he
was accompanied by Mr. Lanman. They approached
the place in silent reverence, and, whilst standing
there, Mr. Webster, pointing to the tomb and the
enclosed green spot, said, in a deliberate and im
pressive manner, —

"This will be my home ; and here three monu
ments will soon be erected — one for the mother of
my children, one each for Julia and Edward, and
there will be plenty of room in front for the little
ones that must follow them."

These were the only words he uttered. They
were enough to indicate the current of his thoughts
and feelings. He was thinking, with tender interest,
of the dead and of the living, — of those who had
gone, and of those who were to follow, — not for-
getting himself. "This will be my home." Alas!
how soon was this verified! The monuments to
which he referred are now there. They are simple
columns, with granite bases and marble caps, containing the following inscriptions : —

"Grace Webster,
Wife of DANIEL WEBSTER :
Born January 16, 1781 ;
Died January 21, 1828.
Blessed are the pure in heart, for they shall see God."

"Julia Webster,
Wife of
SAMUEL APPLETON APPLETON :
Born January 16, 1818 ;
Died April 18, 1848.
Let me go, for the day breaketh."

"Major Edward Webster :
Born July 28, 1820 ;
Died at San Angel, in Mexico,
In the military service of his country,
January 23, 1848.
A dearly beloved son and brother."

Over the door of the tomb is a plain marble slab, on which is inscribed, in bold, deep letters, the name of

"DANIEL WEBSTER."

We see, from the above facts, that intellectual greatness is in perfect harmony with delicate sensibility. A man may, at one time, hold a nation spellbound by his eloquence, or in senates, or with foreign ambassadors, be discussing, in the profoundest manner, the most intricate questions of international law, and at another time may be giving exercise, in the most delicate manner, to the tenderest sentiments of affection. There is nothing unmanly in the strongest attachment, even though it finds its expression in a tear.

When Mr. Webster was in England, he wrote the following .lines, in which he doubtless refers to his own experience of

"THE MEMORY OF THE HEART.

" If stores of dry and learned lore we gain,
  We keep them in the memory of the brain ;
  Names, things, and facts — whate'er we knowledge call,
  There is the common leger for them all ;
  And images on this cold surface traced
  Make slight impressions, and are soon effaced.

" But we've a page more glowing and more bright,
  On which our friendship and our love to write ;
  That these may never from the soul depart,
  We trust them to *the memory of the heart*.
  There is no dimming — no effacement here ;
  Each new pulsation keeps the record clear ;
  Warm, golden letters all the tablet fill,
  Nor lose their lustre till the heart stands still.

" LONDON, November 19, 1839."

CHAPTER XII.

To see Mr. Webster in some grave debate, or
when pleading an important case before a jury, an
individual might infer, from the dignity and seriousness of his manner, that cheerfulness was not an
element of his nature. Nothing could be farther
from the truth. Among the strata which entered
into the composition of his character was a vein of
mirthfulness, that ofttimes *cropped* out above the surface of his habitual gravity, revealing the rich stores
that were concealed beneath. Sometimes this playful humor was mingled with his professional duties.
It is conspicuous in the first part of his great reply
to Hayne.

On one occasion he conducted a case in Boston,
before the Circuit Court, having reference to the
violation of some patent for a wheel. Whilst the

15   217

case was in progress, he wrote the following letter
to a friend, who says of it, "The letter is not, of
course, written for the public eye; but I have permission to use it, and make extracts from it. You
will see, from its half serious and half ironical character, how playful he can be, even while sitting at
the bar, waiting for his turn to be heard in a cause.
He speaks of himself in it as he supposes others
will speak of him. To show you that he is not always cold and unbending, I will give you an extract
from the letter." The following is the extract: —

"Boston, Jan. 15, '49 — Monday, 12 o'clock,
In C. Court, United States.

"*Marcy* vs. *Sizer* being on trial, and *Tabero dicente in longum;**
and another snow storm appearing to be on the wing.

"My dear Sir: We are in court yet, and so
shall be some days longer. We have the evidence
in, and a discussion on the law, preliminary to our
summing up, is now going on. I think it will con-
sume the remainder of this day, if it lasts no longer.
Mr. Choate will speak to-morrow, and I close immediately after. . . .

"I am afraid my luck is always bad, and I fear
is always to be so." . . . Here Mr. Webster
speaks of what he expects, and about which he fears
he may be disappointed, and the consequences of
it. He then goes on to say, —

* Taber making a long plea.

"It will be said, or may be said, hereafter, Mr. Webster was a laborious man in his profession and other pursuits. He never tasted of the bread of idleness. His profession yielded him, at some times, large amounts of income; but he seems never to have aimed at accumulation, and perhaps was not justly sensible of the importance and duty of preservation. Riches were never before his eyes as a leading object of regard. When young and poor, he was more earnest in struggling for eminence than in efforts for making money; and in after life, reputation, public regard, and usefulness in high pursuits, mainly engrossed his attention. He always said, also, that he was never destined to be rich; that no such star presided over his birth; that he never obtained any thing by any attempts or efforts out of the line of his profession; that his friends, on several occasions, induced him to take an interest in business operations; that, as often as he did so, loss resulted, till he used to say, when spoken to on such subjects, 'Gentlemen, if you have any projects for money-making, I pray you keep me out of them; my singular destiny mars every thing of that sort, and would be sure to overwhelm your own better fortunes.'" After this he says, —

"Mr. Webster was the author of that short biography of most good lawyers, which has been ascribed to other sources, viz., that they *lived well, worked hard, and died poor.*"

And in the same letter he tells the following anecdote of himself : —

Sitting one day at the bar in Portsmouth, with an elderly member of the bar, his friend, who enjoyed with sufficient indulgence that part of a lawyer's lot which consists "in living well," Mr. Webster made an epitaph, which would not be unsuitable : —

> " Natus consumere fruges ;
>   Frugibus consumptis,
>   Hic jacet
>   R. C. S." *

At the close of the letter, he added the following postscript, relative to the case on trial : —

" *Half past 2 o'clock — Cessat* Taber ; Choate *sequitur, in questione juris, crastino die.* †

> " Taber is learned, sharp and dry ;
>   Choate full of fancy, soaring high ;
>   Both lawyers of the best report,
>   True to their clients and the court ;
>   What sorrow doth a Christian feel,
>   Both should be ' *broken on a wheel !* ' "

The same gentleman says, " I have many letters like this, and I have always found him, throughout all my travelling, sojourning, and sports with him, one of the most agreeable men, one of the most amiable and playful I ever met with. No one has

---

* Being born to eat fruit ; and having consumed all, here lies R. C. S.

† Taber ceases ; Choate follows, on the question of equity, to morrow

known him more intimately, or has seen him oftener, under every variety of circumstances, for fifteen years."

We were in the Circuit Court in Boston on a similar, perhaps on the very same occasion, when he and Mr. Choate were pitted against each other in a case in which the violation of a patent for the protection of a new kind of wheel for rail cars was the question at issue. Mr. Choate, after pleading nearly three days, closed with a very pathetic appeal to the sympathies of the jury in behalf of his client. He begged them to consider the condition of his client, and the effect which would be produced upon him and his family if their verdict was against him. The peroration produced a decided impression.

Mr. Webster was to follow immediately. It was his first object to dispel the effect of Mr. Choate's closing appeal. This he did most effectually by a practical joke, which produced a sensation of hilarity throughout the whole court room. To appreciate its point, it should be known that a short time prior to this trial, Mr. Choate had been invited to give an address on some public occasion in a distant town. When his reply reached the committee from whom he had received the invitation, such was the peculiarity of the chirography, or so badly was the reply written, that none of them could read it. They were obliged to send for some one well skilled in deciphering difficult penmanship to translate the document. This anecdote was at that very time going the rounds of the papers. It had been read by many, if not by all, in the court room. After Mr. Choate had finished his plea, and had gone away from the table, where he had left his *brief*, or outline of argument, which was written on a number of loose sheets of paper, Mr. Webster, after a moment's whisper with his distinguished opponent, took up these loose sheets, and turning to the spectators, said, in a very gentlemanly manner, " Ladies, would you like to see a specimen of Mr. Choate's writing ? " and then with his own hands distributed them among the audience. This ingenious ruse was successful. The general burst of laughter, and the universal rush and scrambling after Mr. Choate's hieroglyphics, which were flying like mammoth snow flakes about the room, effectually dispelled the tender, sympathetic emotions which had been awakened by the moving peroration of his plea. The mirthfulness did not immediately subside. As each individual who obtained a piece of the mysterious paper looked upon it, his countenance was immediately wreathed in smiles. We were successful in obtaining a sheet, and, tearing it in two, gave half of it to a lady, who seemed to be as anxious for an autograph as ourselves. Upon casting our eye upon it, we had no difficulty in discovering the cause of the pleasantry

which all seemed to experience.   True, there were
on the paper plenty of lines, curves and angles; but
how to put them together so as to make out a single
sentence we found impossible.   We no longer wondered at the continued tittering of the audience.

While his brief was flying around among the audience, Mr. Choate was standing by the stove, with
his back to the spectators.   A friend stepped up to
him, and, we presume, told him what was going on.
He looked around, and when he saw how the audience were employed, he stroked his chin, smiled,
and turned again towards the stove, apparently enjoying the joke as highly as any.

As another specimen of Mr Webster's pleasantry,
we refer to a passage in a speech which he gave at
Syracuse : —

"It has so happened that all the public services
which I have rendered to the world, in my day and
generation, have been connected with the general government.   I think I ought to make an exception.   I
was ten days a member of the Massachusetts legisla-
ature, [laughter,] and I turned my thoughts to the
search of some good object in which I could be useful
in that position ; and after much reflection, I introduced a bill, which, with the general consent of both
houses of the Massachusetts legislature, passed into
a law, and is now a law of the state, which enacts
that no man in the state shall catch trout in any

other manner than in the old way, with an ordinary hook and line. [Great laughter.] With that exception, I never was connected for an hour with any state government in my life. I never held office, high or low, under any state government. Perhaps that was my misfortune.

" At the age of thirty, I was in New Hampshire practising law, and had some clients. John Taylor Gilman, who for fourteen years was governor of the state, thought that, a young man as I was, I might be fit to be an attorney general of the State of New Hampshire, and he nominated me to the council ; and the council taking it into their deep consideration, and not happening to be of the same politics as the governor and myself, voted, three out of five, that I was not competent ; and very likely they were right. [Laughter.] So you see, gentlemen, I never gained promotion in any state government."

The New York Daily Times relates the following, which is a kind of practical joke upon Mr. Webster himself : —

" Some years ago he started off from Marshfield on a trouting expedition to Sandwich, a neighboring town on Cape Cod. On approaching a fine stream, he alighted from his wagon ; and just then he met the owner of the farm, whose stream ran through it. 'Good morning,' says Webster ; 'is there any trout here ?' 'Well,' says the farmer, 'some people fish here, but I don't know what they do get.' 'I'll throw my line in,' says Webster, 'and see what there is.'

"Webster walked the banks of the stream, trying his luck, and the old farmer followed him. Soon Webster remarked, 'You have some bog on your farm.' 'Yes,' says the farmer ; 'that ain't the worst of it.' Fishing still farther along, Webster says, 'You seem to have plenty of mosquitoes here.' 'Yes,' he replied, 'that ain't the worst of it.' Webster still kept on throwing his line into the deep pools, and then said, 'You have plenty of briers here.' 'Yes,' says the farmer, 'and that ain't the worst of it.' Mr. Webster, getting somewhat discouraged, in a hot August day, bitten by mosquitoes, scratched by briers, and not raising a single fish, dropped his rod, and said, 'he didn't believe there was any trout here.' 'And that ain't the worst of it,' says the farmer. 'Well,' says Mr. Webster, 'I would like to know *what the worst of it is.*' '*There never was any here !*' says the farmer. Mr. Webster enjoyed the joke, and often told it to his particular friends."

In 1841, when he was secretary of state, he came home from the department, where he had been engaged in official interviews with foreign ministers, and taking from his parlor a small basket, very elegantly ornamented, he immediately left the house.

After an absence of half an hour, he returned, and
handed Mrs. Webster the same basket, but with its
weight greatly increased. Imagine her surprise,
when, as she looked in, she found it *filled with
hens' eggs.* Feeling, perhaps, a little mortified
that her distinguished companion should descend to
so inappropriate an employment, she inquired the
reason of his conduct. Her husband replied, that
he had been "all the morning discussing with the
diplomatic corps the affairs of some half dozen of
the principal kingdoms of the world, and, as he was
fond of seeing both ends meet, he only wished to
realize how it would seem for him, a secretary of
state, to turn from such imposing business to the
opposite extreme, of purchasing, within the same
hour, a basket of newly-laid eggs."

On one occasion, many years ago, when Mr. Webster was in the Senate, just as he arose to speak, a
ministerial-looking stranger in the gallery suddenly
cried out, so as to be heard by the whole Senate,
"My friends, the country is on the brink of destruction ; be sure that you act on correct principles. I
warn you to act as your consciences may approve.
God is looking down upon you, and if you act upon
correct principles, you will get safely through."
Having thus discharged what he probably regarded
as a responsible duty, he stepped back, and quietly
disappeared, without giving the officers time to seize

him.   Of course such an unlooked-for interruption
threw the Senate into confusion.   Some laughed,
some conversed jestingly with each other, some left
their seats, and several minutes elapsed before the
chairman succeeded in restoring order.   During all
the excitement Mr. Webster retained his standing
posture, ready to commence so soon as the opportunity should be presented.   The favorable moment
having arrived, the first sentence he uttered was
this : " *As the gentleman in the gallery has concluded,
I will proceed with my remarks.*"   How much better
was this pleasantry than though he had indulged in
an outburst of passion at the disturbance, and insisted that the gallery should be cleared of spectators !   ·

Mr. Webster was good at a rifle shot, as well as
with hook and fly.   When travelling through the
State of Ohio, a number of years ago, in company
with a friend, he came upon a party of Buckeye
farmers, who were testing their skill in the use of
the gun, by firing at a target for turkeys.   Having
reined in his horses, for the purpose of enjoying the
sport as a spectator, he was invited by the free-and-
easy marksmen to try his skill.   He was not unwilling to comply.   It was an amusement with which
he was familiar.   After examining several rifles, in
a manner which evinced his acquaintance with the
instrument, he selected one of the best, and, with

the motley group of rough-looking western farmers standing around him, he raised the weapon to his eye, and in a moment sent a ball directly through the centre of the target. He was acknowledged a good shot, and had one of the finest turkeys in the flock presented to him. Then the questions went round, "Who is this? Where's he from? What's his business? Where is he going?" But no satisfaction could they obtain. They finally invited him to dine with them at an inn near by. He consented. Their curiosity being highly excited to learn who this skilful marksman was, his friend took the liberty of introducing him at the dinner as the Hon. Daniel Webster, member of Congress. Great was their pleasurable astonishment to learn that their stranger guest was the distinguished individual who had recently delivered a famous speech in Congress, of which they had heard, and some of them had read. As he had discoursed so effectively from the rifle's mouth, they wanted to hear some words of eloquence fall from his own. He was, therefore, *called out*, — perhaps by one of the party giving a toast in his honor. In responding to the call, he addressed to them a few appropriate remarks, and then proceeded on his journey. They earnestly endeavored to induce him to fire another rifle; but he was too wise to incur the liability of losing their good opinion of his skill by attempting a second

WEBSTER AND THE BUCKEYES

" crack shot." Not only did he put a ball through the centre of the target, but succeeded in making so favorable an impression upon their hearts, that some of them accompanied him twenty miles on his journey.

This *incog.* character was the occasion of another adventure, but of a somewhat different nature. When in company, Mr. Webster always dressed like a gentleman; but when on his farm, or on a fishing or gunning excursion, his costume was characterized for its appropriateness. He could be mistaken for no other character than the one he had assumed. In his gunning or fishing toggery, no stranger would suspect him of being any thing more than he seemed. On one occasion he was out after wild ducks, in company with his man, Seth Peterson, when they fell in with " a couple of Boston sporting snobs," who were in difficulty because there was a bog in the way, which they could not cross without getting wet. Judging of Mr. Webster from his costume; they supposed him to be one of the rustic farmers of Marshfield, and therefore asked him to carry them on his back to a dry point on the other side of the bog. Without revealing himself to them, Mr. Webster consented. After he had complied with their request, and had received from each of them a quarter of a dollar for the job, they inquired, in a flippant, familiar manner, " Is old

Webster at home ? We've had such miserable luck in shooting, that we should like to honor him with a call." To this question, expressed in such an undignified manner, Mr. Webster calmly replied, "that the gentleman alluded to was not at home just then, but would be as soon as *he* could walk to the house, and *he* would be glad to see them at dinner."

What reply these sporting gentlemen made to this rebuke is not recorded, but evidence is furnished that they did not dine with "old Webster" that day.

Young men should be careful not to form an opinion of others from their external appearance. A noble character is ofttimes concealed under an unfashionable costume. It is especially dangerous, in country places, to infer the social standing of a stranger from the garb in which he appears. The employment of a farmer forbids the wearing of fine broadcloth, French satin, and polished calfskin, when engaged in his daily occupation. And if, because the fabric of his garments is coarse, and their surface soiled, any one should infer that poverty of purse, feebleness of intellect, and a low social position were among his possessions, and should treat him accordingly, he would incur the liability of making a discovery which would very justly overwhelm him with mortification. The wisest course is, to treat every man, whatever may be his appearance, as a gentleman, until we learn his forfeiture of that character.

The natural humor of Mr. Webster, of which we have given several illustrations, manifested itself in early childhood. On one occasion, when he and his brother Ezekiel were boys, after they had gone to bed, they got into a controversy about some passage in the Columbian Orator, a famous school book of that day; they left their pillows, and began some researches in order to settle the dispute; in so doing they managed to set their bedclothes on fire, and narrowly escaped consuming the house. When asked, the next morning, how the accident was caused, Daniel replied, " *We were in pursuit of light, but got more than we wanted.*"

At another time their father gave them a certain piece of work to perform during his absence from the house; but finding, upon his return, that the task was unperformed, he questioned the boys with some degree of sternness concerning their employment : —

" What have you been doing, Ezekiel ? "

" Nothing, sir," was his answer.

" Well, Daniel, what have you been doing ? "

" *Helping Zeke, sir.*"

How much help " Zeke " required to do nothing, we are not informed.

The same native humor peeps out in the reply he

16

gave to a friend who asked him what he intended
to speak about in his historical address, in New
York, on the next day.

"I am going," said he, "to be excessively learned
and classical, and shall talk much about the older
citizens of Greece. When I make my appearance
in Broadway to-morrow, people will accost me thus:
'Good morning, Mr. Webster. Recently from
Greece, I understand. How did you leave *Mr.
Pericles* and *Mr. Aristophanes?*'"

The address alluded to in this playful manner
was one of rare excellence. It was instructive,
'classical, eloquent. So great was the desire to hear
him, that tickets for admission were sold, in some
instances, for a hundred dollars.

Frequently, when Mr. Webster was engaged in
his favorite amusements of riding, gunning, and fishing, his mind would revert to the great themes
which his office or his profession required him to
discuss and settle. Some of the interesting passages
in his addresses were prepared on these occasions.
It is stated that, at one time, when engaged in
angling, as he drew a large trout from the water,
he exclaimed, as if addressing his captive, and re-
garding it as the representative of others, "Venerable men! you have come down to us from a former
generation. Heaven has bounteously lengthened out
your lives, that you might behold this joyous day"

And these very words were afterwards employed in his oration at the laying of the corner stone of the Bunker Hill monument, when he addressed the veterans — the few surviving soldiers of that memorable battle.

It is a great mistake to suppose that cheerful humor and sparkling wit should never be indulged. They are the developments of an element of character which tends greatly to the promotion of human happiness. Ofttimes, when the brow is wrinkled with care, and the heart filled with sadness, some humorous remark, or sparkling repartee, or the relation of some ridiculous incident, or amusing anecdote, will smooth that brow, and neutralize the sadness of the burdened spirit. In the walks of grave professional life, exhibitions of good humor are like beautiful wild flowers, peeping here and there from the rocks and crevices by the roadside, which, by their delicate colors and pleasant perfume, afford delight to the weary traveller, who would otherwise be oppressed with the monotony and gloominess of the way. Flowers of this kind Mr. Webster both culled and cultivated. He knew, also, how to use them. There were few men more genial, more humorous, or who could more easily set " the table in a roar," than he. His relation of anecdotes always produced a decided effect.

He was also exceedingly happy in giving a pleasant turn, in social company, to topics on which he
differed from others. The following is an instance.
In 1847 he visited Charleston, South Carolina. A
dinner was given him. There were present at the
table those with whose political sentiments he had
no sympathy — those whom he had felt it his duty
to oppose, in Congress and elsewhere, with all the
weight of his personal talents and official position.
After being called out by a toast, which was drank
in his honor, he closed his speech in the following
agreeable manner : —

"Gentlemen, allow me to tell you of an incident.
At Raleigh, a gentleman, purposing to call on me,
asked his son, a little lad, if he did not wish to go
and see Mr. Webster. The boy answered, 'Is it
that Mr. Webster who made the spelling book, and
sets me so many hard lessons ? If so, I never want
to see him as long as I live.'

"Now, gentlemen, I am that Mr. Webster who
holds sentiments, on some subjects, not altogether
acceptable, I am sorry to say, to some portions of
the South. But I set no lessons ; I make no spelling books. If I spell out some portions of the Constitution of the United States in a manner different
from that practised by others, I readily concede,
nevertheless, to all others a right to disclaim my

spelling, and adopt an orthography more suitable to their own opinions, leaving all to that general public judgment to which we must, in the end, all submit." And when he took his seat, the following toast was submitted: " Here's to the agreeable schoolmaster — who sets no lessons."

CHAPTER XIII.

A PRACTICE of Mr. Webster, which he seems to have kept up through life, was that of early rising. Long before the first gray streak in the eastern horizon heralded the approach of the " king of day," he was up, dressed, and in the depth of his day's work. It was his uniform practice to despatch his study and correspondence by the middle of the forenoon. On one occasion he said, " What little I have accomplished has been done early in the morning." In a letter to an agricultural convention, he wrote, " When a boy among my native hills of New Hampshire, *no cock crowed so early that I did not hear him.*" During his residence at Washington, he was accustomed to visit the market, make his purchases, and converse familiarly with the butchers and farmers, long before the citizens of the capital were

236

stirring. Strangers in Washington, after learning
this fact, would themselves go to the market in the
early dawn, for the purpose of getting a sight of the
great statesman.

Mr. Lanman says, " Mr. Webster admired, above
all things, to see the sun rise, especially from his
chamber window at Marshfield. He appreciated
the moral sublimity of the spectacle, and it ever
seemed to fill his mind with mighty conceptions.
On many occasions, at sunrise, both in the spring
and autumn, has he stolen into the chamber occupied
by the writer, which looked upon the sea, and, with
only his dressing gown on, has stood by his bedside,
and startled the writer out of a deep sleep, by a
loud shout somewhat to this effect : —

" ' Awake, sluggard ! and look upon this glorious
scene ;. for the sky and the ocean are enveloped in
flames ! '

" On one occasion the writer was awakened in a
similar manner at a very early hour, when, lo, Mr.
Webster, who happened to be in a particularly playful mood, was seen going through the graceful mo
tions of an angler, throwing a fly and striking a
trout, and then, without speaking a word, disappeared. As a matter of course, that day was given
to fishing."

In 1852 Mr. Webster visited Virginia ; he continued his habit there. As one of its results, we have

the following beautifully descriptive account of the morning. None but a passionate lover of the early dawn could have written it.

"RICHMOND, VA.,
. Five o'clock, A. M., April 29, 1852.

"MY DEAR FRIEND: Whether it be a favor or an annoyance, you owe this letter to my early habits of rising. From the hour marked at the top of the page, you will naturally conclude that my companions are not now engaging my attention, as we have not calculated on being early travellers to-day.

"This city has a 'pleasant seat.' It is high; the James River runs below it, and when I went out, an hour ago, nothing was heard but the roar of the falls. The air is tranquil, and its temperature mild. It is morning, and a morning sweet, and fresh, and delightful. Every body knows the morning in its metaphorical sense, applied to so many occasions. The health, strength, and beauty of early years lead us to call that period the 'morning of life.' Of a lovely young woman we say, she is 'bright as the morning,' and no one doubts why Lucifer is called 'son of the morning.'

"But the morning itself, few people, inhabitants of cities, know any thing about. Among all our good people, no one in a thousand sees the sun rise once in a year. They know nothing of the morning. Their idea of it is, that it is that part of the day which comes along after a cup of coffee and a beefsteak, or a piece of toast. With them morning is not a new issuing of light, a new bursting forth of the sun, a new waking up of all that has life from a sort of temporary death, to behold again the works of God, the heavens and the earth ; it is only a part of the domestic day, belonging to reading the newspapers, answering notes, sending the children to school, and giving orders for dinner. The first streak of light, the earliest purpling of the east, which the lark springs up to greet, and the deeper and deeper coloring into orange and red, till at length the 'glorious sun is seen, regent of the day,' —this they never enjoy, for they never see it.

"Beautiful descriptions of the morning abound in all languages ; but they are the strongest, perhaps, in the East, where the sun is often an object of worship.

"King David speaks of taking to himself the 'wings of the morning.' This is highly poetical and beautiful. The wings of the morning are the beams of the rising sun. Rays of light are wings. It is thus said that the Sun of righteousness shall arise 'with healing in his wings ' — a rising sun that shall scatter life, health, and joy throughout the universe.

"Milton has fine descriptions of morning, but not so many as Shakspeare, from whose writings pages

of the most beautiful imagery, all founded on the
glory of the morning, might be filled.

"I never thought that Adam had much the advantage of us, from having seen the world while it
was new.

"The manifestations of the power of God, like
his mercies, are 'new every morning,' and fresh
every moment.

"We see as fine risings of the sun as ever Adam
saw; and its risings are as much a miracle now as
they were in his day, and I think a good deal more,
because it is now a part of the miracle that, for
thousands and thousands of years, he has come to
his appointed time, without the variation of a mil-
lionth part of a second. Adam could not tell how
this might be. I know the morning; I am acquainted with it, and I love it. I love it fresh and sweet
as it is — a daily new creation, breaking forth and
calling all that have life, and breath, and being, to
new adoration, new enjoyments, and new gratitude.

                              "DANIEL WEBSTER."

"We see as fine risings of the sun as ever Adam
saw." How interesting is that thought! By rising
early, and looking from an upper window, or ascending some small eminence which gives us the
command of the horizon, we may behold a scene
of as much magnificence as greeted the eyes of

Adam, when the first rays of the rising sun gilded the beauties of paradise. Try it, young reader. Rise before the sun ; go forth to hail his coming; play in the beams sent forth by his upper edge before his centre makes its appearance; observe carefully the effects produced upon the appearance of the various objects upon hill, tree, cloud, lake, and building, as the darkness flees away, and the gray dawn brightens into the full light of day ; and if you possess a particle of the love of the beautiful, you will acknowledge that no display of the pyrotechnic art can bear any comparison to the gorgeous splendor of the scene before you.

Those who lounge away their time upon their pillow are not aware of the amount which the aggregate of these lost hours would make. Dr. Doddridge has said that the difference between rising at five and seven o'clock in the morning for the space of forty years, supposing a man to go to bed at the same hour at night, is nearly equivalent to the addition of ten years to a man's life.

It follows that he who desires to lengthen his life in respect to its practical influence, should rise earlier than he has been accustomed to. All the time that he thus redeems from the pillow is so much added to active existence.

In addition to this, the freshness of the morning air, and the renovation which the mind has received froin its recent sleep, by which the clearness of its perceptions and the rapidity of its operations are ii creased, render this a peculiarly favorable time fer intellectual pursuits.

Mr. Webster's habit in this respect was similar to that of many other distinguished characters. Buffon, the great naturalist, ascribes the existence of many volumes of his works to his practice of early rising.

We have already remarked that Mr. Webster was a lover of nature. This was evinced in his choice of a residence at Marshfield, where hill, pond, forest, and ocean combine their peculiar beauties to render the place attractive, and also by his assiduous care, with which all the peculiar charms of the place have been developed.

General Lyman, in a letter which he wrote in November, 1843, at Marshfield, says, "Mr. Webster, seeing the interest I manifested yesterday on the subject of the forest, which is periodically cut down for wood, and suffered to grow up again, was kind enough to show me vast numbers of trees, probably one hundred thousand, which he has planted from the seed with his own hands. They are, however, yet small. He said his way had been to sow the seed, in favorable places, of the locust, horsechestnut, catalpa, &c., some of which have been transplanted at an early age, and others left to grow up in thickets. A little belt of wood thus

WEBSTER AT MARSHFIELD

produced, none of the trees of which have been planted more than a dozen or thirteen years, bounding the lawn and pond on one side, is already so high and dense as to afford a perfectly shaded walk through the centre of it, not only making a beautiful promenade, but filling up the background of the landscape, of which the lawn and pond constitute prominent features.

"Mr. Webster spoke in warm terms—terms almost of indignation—of the stupidity of persons who omit to plant trees from an idea that they may not live to see their growth and beauty, or to taste their fruits. He reminded me of Walter Scott's good advice on this subject. He would plant a tree which would be growing while others were sleeping.

"He spoke of the just and excellent taste of Sir Walter Scott, on all subjects of this kind, and referred to two articles written for the London Quarterly Review, some years ago, on planting trees, landscape, &c., as being full of instruction. 'Where is the man,' said Mr. Webster, 'who does not admire the principle which actuated the late Stephen Girard, of Philadelphia, who, when bending over the grave with age, said he would plant a tree to-day if he knew he were to die to-morrow? If every man were actuated by such sentiments, what a change it would produce in the affairs of the world!'

He showed me eight or nine specimens of oak ;
several of them he had obtained from the Southern
States ; all the varieties of pines and cedars, and
the arbor vitæ, from Maine ; various sorts of ash,
maple, and the buckeye from Ohio ; and the sweet
gum from Virginia.

" For these last two, however, the climate was
found somewhat too severe. The whitewood, as
we call it in New York and Ohio, — properly the
liriodendron, or tulip tree, — appears to grow well.
Hedges of buckthorn line the avenue to the house,
stand the climate well, and are very handsome.

" In a few years these trees, according to my
prediction, will be the admiration of every body,
and branches of them will be cut and carried away
by future generations, who will know the biography
of the great man of our time, as branches are now
cut and carried away from the trees which grow on
the plantations of other sages, whose pillars are in
the dust. The handsome wooden eminence near
the house is now beautifully covered with a thicket
of locusts, catalpas, young cherry trees, &c. This
little hill, twelve years ago, was perfectly naked, and
the sand was blown about by the wind. A lady,
visiting Mrs. Webster, begged that so unsightly an
object might be made to mend its appearance. Her
advice was followed, and six years afterwards, visiting Marshfield again, she clapped her hands with

admiration at the success of what she had recommended."

Although Mr. Webster was fond of gunning, and often went out for that purpose, being an "excellent shot," yet he allowed no gun to be fired upon his premises. Such birds and game as approached his house, or made it their home any where on his grounds, he would not allow to be disturbed. The delightful effect of this kind treatment is described as follows by his visitor : —

"I was struck with the tameness of several little animals and birds, which I have elsewhere found quite wild and shy. A squirrel, for instance, sat almost within our reach, eating a nut, and hearing us talk, without the least indication of fear. The birds hopped about, singing their wild notes, as if unconscious of our presence. A brood of quails had actually been hatched between the house and the gate, in the hedge that lines the carriage way to the door. I inquired why this was so ; he said, 'During the whole time I have been there, I have endeavored to cultivate their acquaintance, and have never permitted their nests to be disturbed ; nor do I allow guns to be fired on the premises, nor sticks or stones to be thrown at them, nor any thing done that would frighten them away. They seem to know where they are well treated, and come with the seasons to enjoy my protection.' "

17

On one occasion, Mr. Webster was walking over his grounds with a gentleman from Boston, when a flock of quails darted across the road only a few feet from them. The gentleman was highly excited at the discovery of the game, and longed to try his skill with powder and ball. " O, if I only had a gun," said he, " I could easily kill the whole flock. Have you not one in your house, sir ? "

" Yes, sir," replied Mr. Webster, with his usual calmness — " yes, sir, I have a number of guns ; but no man whatsoever do I ever permit to kill a bird, rabbit, or squirrel, on any of my property." He then proceeded to condemn the indiscriminate slaughtering propensities of the Americans.

" In this country," said he, " there is an almost universal passion for killing and eating every wild animal that chances to cross the pathway of man ; while in England and other portions of Europe these animals are kindly protected and valued for their companionship. This is to me a great mystery ; and so far as my influence extends, the birds shall be protected." Just at this moment one of the little fugitive quails, that the visitor was so anxious to kill, mounted a little eminence, and poured forth a song, as if in gratitude to its humane protector. " There," said Mr. Webster, " does not that gush of song do the heart a thousand fold more good than could possibly be derived from the death of that

beautiful bird?" The stranger returned his thanks
to Mr. Webster for his gentle reproof, and subsequently acknowledged that "this little incident made
him love the man whom he had before only admired
as a statesman."

Mr. Webster, in the earnestness of his desire to
surround his dwelling at Marshfield with the charms
of animated nature, has succeeded in accomplishing, what very few persons in this country have ever
attempted, viz., the taming of wild geese. "The
value and pictorial beauty of Marshfield are greatly
enhanced," says Mr. Lauman, "by the existence, in
the immediate vicinity of the mansion, of a trio of
little lakes, all of them fed by springs of the purest
water. The two smaller ones are the favorite
haunts of the common geese and the duck tribes;
but the larger one, which studs the landscape very
charmingly, is the exclusive domain of a large flock
of wild geese which Mr. Webster had domesticated.
He informed the writer that his first attempts to tame
these beautiful creatures were all unsuccessful, until
the idea occurred to him that perhaps they might be
made contented with their civilized abode, provided
they could have awarded to them small sedgy islands,
such as were found at their breeding-places in the
far north, where they might make their nests and
remain undisturbed by the fox and other prowling
animals. The experiment was tried; and while

the geese were rendered contented with their lot,
the lake itself has been greatly improved in picturesque beauty by its wild yet artificial islands.   Indeed, the rural scenery of Marshfield is all that
could be desired by the painter or poet , but when
they come to add thereto an immense expanse of
marsh land, veined with silver streams, dotted with
islands of unbroken forest, skirted with a far-reach
ing beach, and bounded by the blue ocean, they cannot but be deeply impressed with the magnificence
of its scenery."

Mr. Webster's love of Nature was not superficial.
Whilst he greatly admired all her external features,
he was interested in the study of her laws.   In his library was a collection of rare and valuable works on
the various departments of natural history, and the natural sciences, the perusal of which afforded him great
pleasure whenever he could secure time for the purpose.   On a certain occasion, when these subjects
were made the topics of conversation, he said that
he wished he could live three lives while living this.
"One I would devote to the study of geology —
to reading the earth's history of itself.   Another life
I would devote to astronomy.   I have recently read
the history of that science. written so clearly, that,
although I am no mathematician, I could understand
it, and was astonished at seeing to what heights it

had been pushed by modern intellects. The other I would devote to the classics."

It is an interesting fact, and one on which the young would do well to ponder, that, as Mr. Webster advanced in years, his mind was withdrawn from themes and speculations which interested him in the earlier periods of his life, and was devoted, with increased pleasure, to the contemplation and study of nature.

Amongst all the visitors who were honored with the hospitality of his elegant mansion, there were few so cheerfully welcomed as those who were devoted to the investigation of natural objects. With these Mr. Webster loved to converse, and exchange items of information. He also furnished such individuals every facility in his power for the prosecution of their studies. The celebrated Audubon was one of his personal friends; and on one occasion, when the great ornithologist was visiting Marshfield, "he was presented by Mr. Webster with a wagon load of miscellaneous birds, which the latter had ordered to be killed by his hunters all along the coast, and among them was the identical Canada goose which figures so beautifully in the 'Birds of America.' Mr. Webster has said that the delighted naturalist studied the attitude of that single goose for an entire day, and that he was three days in taking its portrait.'

At another time, in conversation with a clergyman, —Rev. Dr. Choules, — he gave utterance to the following beautiful sentiments : —

"When I was in England I was greatly pleased with the wallflower, so often seen upon the walls of ruins and decaying buildings. The country people call it the bloody wallflower. I seldom picked this sweet-scented flower without thinking of the hopes and wishes of life — the best and sweetest of my life all surrounded with ruin and decay : still we must look out for the blossoms of hope."

"I have been reading White's Selbourne once more. What moral beauty there was in White's mind! How he revelled in quiet country life! and when he became deaf, and could no longer hear the birds sing, yet he thanks God that his eyesight is still quick and good."

Walking in the evening at Marshfield, and gazing at the sea, Mr. Webster stopped, and placing his hand upon the shoulder of the same gentleman, recited several verses of Mrs. Hemans's impressive poem on the Sound of the Sea :

"Thou art sounding on, thou mighty sea,
  Forever and the same ;
The ancient rocks yet ring to thee,
  Whose thunders nought can tame.

"O, many a glorious voice is gone
  From the rich bowers of earth.

And hushed is many a lovely one
Of mournfulness or mirth.

" But thou art swelling on, thou deep,
Through many an olden clime,
Thy billowy anthems ne'er to sleep
Until the close of time."

The study of nature is one of the noblest employ-ments of the human mind. We are then brought into direct contact with the works of the Creator. We are furnished with conclusive evidences of his existence and attributes. Not only by these pursuits is the taste refined, and the love of the beautiful strengthened, but an influence is exerted favorable to the cultivation of moral character.

Besides, in the study of nature we need not go far for lessons. They spring up in the beautiful flowers which ornament our path; they smile upon us in the stars above our head; we may read them upon the tapestry of the ever-changing clouds, in the architecture of mountains, and the solemn grandeur of ancient forests; they whisper around us in the buzzing of insects; they charm us in the melody of birds; they fill us with awe in the howling of the storm, the roaring of the angry ocean, and the ter-rific tones of the threatening thunder. They are spread out all around us on nature's ample page, and whenever so disposed, we may study them to our " heart's content." We are aware of a class of in-

dividuals in the community who look with a feeling
bordering upon contempt on pursuits of this nature
Picking weeds to pieces, or carefully examining the
formation of an insect, or a reptile, they seem to
regard as totally unworthy so exalted a being as
man.

They cherish a feeling of pity bordering on contempt for those who are devoted to such pursuits.   It would be well for such persons to consider
whether any thing, which the all-wise Creator has
not deemed as beneath himself to make, can be unworthy for us to examine and admire, and whether
it may not exhibit a want of suitable regard for the
Creator himself, when the displays of his power and
glory, as exhibited in the works of his hand, fail of
attracting attention, or of awakening admiration.

THE nobleness of Mr. Webster's nature was exhibited in a striking manner on different occasions, when he endeavored to prevent the perpetuity of personal feuds. In the exciting debates of Congress it was natural, under the influence of temporary impulse, that language should be used, which, in a calmer mood, the speaker himself would not justify. Such instances, however, were exceedingly rare in the speeches of Mr. Webster. He seemed always to appreciate the dignity of his character as a senator of the most powerful republic on earth, and evinced an unwillingness to do or say any thing that was unbecoming his exalted position. He was not insensible to the high standing of his opponents, neither was he unwilling to accord to them his meed of praise for their genius and learning.

Hiram Ketchum, Esq., of New York, in a brief eulogy upon Mr. Webster, among other things, said,

253

"I have known him in private and domestic life.
During the last twenty-five years I have received
many letters from him, some of which I retain,
and some have been destroyed at his request. I
have had the pleasure of meeting him often in private circles, and at the festive board, where some
of our sessions were not short; but neither in his
letters nor his conversation have I ever known him
to express an impure thought, an immoral sentiment,
or use profane language. Neither in writing nor
in conversation have I ever known him assail any
man. No man in my hearing was ever slandered
or spoken ill of by Daniel Webster. Never in my
life have I known a man whose conversation was
uniformly so unexceptionable in tone and edifying
in character. No man ever had more tenderness of
feeling than Daniel Webster. He had his enemies
as malignant as any man; but there was not one of
them, who, if he came to him in distress, would not
receive all the relief in his power to bestow."

Another illustration of his magnanimity is furnished in his direction to the Hon. Edward Everett,
when carrying Mr. Webster's Works through the
press, to suppress all allusions which were adapted
to perpetuate personal feuds. In allusion to this
fact, Mr. Everett, in his beautiful eulogy upon Mr.
Webster, says, —

"In preparing the new edition of his works, he

thought proper to leave almost every thing to my discretion — as far as matters of taste are concerned. One thing only he enjoined upon me, with an earnestness approaching to a command. 'My friend,' said he, 'I wish to perpetuate no feuds. I have sometimes, though rarely, and that in self-defence, been led to speak of others with severity. I beg you, where you can do it without wholly changing the character of the speech, and thus doing essential injustice to me, to obliterate every trace of personality of this kind. I should prefer not to leave a word that would give unnecessary pain to any honest man, however opposed to me.'

"But I need not tell you, fellow-citizens, that there is no one of our distinguished public men whose speeches contain less occasion for such an injunction. Mr. Webster habitually abstained from the use of the poisoned weapons of personal invective or party odium. No one could more studiously abstain from all attempts to make a political opponent personally hateful. If the character of our congressional discussions has of late years somewhat declined in dignity, no portion of the blame lies at his door."

A gentleman who was on familiar terms with him for years says, "In all the interviews which I had the happiness and honor to enjoy with this great man, I cannot remember that I ever heard him utter an unkind, acrimonious, or uncharitable remark upon any man. Once, when a gentleman had named some violent censures heaped upon him in his public character, Mr. Webster calmly replied, 'Perhaps my calumniator's misfortunes have soured his temperament, for I remember him a very kindly-disposed person; we must make allowances for the infirmities of age.' The provocation had been very great, and his motives had been wantonly assailed, yet his considerate and magnanimous spirit triumphed nobly upon this occasion." *

As another instance, we relate the following. After the negotiation of the Ashburton treaty, by which very complicated and threatening difficulties between this and the mother country were adjusted, Mr. Webster had serious charges alleged against him in the United States Senate by Hon. Mr. Dickenson. These charges he repelled in strong language. When, in 1850, Mr. Webster left the Senate in order to enter upon his duties as Secretary of State, he addressed the following letter to Mr. Dickenson. The painful occurrences to which he refers are those connected with that debate.

" WASHINGTON, Sept. 27, 1850.

" MY DEAR SIR : Our companionship in the Senate is dissolved. After this long and most impor-

---

* Rev. Dr. Choules.

tant session, you are about to return to your home, and I shall try to find leisure to visit mine. I hope we may meet each other again two months hence, for the discharge of our duties in our respective stations in the government. But life is uncertain, and I have not felt willing to take leave of you without placing in your hands a note containing a very few words which I wish to say to you.

" In the earlier part of our acquaintance, my dear sir, occurrences took place which I remember with constantly-increasing regret and pain, because, the more I have known of you, the greater have been my esteem for your character and my respect for your talents. But it is your noble, able, manly, and patriotic conduct in support of the great measure of this session which has entirely won my heart, and secured my highest regard. I hope you may live long to serve your country ; but I do not think you are ever likely to see a crisis in which you may be able to do so much either for your own distinction or the public good. You have stood where others have fallen ; you have advanced with firm and manly step where others have wavered, faltered, and fallen back ; and for one, I desire to thank you, and to commend your conduct, out of the fulness of an honest heart.

" This letter needs no reply ; it is, I am aware, of very little value ; but I have thought you might be

willing to receive it, and, perhaps, to leave it where
it would be seen by those who shall come after you.
I pray you, when you reach your own threshold, to
remember me most kindly to your wife and daughter.
I remain, my dear sir, with the truest esteem,

" Your friend and obedient servant,

" DANIEL WEBSTER.

" HON. D. S. DICKENSON, U. S. Senate."

Another interesting illustration of his noble high
mindedness was furnished in his eulogy upon Mr.
Calhoun, of South Carolina.   On some of the most
important questions ever discussed by Congress, and
in some of the most intensely-exciting debates, he
and Mr. Calhoun were opponents.   On the floor of
the Senate, that great arena for intellectual chivalry,
they measured lances.   A spectator might have imagined that in heart, as well as in political opinion,
they were strongly hostile to each other.   Yet when
it was announced in the Senate by Mr. Butler,
his colleague, that Mr. Calhoun had deceased, Mr.
Webster arose and delivered a beautiful eulogy, from
which we make the following extracts, which show
how highly he could appreciate the talents and
character of an honorable opponent, and with what
felicity he could express his admiration.

   " I hope the Senate will indulge me in adding a
very few words to what has been said.   My apology

for this presumption is the very long acquaintance which has subsisted between Mr. Calhoun and myself. We were of the same age. I made my first entrance into the House of Representatives in May, 1813. I found there Mr. Calhoun. He had already been a member of that body for two or three years. I found him there an active and efficient member of the House, taking a decided part, and exercising a decided influence in all its deliberations.

" From that day to the day of his death, amidst all the strifes of party and politics, there has subsisted between us always, and without interruption, a great degree of personal kindness.

" Differing widely on many great questions respecting our institutions and the government of the country, those differences never interrupted our personal and social intercourse. I have been present at most of the distinguished instances of the exhibition of his talents in debate. I have always heard him with pleasure, often with much instruction, not unfrequently with the highest degree of admiration.

" Mr. Calhoun was calculated to be a leader in whatsoever association of political friends he was thrown. He was a man of undoubted genius and of commanding talent. All the country and all the world admit that. His mind was both perceptive and vigorous. It was clear quick, and strong.

" Sir, the eloquence of Mr. Calhoun, or the manner in which he exhibited his sentiments in public bodies, was part of his intellectual character. It grew out of the qualities of his mind. It was plain, strong, terse, condensed, concise, sometimes impassioned, still always severe. Rejecting ornament, not often seeking far for illustration, his power consisted in the plainness of his propositions, in the closeness of his logic, and in the earnestness and energy of his manner. These are the qualities, as I think, which have enabled him through such a long course of years to speak often, and yet always command attention. His demeanor as a Senator is known to us all — is appreciated, venerated, by us all. No man was more respectful to others; no man carried himself with greater decorum, no man with superior dignity. I think there is not one of us, when he last addressed us from his seat in the Senate, — his form still erect, with a voice by no means indicating such a degree of physical weakness as did in fact possess him, with clear tones, and an impressive, and, I may say, an imposing manner, — who did not feel that he might imagine that we saw before us a Senator of Rome while Rome survived.   .   .   .

" Mr. President, he had the basis, the indispensable basis, of all high character — and that was unspotted integrity and unimpeached honor. If he had aspirations, they were high, and honorable, and noble.

There was nothing grovelling, or low, or meanly selfish that came near the head or heart of Mr Calhoun. . . . .

"He has lived long enough, he has done enough; and he has done it so well, so successfully, so honorably, as to connect himself for all time with the records of his country. He is now an historical character. Those of us who have known him here will find that he has left upon our minds and our hearts a strong and lasting impression of his person, his character, and his public performances, which, while we live, will never be obliterated. We shall hereafter, I am sure, indulge it as a greatful recollection that we have lived in his age, that we have been his contemporaries, that we have seen, and heard him, and known him. We shall delight to speak of him to those who are rising up to fill our places. And when the time shall come that we ourselves must go, one after another, to our graves, we shall carry with us a deep sense of his genius and character, his honor and integrity, his amiable deportment in private life, and the purity of his exalted patriotism."

Mr. Hayne was a far more violent controversialist than Mr. Calhoun. His attack upon Mr. Webster and upon Massachusetts in the Senate on Mr. Foot's resolution, so unprovoked, so gracefully

18

acrimonious, called forth from Mr. Webster what
has been termed his "great speech," yet when Mr.
Webster visited South Carolina, subsequently to
the death of Mr. Hayne, he took occasion to speak
publicly of his deceased opponent in the most respectful manner.   His animosities, if he had any,
seemed to have been buried in the grave of his
distinguished competitor.

We have dwelt upon this trait of character the
longer, because we desire to commend it strongly to
the imitation of the young.   We all have opponents.
Where the opposition is merely one of opinion, it is
comparatively harmless.   We may differ in sentiment without any interruption·of friendly relations.
Yet in that case it is eminently desirable that each
should treat his opponent with great courtesy.   They
should be careful not to impugn each others motives,
not to indulge in criminations and recriminations, not
to exhibit in tone or gesture an acrimonious spirit.
Each should strive to present the opinions of the
other with perfect fairness, to put upon them the
most favorable construction, and to discuss them with
great candor.   No permanent advantage is ever
gained by misrepresentation.

But when the opposition extends beyond that of
opinion, when there is an evident intention on the
part of an opponent to inflict upon us injury, then an

opportunity is offered for the exercise of magnanimity. When a foe has fallen, attempt not his
ruin, but extend towards him the hand of kindness.
Having defended yourself, there pause. Follow not
your vanquished opponent with invective. Give him
credit for all the commendable qualities he possesses,
and make all the allowances charity can suggest for
the imperfections of his character and the incorrect-
ness of his opinions.

CHAPTER XV.

THE human family constitutes one great brotherhood. Each should feel an interest in each. When ever an opportunity exists of removing the difficulties in others' paths, of lightening their burdens, or of promoting their elevation, improvement, and happiness, the assistance should be cheerfully rendered.

As human happiness and misery are made up of the aggregate of things in themselves comparatively trivial, encouragement is offered for all to labor in the field of benevolence. Every kind word, or gentle smile, or unexpensive gift exerts a beneficent influence. It is like a gleam of sunshine. breaking through the clouds in a dark and stormy day. Unexpected acts of favor towards our fellow-pilgrims in the journey of life are ofttimes like the notes of

264

some familiar tune sweetly falling upon the ear of the weary traveller when resting upon the fragments of hoary ruins in some remote wilderness, where he supposed himself excluded, by many a tedious league, from all civilized beings. That favorite tune dispels the illusion, by the conviction which it awakens that sympathetic companionship is at hand. By the power of association, those time-honored ruins seem peopled with familiar forms. The feeling of loneliness is entirely gone. How many of life's pilgrims there are, who, though surrounded by a multitude, feel alone ! To them it seems as if there was " no flesh in man's obdurate heart ; it does not feel for man " — as if a great gulf separated them from the mass of unfeeling humanity moving around them. Slight attentions, kind words, offices of friendship bridge this gulf, and make them feel that they are in sympathetic communication with the race. These labors of love, like rays of heavenly light, banish the darkness of their hearts ; the air seems filled with the melody of household tunes, awakening in the otherwise desolate soul a sense of brotherhood with man.

Among the incidents in the life of Mr. Webster which have been made public are a number illustrative of his thoughtful friendship and benevolence.

When in England, some dozen years ago, he was in company with Mary Russell Mitford. In her

" Recollections of a Literary Life," this lady relates the following pleasing reminiscence of that occasion : —

" During this visit a little circumstance occurred, so characteristic, so graceful, and so gracious, that I cannot resist the temptation of relating it. Walking in my cottage garden, we talked naturally of the roses and pinks that surrounded us, and of the different indigenous flowers of our island and of the United States. I had myself had the satisfaction of sending to my friend Mr. Theodore Sedgwick a hamper containing roots of many English plants familiar to our poetry : the common ivy, (how could they want ivy who had had no time for ruins ?) the primrose, and the cowslip, immortalized by Shakspeare and by Milton ; and the sweet-scented violets, both white and purple, of our hedgerows and our lanes ; that known as the violet in America, (Mr. Bryant somewhere speaks of it as 'the yellow violet,') being, I suspect, the little wild pansy, (viola tricolor,) renowned as the love-in-idleness of Shakspeare's famous compliment to Queen Elizabeth. Of these we spoke ; and I expressed an interest in two flowers, known to me only by the vivid description of Miss Martineau — the scarlet lily of New York and of the Canadian woods, and the fringed gentian of Niagara. I observed that our illustrious guest made some remark to one of the ladies of the party ; but I little expected that, as soon after his return as seeds of these plants could be procured, I should receive a package of each, signed and directed by his own hand. How much pleasure these little kindnesses give! And how many such have come to me from over the same wide ocean!"

Here an interest in certain flowers, expressed by a lady in casual conversation, was remembered for months, and was the means of inducing him to send, unasked, a package three thousand miles, signed and directed by his own hand, that she might enjoy the gratification of raising the flowers for herself. The plants produced by those seeds were no doubt highly prized by the gifted authoress; and now that he who sent them has passed away, they will be held in higher estimation than ever. How strange it is that the death of a friend enhances the value of all the tokens of his kindness! Gifts, of which we were unmindful while their donor was alive, become treasured mementoes of his love, when the hand that gave them is mouldering in the tomb. In such treasures not a few have been made rich by the demise of the great statesman. Trees of grafts cut from his orchards, animals reared from stock on his farm, plants raised from seed received from his hands, to say nothing of tokens of other kinds, and especially letters in which he has poured out the fulness of his heart, though valued before, will now be more highly prized than ever.

When Mr. Webster was in Congress, he was ac
customed to receive from different quarters seeds of
various kinds. These he neither sold nor monopo-
lized for himself. Being greatly interested in agricultural pursuits, he was desirous of diffusing as far
as possible all kinds of crops. For this reason he
gave away the seeds which he received, that the
farmers might experiment with them upon their
different kinds of soil. In that beautiful letter to
John Taylor, containing such a mingling of gravity
and cheerfulness, sober politics and minute farming
directions, where there is such a singular blending
of incongruous objects as " pennyroyal crops,"
" little wife," "my mother's garden," and " the
graves of my family," he says, " I have sent you
many garden seeds. *Distribute them among your
neighbors.* Send them to the stores in the village,"
(not to sell ; no, no, but) " that *every body may have
part of them without cost.*"

It would be interesting to know the history of
some of those seeds. What were they ? which of
them were successfully raised ? how did they compare with other crops of the same kind ? did any
of them introduce new species? in what respects
was their introduction an improvement ? has a suc-
cession of crops been raised from these seeds ? how
have those crops turned out as to quality and
quantity ?

If we had the means of answering these questions, it would not be at all surprising to learn that new and important additions had been made to certain departments of the agricultural interest by seeds received through the thoughtful attention of the farmer statesman.

But Mr. Webster not only gave away seeds. When occasion required it, he was willing to part with more important articles. He was especially considerate towards his unfortunate neighbors. Such was his accessibleness when at home, that the farmers in his vicinity freely approached him and related their embarrassments. Those who had been acquainted with him in his early years made capital of their former friendship in appealing to his benevolence.

On one occasion, when confined by illness to his room at Marshfield, an old friend who resided at a distance of thirty miles called to see him. He was at once admitted to the chamber. At first the conversation was upon " days of auld lang syne." They each drew upon their store of reminiscences, and lived old scenes over again. After some time had been spent in this delightful manner, the visitor entered upon his tale of woe, and related the various misfortunes which he had experienced. He seems to have been in reduced circumstances, for in the conversation he incidentally expressed his earnest

desire to obtain a good cow. The invalid listened
attentively to every word he uttered, but made no
reply. When the friend had finished the story of
his sorrows, and arose to leave, Mr. Webster called
Mr. Porter Wright, the superintendent of his farm,
into his presence, and gave him instructions to show
his friend the cattle which were on the farm, and
then present him with any cow which he might
be pleased to select from the number. The herd
was examined, and the visitor made choice of a fine
Alderney, valued at fifty dollars, which was cheerfully given him by his invalid friend. He went
away rejoicing. "And this is only one of many
similar instances which might and will be recorded
of the astonishing liberality of Mr. Webster."

We have already referred to the fact that when
his early teacher, Mr. Tappan, was reduced to
poverty, in his old age, he sent him at one time fifty,
and at another time twenty dollars for his relief.
The delicacy with which it was done — the words
of affectionate sympathy which accompanied these
substantial tokens of friendship — must have rendered
the donation doubly acceptable.

On the Elms Farm, at Franklin, Mr. Webster had
a bull of the Hungarian breed. It was young,
large, and beautiful, weighing about two thousand
pounds, with a neck more than six feet in circum-
ference, and of a delicate light slate color. It was an

object of special interest to those who visited the place. On one occasion, Mr. John Taylor was in the field with it, when, without provocation, the animal suddenly became enraged, rushed upon him, gored him with his horns, tossed him high in the air, and, after he had fallen, trampled him under his hoofs, injuring him severely. He would probably have been wounded much more dangerously if he had not seized and held on to the ring which ornamented the bull's nose. As it was, he had a very narrow escape from death.

Mr. Webster heard in Boston that the superintendent of his farm was injured, but he knew not the particulars. It being the season of the year when he was accustomed to make his annual visit there, he was soon on his way to Franklin. When he reached Concord, where he heard the particulars of the affair, and learned that his life was considered in danger, he was deeply afflicted, and manifested great anxiety to pursue his journey. As soon as he arrived at home, he hastened to the house of Mr. Taylor, whom he found prostrate upon his bed, enduring the severe sufferings of a dislocated shoulder, a dreadfully bruised breast, and a deep wound in his thigh, some seven inches long. Mr. Webster was filled with solicitude for his friend. He inquired the opinion of the physician, and when he learned that he had pronounced him out of danger, he was greatly relieved.

Mr. Taylor, doubtless, in order that he might allay the anxiety of Mr. Webster, gave quite an amusing narrative of his rencounter with the enraged animal, and of other feats which it had performed. " Do you think the creature is dangerous ? " asked Mr. W., "and ought to be chained ? "

" Why," replied Taylor, " he is no more fit to go abroad than your friend Governor Kossuth himself."

" Rather strong language this," humorously replied Mr. W. ; " but when a man has been gored almost to death by an Hungarian bull, it is not strange that he should be severe upon the Hungarian governor."

We have related this painful incident in order to say that when Mr. W. first heard of it in Boston, not, however, imagining the extent of its severity, he immediately determined to take Mr. Taylor a present of something which he supposed would be appropriate to one in his condition. He looked around, and made the necessary purchase. When he arrived at Elms Farm, he gladdened the heart of the wounded man by the donation of a *basket of grapes* and a *fresh salmon*, brought purposely for him from Boston. The present was worthy of a nobleman, and they were noblemen of nature's mould who gave and received it.

O, how greatly such acts of friendly attention smooth the sharp asperities of life! How they pour the oil of gladness into the wounded spirit! A bouquet of flowers, a little fruit, or pleasant confection, sent into the room of the invalid, are odorous with the fragrance of affection they are little tokens of remembrance ; they show the sufferer that he is not forgotten by the absent, but is thought of with interest, and his happiness desired.

Mr. Webster seems to have been particularly kind to those in his employ. He had in Washington a colored man of the name of Charles Brown, who was his servant for nearly thirty years. He was a worthy, trusty person. Mr. Webster appreciated his qualities, and was accustomed to give him money to spend on holidays and other times, in addition, as we suppose, to his support. A few years ago he ascertained that this servant had bought a piece of land, and had erected a small, yet comfortable house.

" Where did you get money to purchase so fine a house ? " asked he.

" I am glad to say, sir," replied Brown, " that it all came out of your pocket. It is the money which you have given me on holidays and at other times."

It would seem from this that the spending-money

given to this servant must have been somewhat liberal.

A similar spirit was developed by Mr. Webster in the following "items" in his last will and testament : —

"Item. My servant William Johnson is a free man. I bought his freedom not long ago for six hundred dollars. No demand is to be made upon him for any portion of this sum, but so long as is agreeable, I hope he will remain with the family.

"Item. Monicha McCarty, Sarah Smith, and Ann Bean, colored persons, now, also, and for a long time in my service, are all free. They are very well deserving, and whoever comes after me must be kind to them."

Public men, especially if they have the reputation of wealth and liberality, are frequently called upon by private individuals for donations to various objects. In these calls the proprieties of time and circumstance are not always regarded. Sometimes, instead of donations, reproofs are received. On one occasion, Mr. Webster gave both. The following are the facts : —

A lady called upon him in Washington, and related a long and mournful story about her afflictions, stating that she was very poor ; that she resided in a western city ; that she had not sufficient money to

reach her home, and then asked him to assist her.
He listened with some degree of impatience to her
tale, expressed his surprise that she, a total stranger,
should feel at liberty to call on him for the purpose
of soliciting charity, simply because he was connected with the government ; and, after administering a plain reprimand for her improper conduct, he
closed the interview by *presenting her with fifty
dollars.*

It is sometimes a difficult task to decide upon the
path of duty in such cases.   It is so easy to be de-
ceived by impostors, and such deceptions occur so
frequently, that we know not, when a stranger asks
for assistance, whether it may not be one of this class.
A safe course would be to require corroborating
evidence of the facts in the case, in addition to the
statements of the solicitor.   And even then decep-
tion would not be impossible ; for such corroborating evidence might be abundantly furnished, and the
whole be based upon falsehood.

To another woman he gave a similar amount, but
under very different circumstances.   The incident is
highly interesting.

In the early part of his professional career, when he
was practising law in Portsmouth, one of his clients,
whom he had conducted successfully through a somewhat difficult suit, was unable to pay him his fees.
He therefore insisted upon giving him the deed of a

certain lot of land in a neighboring county. The matter was adjusted by the acceptance of this deed. Where the land was, or what was its quality, Mr. Webster knew not. After many years had passed away, he had occasion to visit this county. It occurred to him that perhaps it would be well to look up the land, and ascertain its condition. He went to work for that purpose. He made his inquiries, and, after following the directions which were given him, he discovered the property. Upon it was an old house, built among the rocks, which appeared to be inhabited. He knocked at the door, and entered. He found it was occupied by an old woman, who, hermit-like, lived there all alone. He entered into familiar conversation with her, and asked who owned the place. She told him that it belonged to a lawyer, by the name of Webster; and she was expecting every day that he would come and turn her out of doors. She little knew the character of that Webster. After some further inquiries, he surprised the old lady by the announcement that he was lawyer Webster, the owner of the place, but that she need not fear that he had come to warn her out. That was far from his intention. After allaying her apprehensions, he sat down at her table, partook of such refreshments as the humble hut afforded, and then departed, *leaving the old lady a donation of fifty dollars.*

Ever since then, that rocky spot has been desig
nated " Webster's Farm."

This, however, was not the limit of his donations.
When occasion required, he gave more largely.
He was a large-hearted man. Says Mr. Lanman,
— " The following well-authenticated fact was related to the writer by an eye witness, and is only a
specimen of many that might be mentioned, tending
to illustrate the character of Mr. Webster's heart.
Somewhere about the year 1826, a certain gentleman
residing in Boston was thrown into almost inextricable
difficulties by the failure of a house for which he had
become responsible to a large amount. He needed
legal advice, and being disheartened, he desired the
author of this anecdote to go with him and relate his
condition to Mr. Webster. The lawyer heard the
story entirely through, advised his client what to do,
and to do it immediately, and requested him to call
again in a few days. After the gentlemen had left
Mr. Webster's office, he came hurriedly to the door,
called upon the gentlemen to stop a moment, and
having approached them with his pocket book in
hand, he thus addressed his client : ' It seems to
me, my good sir, if I understood your case rightly,
you are entirely naked; is it so ? '

The client replied that he was indeed penniless,
and then of course expected a demand for a retain-
ing fee. Instead of that demand, however, Mr

19

Webster kindly remarked, as he handed the client a
bill for *five hundred* **dollars**, —

"'Well, there, take that: it is all I have by me
now.   I wish it was more ; and if you are ever able,
you must pay it back again.'

"The client was overcome, and it may be well
imagined that he has ever since been a 'Webster
man.'   Surely a man who can command the admiration of the world by the efforts of his gigantic
intellect, and also possesses the above self-sacrificing
habit of making friends, must indeed be a great and
a good man."

To all intents this was a donation.   He knew not
that the man would ever be in a condition to refund
the money ; he let him have it subject to that contingency.   It was to be a loan if the man ever had
the ability to return it ; if otherwise, it was a gift.

This chapter cannot be more appropriately closed
than with the following deeply-affecting narrative
which is equally illustrative of Mr. Webster's benevolence and piety.   Rather than mar the account by
presenting it in our own language, we give it as it
appeared in the National Intelligencer.

"In answer to some fanatical imputations on Mr.
Webster's religious principles, because of his support
of the compromise measures, a widow lady, who
resided in the vicinity of Mr. W.'s early home, said, —

"'Mr. Webster an infidel !   I cannot believe that.

I have known him long, and, if it would not savor
too much of egotism, I could relate some incidents
that would, I think, convince you that, whatever his
political views may have been, he certainly was not
an infidel.'

"She was requested to do so, and accordingly
wrote the following : —

"'Mr. Webster and my husband became acquainted in early life, and the friendship of youth extended
to riper years.   They were truly congenial spirits,
and sought each other's society as much as possible.
But the cares of business at length separated them,
and for many years they seldom met.   My husband
settled down in this place, and Mr. Webster went
forth to battle for the right in the councils of the
nation.

"'For some time we were greatly prospered.   A
lucrative business brought us wealth almost beyond
our hopes.   Two children came like a sunbeam to
light up our happy home with their joyous smiles,
and to cheer our spirits with their innocent prattle.
Those were happy days, and I love to recall them.
But alas! they were soon covered with clouds of
darkness, that even the eye of faith could hardly
penetrate.   .

"'Some of the firms in which my husband's funds
were placed became involved, and our little all was

swept from our grasp. When he found that every effort to recover it but plunged him deeper into difficulty, he became disheartened. Soon his health failed, and he was compelled to give up his business entirely. He then sold the shop, and what else we could spare, and with the avails paid every debt except one. This was due to a friend who chose to wait for his money rather than take from us the cottage where we lived, the only property we could then call our own.

" ' But hardly was the arrangement made when the gentleman died, leaving the note in the hands of one who knew not how to show mercy. He demanded immediate payment, and we were about to sell our house when our oldest child was taken down with a fever, and soon left us, as we hope, for a better world. The same disease prostrated my husband; and when the physician told me he must die, I felt that my cup of sorrow was full. But no; I was mistaken.

" ' There was yet another drop to be mingled in that cup of bitterness. While my husband yet lingered between life and death, my daughter, the only remaining child, was taken sick also, and after five days' suffering, she too left us, to rejoin her brother in the " spirit land."

" ' Do you ask how I bore this second bereave-

ment? I believe I had not leisure to think of it.
All my time, all my attention, were given to my
husband, who was slowly but surely going down to
the grave. I had even forgotten the hard-hearted
creditor. But he did not forget. Inexorable as
death itself, he came at the time appointed, and
demanded the money. I think he must have
been intoxicated, for I am sure no man in his
sober senses could have been so cruel. I told him
my husband was dying; but he replied, "Sorry,
sorry to hear it. He won't earn any more money,
and, as you can't pay up, I'll just take the house.
You can live somewhere else, as you have no one to
look after." I interrupted his cruel remarks, and,
thinking to move his feelings, I led him to the room
where lay the cold form of my child.

"'Vain hope! I might as well have tried to
move an iceberg. After much entreaty, I obtained
permission to remain in the house while my loved
one lived, on condition that I gave up the furniture.
This I promised, that I might no more be troubled
with his loathsome presence.

"'The man left me, and I sank into a chair,
utterly overcome at the prospect of the desolation
before me. At that moment I heard a rap at the
door. I could not rise to obey the summons. I
felt that my heart was breaking But the door

slowly opened, and Mr. Webster stood before me.
He had come home on a visit, and, without knowing any thing of our sorrows, he rode over to see
and embrace his early friend. What was his surprise to find him thus! And when the story of our
troubles had been told, when he had assured himself
that his long-cherished friend had but a few more
hours to live, he sat down and wept.

" 'Then he asked to see the corpse of his little
pet, who, when he last visited us, sat upon his knee
and played with his watch. As he rose to leave the
bed, my husband said in a whisper, " Fetch her to me,
that I too may look upon her sweet face once more."

" 'We placed the still beautiful form beside the
bed, and standing near it, gave ourselves up to un-
controllable grief. When able to command his
voice, Mr. W. said, "Let us pray." And kneeling
there, beside the dying and the dead, he prayed as
none but a Christian can pray. Sure I am that a
prayer so earnest, so full of faith and hope in the
Redeemer, was never poured forth from the lips of
an infidel.

" 'Gladly would he have stopped with us through
the night; but business forbade his stay. He left
us, and as he grasped for the last time the hand of
his dying friend, those pale features were lighted up
with a smile of hope, such as they had not worn for

many a day. The troubled spirit was at rest, for the assurance had been given that the widow should be provided for in her affliction.

"'My husband died the next day. I saw no more of the hard-hearted creditor, and the house remained unsold. I still occupy it, and the room where Mr. Webster kneeled in prayer is to me a sacred place.'"

A QUESTION in which a large portion of the community cherish a deep interest is that which has respect to the religious opinions and character of our most eminent statesmen. That there are any among them addicted to profanity, drunkenness, and other immoralities, is an occasion of grief and humiliation. An account of the disgraceful, belligerent scenes which have occasionally transpired in Congress has sent a wave of sadness throughout the land. Such occurrences have been deplored both publicly and privately. They have furnished topics for penitential confession and earnest prayer in the services of the sanctuary, and in the private devotions of the closet. It will be a fortunate day for our country when immorality of character, or a positive disregard for Christianity, shall be sufficient to prevent the election of any individual, however eminent he may be in other respects, to any office of responsibility. In canvassing the qualifications of candidates, the time has come when a higher estimate should be placed upon moral requisites. We need men of good hearts, as well as strong minds. Integrity of character should be the ballast of the ship of state ; and this should be developed not only in the laws which are passed, but in those who enact and execute them.

With reference to Mr. Webster, it is stated that during his long congressional career, though he was frequently placed in circumstances of the most exciting character, and was ofttimes the subject of personal and irritating allusion, he never departed from the proprieties of debate. *He was never called to order.* If this rigid adherence to the rules of parliamentary decorum had been imitated by others, the various scenes of congressional rowdyism which have dishonored the halls of our national legislation would have been avoided.

But Mr. Webster was governed by something higher than a mere regard to decorum. He knew that the character of his country was, in the opinion of foreign nations, implicated in these scenes of

disorder, and that they were at variance with that
spirit of good will towards others which is so prominent and beautiful an element of Christianity.
Patriotism and religion combined to guide his
course.

His parents, as we have seen, were Christians of
the Puritan stock. His "excellent mother" in-
stilled into his mind, from his earliest childhood,
sentiments of piety. He was, when quite young,
taught the Catechism and the hymns of Dr. Watts.
The history and precepts of the Scriptures were
also impressed upon his mind. He was taught to
regard the Sabbath and to reverence the institution
of Christianity. These early influences were not in
vain. He became hopefully pious, and, when· a
young man, united with the Orthodox Congregational Church. He had, even at that time, attained
to such a reputation, that the following incident.
comparatively trifling in itself, which occurred then,
is remembered to the present day. On the occasion
of his making a public profession of religion, the
only occupant of the same pew with him was a
" very poor, and a very old, woman." The service
was closed with singing. After Mr. Webster had
found the hymn, he offered a part of the book to
the poor woman, and they both sang together from
the same page — a beautiful symbol of the union
existing between the piety of youth and that of age.

Even though their voices might have been discord-
ant, they were one in spirit. This pleasant incident
is still a topic of fireside conversation among the
members of the parish.

When he delivered his Fourth of July Oration at
Hanover, during his collegiate course, he took occasion to express the obligations of the people to cherish sentiments of thanksgiving towards the Ruler of
nations for the blessings they enjoyed. His language was as follows: "If piety be the rational
exercise of the human soul, if religion be not a
chimera, and if the vestiges of heavenly assistance
are clearly traced in those events which mark the
annals of our nation, it becomes us on this day, in
consideration of the great things which have been
done for us, to render the tribute of unfeigned
thanks to that God who superintends the universe,
and holds aloft the scale that weighs the destinies
of nations."

These sentiments are important. They are worthy of being incorporated in every oration on our
national anniversary. We should never forget our
indebtedness to the Ruler of nations for the political
freedom with which he has blessed us. The Fourth
of July ought to be a day of national thanksgiving.
With our various demonstrations of joy there should
be mingled feelings of devout gratitude. Of this

the youthful orator was convinced, and has earnestly expressed it in the quotation we have given.

Being a firm believer in the divine origin of the Scriptures, he has on various occasions expressed himself warmly upon the importance of making them a subject of study.

A correspondent of the Commercial Advertiser says, —

" Some years ago we had the pleasure of spending several days in company with Mr. Webster at the residence of a mutual friend, Harvey Ely, Esq., at Rochester. During that intercourse, we had more than one opportunity of conversing on religious subjects — sometimes on doctrinal points, but more generally on the importance of the Holy Scriptures, as containing the plan of man's salvation, through the atonement of Christ. So far as our knowledge of the subject extends, Mr Webster was as orthodox as any we ever conversed with.

" On one occasion, when seated in the drawing room with Mr. and Mrs. Ely, Mr. Webster laid his hand on a copy of the Scriptures, saying, with great emphasis, ' This is the book ! ' This led to a conversation on the importance of the Scriptures, and the too frequent neglect of the study of the Bible by gentlemen of the legal profession, their pursuits in life leading them to the almost exclusive study of works having reference to their profession. Mr

Webster said, ‘ I have read through the entire Bible
many times. I now make a practice to go through
it once a year. It is the book of all others for lawyers as well as for divines ; and I pity the man that
cannot find in it a rich supply of thought, and of
rules for his conduct ; it fits man for life — it pre-
pares him for death.’

“ The conversation then turned upon sudden
deaths ; and Mr. Webster adverted to the then recent death of his brother, who expired suddenly at
Concord, N. H. ‘ My brother,’ he continued, ‘ knew
the importance of Bible truths. The Bible led him
to prayer, and prayer was his communion with God.
On the day on which he died, he was engaged in an
important cause in the court then in session. But this
cause, important as it was, did not keep him from his
duty to his God ; he found time for prayer, for on the
desk which he had just left was found a paper written by him on that day, which for fervent piety, a
devotedness to his heavenly Master, and for expressions of humility, I think was never excelled.’

“ Mr. Webster then mentioned the satisfaction he
had derived from the preaching of certain clergymen,
observing that ‘ men were so constituted, that we
could not all expect the same spiritual benefit under
the ministry of the same clergymen.’ He regretted
that there was not more harmony of feeling among
professors generally, who believed in the great truths

of our common Christianity. Difference of opinion, he admitted, was proper; but yet, with that difference, the main objects should be love to God — love to our fellow-creatures. In all Mr. Webster's conversations, he maintained true catholicity of feeling."

The editor of the Boston Atlas, as quoted by General Lyman, in his Memorials, says, —

"It was our fortune to pass several days at his home in Marshfield, some six or seven years ago; and well we remember one beautiful night, when the heavens seemed to be studded with countless myriads of stars, that about nine o'clock in the evening, we walked out, and he stood beneath the beautiful weeping elm which raises its majestic form within a few paces of his dwelling, and, looking up through the leafy branches, he appeared for several minutes to be wrapped in deep thought, and, at length, as if the scene, so soft and so beautiful, had suggested the lines, he quoted certain verses of the eighth Psalm, beginning with the words, 'When I consider thy heavens, the work of thy fingers, the moon and the stars, which thou hast ordained, what is man, that thou art mindful of him? and the son of man, that thou visitest him? For thou hast made him a little lower than the angels, and hast crowned him with glory and honor,' &c. The deep, low tone in which he repeated these inspired words, and the deep, rapt attention with which he gazed up through the branches of the elm, struck us with a feeling of greater awe and solemnity than we ever felt, when, a year or two later, we visited some of the most magnificent cathedrals of the old world, venerable with the ivy of centuries, and mellowed with the glories of a daily church service for a thousand years.

" We remained out beneath the tree for an hour, and all the time he conversed about the Scriptures, which no man has studied with greater attention, and of which no man whom we ever saw knew so much, or appeared to understand and appreciate so well. He talked of the books of the Old Testament especially, and dwelt with unaffected pleasure upon Isaiah, the Psalms, and especially the Book of Job. The Book of Job, he said, taken as a mere work of literary genius, was one of the most wonderful productions of any age, or in any language. As an epic poem, he deemed it far superior to either the Iliad or Odyssey. The two last, he said, received much of their attraction from the mere narration of warlike deeds, and from the perilous escape of the chief personages from death and slaughter; but the Book of Job was a purely intellectual narrative. Its power was shown in the dialogue of characters introduced. The story was simple in its construction, and there was little in it to excite the

imagination or arouse the sympathy.   It was purely
an intellectual production, and depended upon the
power of the dialogue, and not upon the interest of
the story, to produce its effects.   This was considering it merely as an intellectual work.   He read it
through very often, and always with renewed delight.
In his judgment, it was the greatest epic ever
written.

"We well remember his quotation of some of the
verses in the thirty-eighth chapter: 'Then the
Lord answered Job out of the whirlwind, and said,
Who is this that darkeneth counsel by words without
knowledge ?   Gird up now thy loins like a man ;
for I will demand of thee, and answer thou me,
Where wast thou, when I laid the foundations of the
earth ?   Declare, if thou hast understanding,' &c.
Mr. Webster was a fine reader, and his recitation of
particular passages, to which he felt warm, were
never surpassed, and were capable of giving the
most exquisite delight to those who could appreciate
them."

With regard to this attachment to the Bible, the
author of Mr. Webster's Private Life says, —

" Indeed, he loved and he read that priceless volume as it ought to be loved and read ; and he once
told the writer that he could not remember the time
when he was unable to read a chapter therein.   He
read it aloud to his family on every Sunday morning,

and often delivered extempore sermons of great
power and eloquence. He never made a journey
without carrying a copy with him, and the writer
would testify that he never listened to the story of
the Savior, or heard one of the prophecies of Isaiah,
when it sounded so superbly eloquent as when coming from his lips. Those admitted to the intimacy of his conversation alone can tell of the
eloquent fervor with which he habitually spoke of
the inspired writings; how much light he could
throw on a difficult text; how much beauty lend
to expressions that would escape all but the eye
of genius; what new vigor he could give to the
most earnest thought; and what elevation even to
sublimity.

"It would be impossible, as C. W. March has
said, for any one to listen half an hour to one
of his dissertations on the Scriptures, and not believe
in their inspiration or *his*. And yet, while his
private conversations and public productions attest
how deeply he was imbued with the spirit of the
Scriptures, neither the one nor the other ever contained the slightest irreverent allusion to any passage
in them, any thing in the way of illustration, anal-
ogy, or quotation, which would seem to question
their sanctity. He was scrupulously delicate in this
regard, and therein differed widely from most of
his contemporaries in public life; as he read and

20

admired the Bible for its eloquence, so did he vener
ate it for its sacredness."

At a dinner table at the Revere House, Boston,
one of the party made a remark upon the poetry of
the Scriptures. "Ah, my friend," immediately replied Mr. Webster, "the poetry of Isaiah, and Job,
and Habakkuk is beautiful indeed; but when you
reach your sixty-ninth year, you will give more for the
fourteenth or the seventeenth chapter of John's Gospel, or for one of the Epistles, than for all the poetry
of the Bible."

It may be asked, If Mr. Webster was so deeply
impressed with the value of the sacred Scriptures,
why did he never give expression to his views at the
anniversary of some of the Bible Societies? He
stated in the above interview, that he had declined
speaking at Bible Societies, "from fear that the motives prompting to such a step would be regarded as
sinister." * He expressed deep regret that he had
never recorded his opinion of the word of God in
some public manner, and intimated a willingness to
comply, if invited to speak at the anniversary of the
American Bible Society. But the arrangement was
never made, owing, probably, to the speedy decease
of the clergyman to whom the matter was suggested.

It is reasonable to suppose that one who was so

* Rev. Dr. Choules's Sermon.

sincerely a lover of the Bible would not be uninterested in the public services of the sanctuary. The following fact will illustrate Mr. Webster's views and practice upon this point : —

He was accustomed, at one period of his life, to spend his months of summer recreation in Dorchester, Massachusetts. The late Rev. Dr. Codman was, at that time pastor of the Orthodox Congregational Church in that town. At the time he became a resident of the place, Mr. Webster called upon Dr. Codman, "with whom he held similar religious opinions," and said to him, —

"Sir, I am come to be one of your parishioners. Not one of your fashionable ones ; but you will find me in my seat both in the morning and in the afternoon."

He is said to have been true to his word. His example in this respect furnishes an impressive rebuke to those " fashionable " worshippers whose conscience and heart are satisfied with a single attendance upon the public services of the Sabbath. May we not see in it, also, the influence of home education ? Being taught, when a boy, to be in his seat on both parts of the day, he continued the practice in subsequent years. He did not go there for amusement, nor to while away an hour that would have otherwise hung heavily on his hands. Indeed, any thing in the form of a sermon which furnished *mere* intellectual entertainment seemed to him out of place.

To Rev. Mr. Alden, of Marshfield, the pastor whose ministrations he attended when at home, he said with emphasis, " When I attend the preaching of the gospel, I wish it to be made a *personal matter,* A PERSONAL MATTER, A PERSONAL MATTER."

On another occasion he expressed his views of preaching to a gentleman who afterwards gave them to the public in the Congregational Journal, in the following article : —

" A few evenings since," says this writer, " sitting by his own fireside, after a day of severe labor in the Supreme Court, Mr. Webster introduced the last Sabbath's sermon, and discoursed in animated and glowing eloquence for an hour, on the great truths of the gospel. I cannot but regard the opinions of such a man in some sense as public property. This is my apology for attempting to recall some of those remarks which were uttered in the privacy of the domestic circle.

" Said Mr. Webster, ' Last Sabbath I listened to an able and learned discourse upon the evidences of Christianity. The arguments were drawn from prophecy, history, with internal evidence. They were stated with logical accuracy and force ; but, as it seems to me, the clergyman failed to draw from them the right conclusion. He came so near the truth that I was astonished he missed it. In summing up his arguments, he said the only alternative presented by these evidences is this: Either Christianity is true, or it is a delusion produced by an excited imagination. Such is not the alternative,' said the critic ; 'but it is this : the gospel is either true history, or it is a consummate fraud ; it is either a reality or an imposition. Christ was what he professed to be, or he was an impostor. There is no other alternative. His spotless life in his earnest enforcement of the truth, his suffering in its defence, forbids us to suppose that he was suffering an illusion of the heated brain.

" 'Every act of his pure and holy life shows that he was the author of truth, the advocate of truth, the earnest defender of truth, and the uncomplaining sufferer for truth. Now, considering the purity of his doctrines, the simplicity of his life, and the sublimity of his death, is it possible that he would have died for ar illusion ? In all his preaching the Savior made no popular appeals. His discourses were all directed to the individual. Christ and his apostles sought to impress upon every man the conviction that he must stand or fall alone — he must live for himself, and die for himself, and give up his account to the omniscient God, as though he were the only dependent creature in the universe. The gospel

leaves the individual sinner alone with himself and
his God. To his own Master he stands or falls.
He has nothing to hope from the aid and sympathy
of associates. The deluded advocates of new doctrine do not so preach. Christ and his apostles,
had they been deceivers, would not have so preached.

"'If clergymen in our days would return to the
simplicity of the gospel, and preach more to individuals and less to the crowd, there would not be so
much complaint of the decline of true religion.
Many of the ministers of the present day take their
text from St. Paul, and preach from the newspapers.
When they do so, I prefer to enjoy my own thoughts
rather than to listen. I want my pastor to come to
me in the spirit of the gospel, saying, "You are
mortal! your probation is brief; your work must be
done speedily. You are *immortal*, too. You are
hastening to the bar of God; the Judge standeth
before the door." When I am thus admonished, I
have no disposition to muse or to sleep. These
topics,' said Mr. Webster, 'have often occupied my
thoughts; and if I had time I would write on them
myself.'

"The above remarks are but a meagre and imperfect abstract, from memory, of one of the most
eloquent sermons to which I ever listened."

These are the true, common-sense views to be
taken of the subject. It will be a most desirable

change in public opinion when these views become popular. There are many to whom no preaching is so interesting as that which indulges in all kinds of flowery and imaginative description of scenes, circumstances, and characters, but which leaves the conscience unaddressed. To hold the mirror of divine truth before them, and show them the moral deformities of their character, is to perform a most unwelcome service. But instead of censuring themselves, and striving for amendment, they make the preacher the subject of their complaints, or else find fault with the truth he utters. Probation, mortality, and eternity are themes too sombre for the contemplation of such. They take no pleasure in them. How widely different was it with Mr. Webster! " I want my pastor to come to me in the spirit of the gospel, saying, ' You are *mortal!* your probation is brief; your work must be done speedily. You are *immortal,* too. You are hastening to the bar of God; the Judge standeth at the door.' " A great mind wants great themes for its contemplation. No wonder that he added, " These topics have often occupied my thoughts."

Reader, permit them to occupy your thoughts. You can dwell upon nothing invested with more profound interest. In comparison with these, all other subjects dwindle into insignificance. Your present life is brief. Yet for all your conduct here

you are accountable at the tribunal of your Maker
It is appointed unto men once to die, and after that
the judgment. Then will follow your immortality,
the character of which will depend upon the course
of life which you have followed here. How ex-
plicit is the language of revelation!—" Be not de-
ceived; God is not mocked. Whatsoever a man
soweth, that shall he also reap. He that soweth to
the flesh shall of the flesh reap corruption. He
that soweth to the spirit shall of the spirit reap life
everlasting." Let the young especially remember
that this life is their seedtime ; that the harvest will
be reaped in another world, and the nature of that
harvest will depend upon the character of the seed
sown here.

Being a believer in the Bible, Mr. Webster was
convinced of the efficacy of prayer. The last time
he attended church, this was the subject of discourse.
It was delivered by that warm-hearted, earnest
preacher, and indefatigable laborer in the vineyard
of Christ, Rev. E. N. Kirk, of Boston.

Hearing that this gentleman was to preach in
Duxbury, a few miles from Marshfield, Mr. W., with
some of his guests, rode over to hear him. Mr.
Charles Lanman, who was one of the number, has
given the following account of the circumstance, with
some additional remarks, of which we gladly avail
ourselves, coming as they do from one who was

favored with the enjoyment of a close personal intimacy with the great statesman.

"The last time that he ever attended church, it was my rare fortune to be his companion. He had been informed that the Rev. E. N. Kirk, of Boston, was expected to preach in Duxbury, some three miles from Marshfield; and packing off his guests and a part of his household in a couple of carriages, he reserved a gig for himself, and in this did we attend. The sermon was on the efficacy of prayer, and was distinguished not only for its eloquence, but for its powerful arguments. It dealt in nothing but pure Bible doctrines, as understood by the orthodox church. Mr. Webster listened with marked attention to the whole discourse, and, after the services were closed, went up and congratulated the preacher. On our return home, his conversation turned upon the sermon, and he said it was a remarkable, a great effort. He said the arguments adduced were unanswerable, and that if a man would only live according to the lessons of such preaching, he would be a happy man both in this world and the world to come. He said, moreover, 'There is not a single sentiment in that discourse with which I do not fully concur. And this remark, when appended, as it ought to be, to the sermon when hereafter published, will serve to convince the world that his views of religion were most substantial and satisfactory.

During the whole of our ride home, he conversed upon matters contained in or suggested by the discourse; and I deeply regret that I did not take more ample notes of what he said on the occasion. The distinct impression left upon my mind, however, was, that if he were not a genuine Christian, the promises of the Bible were all a fable; and God knows that I would rather die than, for a moment, even imagine such a state of things.

" He was a believer in the great atonement; and though, living as he did in a sphere of peculiar temptations, he may have committed errors, he needed no promptings to lead him to a speedy repentance. He was actuated by a spirit of charity which knew no bounds. He treasured no animosities to his fellow-men, and when once wronged by those in whom he had confided with all the guilelessness of a child, he did not retaliate, but simply moved in another sphere beyond their reach. He was a student of the Bible, and read it habitually in his family whenever the annoyances of his official position did not prevent; and never sat down, when with his family alone, to enjoy the bounties of his table, without first imploring a blessing. No man ever thought or talked with more reverence of the power and holiness of God. He came of a race of good men; was baptized into, and became a member, in his college days, of the Congregational church, but died in the communion

of the Protestant Episcopal Church, of which he
was a devout member; and one of the most impressive scenes that I ever witnessed, going to prove
the matchless beauty of our religion, was to see him,
in full view of the Capitol, the principal theatre of
his exploits, upon his knees before the altar, partak-
ing of the sacrament of the Lord's supper. That
spectacle, and the grandeur of his death, are to me
more eloquent than a thousand sermons from human
lips."

The sermon alluded to, preached by Mr. Kirk,
will ever be interesting, not only on account of
its intrinsic merits, but as being the last which
Mr. Webster ever heard, and as drawing from
him the sentiments he then uttered.

He was a believer in the efficacy and the obligation of prayer. He has given the whole weight of
his influence to sanction a practice which not a few
affect to despise.

"Many years ago," says Rev. Dr. Choules,
" 1834, in passing through the Sound, we occupied
the captain's state room. At night Mr. Webster took
up my Bible and read the twenty-third Psalm, and
then made some fine remarks upon the character of
David, observing that the varied experience of
David as a shepherd boy, a King, victorious and
vanquished, had made him acquainted with all
the diversified feelings of human nature, and had

thus qualified him to be the chorister of the church in all future ages. After this, he asked me to commend ourselves to God, remarking that none needed prayer more than ' the wayfaring man.' "

" How absurd," says one, " to imagine that our poor requests receive any attention from the Sovereign of the universe, or secure any benefit to ourselves!" " How superstitious," says another, " to withdraw to some place of retirement, and there pretend to talk to some unseen God ! " The spirit of such harmonizes with certain ones of old, who impiously said, " It is vain to serve God," and " What is the Almighty, that we should serve him ? and what profit should we have if we pray unto him ? "

Not so thought Mr. Webster. If his opinion on other subjects be valuable, it is certainly not worthless on this. He was a believer in the importance of prayer, and performed the duty with more or less frequency.

And why should not you, my young reader ? The Bible enjoins the duty with great frequency. It promises that it shall not be performed in vain. Various interesting instances are given when prayer was answered. How reasonable is it that feeble creatures like ourselves should, in this way, manifest our dependence upon that great and good Being who called us into existence, and who supplies our daily wants   Even if it were not true that prayer is answered, its reflex influence upon the worshipper's mind and heart would justify its performance. To draw voluntarily near to God ; to hold, in the exercise of faith, converse with him ; to acknowledge our weaknesses ; to confess our sins ; to render thanksgiv ing for the innumerable blessings we have received, and earnestly to implore more, — all this has a tendency to deepen within us feelings of humility, penitence, gratitude, and devotion. It makes us more sensible of our weakness and our dependence upon Him who is the object of our prayers.

In respect to his religious sentiments, in addition to what Mr. Lanman has said, Rev. Mr. Kirk, in his sermon on the death of Mr. Webster, entitled Great Men are God's Gift, uses the following language : —

" Having noticed that on several occasions gentlemen have endeavored to show that his religious views were not definite, but indefinite, or, as some would term it, liberal, I would here mention an anecdote, which, from his own lips, I am authorized to say is authentic. Being asked by a Unitarian gentleman, as he was coming out of an Episcopal church in this city, whether he believed that three and one are the same thing, he replied in a manner perfectly characteristic, as it properly disposes of the real difficulty of the Trinity, ' Sir, I believe you and I do not understand the arithmetic of heaven.' "

In further illustration of his religious sentiments, we mention the following incident, as related by Rev. Dr. Choules, in his sermon on Mr. Webster's death : —

"That evening I asked Mr. Webster if his religious views were those of the Orthodox Congregational ists, with whom I had heard that he united in early life. 'Yes,' he said, 'he thought that he had never changed his religious opinions ; that he regarded Jonathan Edwards as being as nearly the stamp of truth as any mere human writer. He spoke of his History of Redemption as having greatly interested him, and added, 'But I prefer to find truth as it is conveyed to us in the word, without system, yet so clear and lucid.' In regard to the atonement, he expressed the most abiding confidence, observing that it seemed to him the great peculiarity of the gospel, to deny which, was to reduce it to a level with other systems of religion. He observed that he had 'no taste for metaphysical refinement in theology, and preferred plain statements of truth.' He thought the pulpit had much to answer for in pro- ducing differences of opinion among Christians, and pressed with the remark, 'I take the Bible to be in- spired, and it must not be treated as though it mere ly *contained* a revelation; *it is a revelation.* You ministers make a great mistake in not dwelling more upon the great *facts* of Christianity; they are the foundations of the system, and there is a power connected with their statement; it seems to me that Peter and Paul understood this. Plain preaching is what we all want, and as much illustration as you can bring up. I once heard Dr. Beecher, in Hanover Street, Boston, talk for an hour on God's law, in its application to the heart and life; he did it in my idea of good preaching.'"

Mr. Webster was particularly pleased with those psalms and hymns by Dr. Watts which dwelt upon the atonement and salvation by faith in Christ. He regretted the modern alteration in some of them, by which, he said, their classic beauty, not less than their devotional character, has suffered. The hymn now commencing, —

> "Here at thy cross, my dying Lord," &c.

he would have read, as in the original, —

> "Here at thy cross, my dying *God*," &c.

The beautiful hymn on the Christian Sabbath, closing with the stanza, as now altered, —

> "My willing soul would stay
> In such a frame as this,
> Till called to rise and soar away
> To everlasting bliss," —

he would have, as Watts wrote it, —

> " My willing soul would stay
>   In such a frame as this,
>   *And sit and sing herself away*
>   To everlasting bliss ; "

the last two lines having a fine classic allusion to the
swan, thus indicating, more effectively, the devotional
spirit.   He often repeated the fifty-first psalm, **and**
referred particularly to the stanza, —

> " No blood of beasts, nor heifers slain,
>   For sin could e'er atone,
>   The blood of Christ must still remain,
>   Sufficient and alone."

Rev. Mr. Alden, the minister of Marshfield, in his
address at Mr. Webster's funeral, said, —

"Those who were present upon the morning of
that Sabbath upon which this head of a family conducted the worship of his household will never forget, as he read from our Lord's Sermon on the
Mount, the emphasis which he alone was capable of
giving to that passage which speaks of the divine
nature of forgiveness. They saw beaming from
that eye, now closed in death, the spirit of Him who
first uttered that godlike sentiment.

"And he who, by the direction of the dying man,
upon a subsequent morning of the day of rest, read
in their connection these words, 'Lord, I believe ;
help thou my unbelief ; ' and then the closing chap-

ter of our Savior's last words to his disciples, being particularly requested to dwell upon this clause of the verse, 'Holy Father, keep through thine own name those whom thou hast given me, that they may be one, as we are,' beheld a sublime illustration of the indwelling and abiding power of Christian faith.

"And if these tender remembrances only cause our tears to flow more freely, it may not be improper for us to present the example of the father, when his great heart was rent by the loss of a daughter whom he most dearly loved. Those present on that occasion well remember, when the struggle of mortal agony was over, retiring from the presence of the dead, bowing together before the presence of God, and joining with the afflicted father as he poured forth his soul, pleading for grace and strength from on high.

"As upon the morning of his death we conversed upon the evident fact that, for the last few weeks, his mind had been engaged in preparation for an exchange of worlds, one who knew him well remarked, 'His whole life has been that preparation.' The people of this rural neighborhood, among whom he spent the last twenty years of his life, among whom he died, and with whom he is to rest, have been accustomed to regard him with mingled veneration and love. Those who knew him best can the most truly appreciate the lessons both from his

21

lips and example, teaching the sustaining power of the gospel.

"A mind like Mr. Webster's, active, thoughtful, penetrating, sedate, could not but meditate deeply on the condition of man below, and feel its respon-sibilities. He could not look on this mighty sys-tem, —

       ' This universal frame, thus wondrous fair,

without feeling that it was created and upheld by an Intelligence to which all other intelligence must be responsible. I am bound to say that in the course of my life I never met with an in-dividual, in any profession or condition, who al-ways spoke and always thought with such awful reverence of the power and presence of God. No irreverence, no lightness, even no too familiar allusion to God and his attributes ever escaped his lips. The very notion of a Supreme Being was, with him, made up of awe and solemnity. It filled the whole of his great mind with the strongest emo-tions. A man like him, with all his proper senti-ments and sensibilities alive in him, must, in this state of existence, have something to believe, and something to hope for ; or else, as life is advancing to its close, all is heart-sinking and oppression. De-pend upon it, whatever may be the mind of an old man, old age is only really happy when, on feeling the enjoyments of this world pass away, it begins to lay a stronger hold on the realities of another.

" Mr. Webster's religious sentiments and feelings were the crowning glories of his character."

The Hon. Mr. Barstow, mayor of Providence, when alluding to the demise of Mr. Webster, related the following interesting facts : —

" He also recognized God in his providence. Who does not remember, after the sad catastrophe of the steamer Atlantic, of his rising in his seat in the American Senate, and recording there three providential deliverances from impending death ? The first I have forgotten.   The second was on the occasion of the loss of the Lexington.   He was in New York, and had engaged passage home in her, and, if I mistake not, went to the boat, but was led, for some cause which then appeared slight, to change his mind.   He went back to his hotel, and his life was saved.   The third was on that fatal thanksgiving eve when the Atlantic was lost.   He was on his way to Washington, and had taken passage in her at Norwich.   When the boat touched at New London, he deemed it unwise to proceed in such a gale. But,' it was replied, 'the boat is new and stanch, and never has stopped for wind or weather; it is the storm line.'   He went on shore, and in one half hour an event occurred which left that strong boat to the mercy of the wind and waves, and sent

mourning through the land.   He did not ascribe
these deliverances to accident, luck, fortune, chance,
but to the good providence of God, who suffers not
the sparrow to fall to the ground without his notice."

It will be appropriate, in this connection, to give
some extracts from an important plea of Mr. Webster, in which he has expressed more fully his sen
timents upon Christianity.

Mr. Stephen Girard, in his devise for the endowment of Girard College, Philadelphia, imposed,
among others, the following restriction: —

"I enjoin and require, that no ecclesiastic, mis-
sionary, or minister of any sect whatever, shall ever
hold or exercise any station or duty whatever in the
said college ; nor shall any such person ever be admitted for any purpose, or as a visitor, within the
premises appropriated to the purposes of the said
college."

The heirs at law were desirous of breaking the
will of Mr. Girard, and for this purpose suit was in-
stituted in the District Court of the Eastern District
of Pennsylvania, where the decision was against
them.   The case was then carried to the Supreme
Court of the United Utates, where Mr. Webster delivered this speech, February 20, 1844.   After giving
his testimony in favor of the exalted character and
deep-toned piety of the American clergy, and speaking of the wrong done by excluding them from

privileges granted even to the basest of men, he proceeds to say, —

"In the next place, this scheme of education is derogatory to Christianity, because it proceeds upon the presumption that the Christian religion is not the only true foundation, or any necessary foundation, of morals. The ground taken is, that religion is not necessary to morality; that benevolence may be insured by habit ; and that all the virtues may flourish, and be safely left to the chance of flourishing, without touching the waters of the living spring of religious responsibility. With him who thinks thus, what can be the value of the Christian revelation ? So the Christian world has not thought ; for by that Christian world, throughout its broadest extent, it has been, and is, held as a fundamental truth, that religion is the only solid basis of morals, and that moral instruction not resting on this basis is only a building upon sand. And at what age of the Christian era have those who profess to teach the Christian religion, or to believe in its authority and importance, not insisted on the absolute necessity of inculcating its principles and its precepts upon the minds of the young ? In what age, by what sect, where, when, by whom, has religious truth been excluded from the education of youth ? Nowhere —· never. Every where, and at all times, it has been, and is, regarded as essential. It is the essence, the

vitality, of useful instruction.   From all this Mr
Girard dissents.   His plan denies the necessity and
the propriety of religious instruction as a part of the
education of youth.   He dissents, not only from all
the sentiments of Christian mankind, from all
common conviction, and from the results of all experience, but he dissents also from still higher authority — the word of God itself.   My learned
friend has referred, with propriety, to one of the
commands of the decalogue ; but there is another, a
first commandment, and that is a precept of religion ;
and it is in subordination to this, that the moral precepts of the decalogue are proclaimed.   This first
great commandment teaches man that there is one,
and only one, great First Cause ; one, and only one,
proper object of human worship.   This is the great,
the ever-fresh, the overflowing fountain of all revealed truth.   Without it, human life is a desert, of
no known termination on any side, but shut in on
all sides by a dark and impenetrable horizon.
Without the light of this truth, man knows nothing
of his origin, and nothing of his end.   And when
the decalogue was delivered to the Jews, with this
great announcement and command at its head, what
said the inspired lawgiver ?   That it should be
reserved as a communication fit only for mature
age ?   Far, far otherwise.   ' And these words, which
I command thee this day, shall be in thy heart ; and

thou shalt teach them diligently unto thy children, and shalt talk of them when thou sittest in thy house, and when thou walkest by the way, when thou liest down, and when thou risest up.'

"There is an authority still more imposing and awful. When little children were brought into the presence of the Son of God, his disciples proposed to send them away; but he said, 'Suffer little children to come unto me.' Unto *me!* He did not send them first for lessons in morals to the schools of the Pharisees, or to the unbelieving Sadducees, nor to read the precepts and lessons *phylacteried* on the garments of the Jewish priesthood; he said nothing of different creeds or clashing doctrines; but he opened at once to the youthful mind the everlasting fountain of living waters, the only source of eternal truths. 'Suffer little children to come *unto me.*' And that injunction is of perpetual obligation. It addresses itself to-day with the same earnestness and the same authority which attended its first utterance to the Christian world. It is of force every where, and at all times. It extends to the ends of the earth, it will reach to the end of time, always and every where sounding in the ears of men, with an emphasis which no repetition can weaken, and with an authority which nothing can supersede. 'Suffer little children to come unto me.'

"And not only my heart and my judgment, my belief and my conscience, instruct me that this great precept should be obeyed, but the idea is so sacred, the solemn thoughts connected with it so crowd upon me, it is so utterly at variance with this system of philosophical *morality* which we have heard advocated, that I stand and speak here in fear of being influenced by my feelings to exceed the proper line of my professional duties. Go thy way at this time, is the language of philosophical morality, and I will send for thee at a more convenient season. This is the language of Mr. Girard in his will. In this there is neither religion nor reason."

It had been Mr. Webster's desire to prepare a work on the evidences of Christianity; but the pressure of public duties prevented. During his last illness at Marshfield, when this subject was made a topic of conversation, and knowing his inability to accomplish it, he resolved to leave, as a substitute, an epitaph to be engraven upon his monument, containing an unequivocal expression of his confidence in the religion of Christ. This was done on Sabbath evening, October 10, 1852. He requested a friend who was then with him to read the ninth chapter of the Gospel by Mark, in which occurs that interesting narrative of a parent bringing his afflicted son to Jesus to be healed, to whom the Savior said, "If thou canst believe, all things are possible to him that

believeth. And straightway the father of the child
cried out, and said with tears, Lord, I believe ; help
thou mine unbelief." He then desired to hear
another passage, commencing John x. 42 — " And
many believed on him there." Both of these portions of Scripture contain instances of faith in
Christ. After the reading of them was finished, he
dictated a few sentences, which, after correction,
were left as follows : —

Lord, I believe; help thou mine unbelief.
Philosophical
Argument, especially
that drawn from the Vastness of
the Universe, in Comparison with the
apparent Insignificance of this Globe, has some-
times shaken my Reason for the Faith which is in me ;
but my Heart has always assured and reassured me that the
Gospel of Jesus Christ must be a Divine Reality. The
Sermon on the Mount cannot be a merely human
Production. This Belief enters into the
very Depth of my Conscience.
The whole History of Man
Proves it.

DANIEL WEBSTER.

This he requested should be dated, and subscribed
with his name. After this he added, " This is the
inscription to be placed on my monument."

In further conversation he remarked, " If I get
well, and write a book on Christianity, about which

we have talked, we can attend more fully to this
matter.   But if I should be taken away suddenly, I
do not wish to leave any duty of this kind unperformed.   I want to leave somewhere a declaration
of my belief in Christianity.   I do not wish to go
into any doctrinal distinctions in regard to the person
of Jesus, but I wish to express my belief in his
divine mission."

We regard the above clear and beautiful inscription as one of the most valuable documents Mr.
Webster ever executed.   We know nothing amongst
all his able pleas, his earnest speeches, and his
dignified state papers, that excels it in importance.
It is the declaration of an eminently profound mind
— a mind which thought for itself, instead of being
carried away by the impassioned appeals or confident assertions of others — a mind capable of detecting sophism under every guise, of exposing the
fallacies of false reasoning, and feeling the power
of all arguments for the truth; it is the declaration
of such a mind "that the gospel of Jesus Christ
must be a divine reality."   By his confession of
faith in the divine mission of Jesus, Mr. Webster
gives the weight of his influence to Christianity; and
in so doing he administers a powerful rebuke to that
flippant, popular infidelity which treats with irreverent familiarity the most sacred truths, which is
filling the land with superficial sceptical theories and

arguments that have been repeatedly overthrown, and by means of which the young and the thoughtless are in danger of being led into the belief that the Bible is nothing more than a mass of cunningly-devised Oriental fables.

CHAPTER XVII.

Mr. Webster's Health fails. — He retires to Marshfield. — His Strength decreases. — Signs his Will. — Returns Thanks. — Encourages Dr. Jeffries. — His Prediction. — It is fulfilled. — Arranges for the Express. — Gives Instructions respecting his Affairs. — His last Interview with his Family. — Peter Harvey. — 24th of October. — Gray's Elegy. — Calls in his Servants. — The Valley. — His Death. — Poetry.

HAVING narrated some of the principal incidents in the life of Mr. Webster, and indulged in a few reflections which they naturally suggested, we come now to the closing scenes of his earthly career.

During the summer of 1852, his health failed, and he retired to his mansion at Marshfield, to obtain some respite from the heavy pressure of his responsible public duties.

Here every thing was done which affectionate solicitude and medical experience could suggest to arrest his disease, but without avail. It was painfully evident that his constitution was gradually yielding to its power. Of this no one was more fully convinced than Mr. Webster himself.

Finding his strength was constantly diminishing, and being impressed with the belief that his life was hastening towards its termination, he made a final disposition of all temporal affairs.

On the evening of the 19th of October, he occupied for the last time his usual seat at his own fireside. After his will was prepared, which he had drawn up himself with great care and minuteness, he had it laid aside, with the intention of delaying a little before affixing to it his signature; but being convinced that he could survive but a short time, he had that important document brought to him, and in the presence of his friends he signed it in a larger and bolder manner than usual. He then folded his hands together, and in an impressive manner said, " I thank God for strength to perform a sensible act." After which he engaged in a most devout manner in audible prayer for several minutes, closing the exercise with the Lord's prayer, and the inscription, "And now unto God the Father, Son, and Holy Ghost be praise forevermore. Peace on earth, and good will to men. That is the happiness," he continued with great emphasis, clasping his hands together as before — " that is the happiness — the essence — good will towards men."

He now requested all but Dr. Jeffries and the nurse to leave the room, that he might, if possible, get a little repose. But before going to sleep, he said, " Doctor, you look sober; you think I shall not be here in the morning, but I shall. I shall greet the morning light.''

His prediction was fulfilled. He did behold the morning light. During the forenoon he said to the physician, who, he thought, appeared sad, "Cheer up, doctor; I shall not die to-day. You will get me along *to-day*." And so he did. But the next morning, conscious that his disease had increased in severity, and that he could not endure it long, he said to his physician in a distinct voice, and with great seriousness, "Doctor, you have carried me through the night. I think you will get me through the day. *I shall die to-night*." To which, after a brief pause, the physician replied, "You are right, sir." Mr. Webster then added, "I wish you, therefore, to send an express to Boston for some younger person to be with you. *I shall die to-night!* You are exhausted, and must be relieved. Who shall it be ? "

The doctor mentioned the name of Dr. J. Mason Warren. " Let him be sent for."

When Dr. Jeffries returned from another room, where he had gone, after the above conversation, to prepare a note to send to Boston, he found that during his absence Mr. Webster had made all the necessary arrangements to send it, even designating the person, the horse, and the vehicle that should go, the route to be pursued, where a fresh horse should be taken, and in what manner the errand should be executed in the city. He also suggested the propriety of mentioning some other physician, in case Dr. Warren could not be obtained. When told that this contingency was provided for, he added, " Right, right."

After obtaining a little rest, he conversed with his wife and son, and with a few others who were " nearest and dearest to him in life, in the most affectionate and tender manner, not concealing from them his view of the approach of death, but consoling them with religious thoughts and assurances, as if support were more needful for their hearts than for his own. On different occasions, in the course of the day, he prayed audibly. Oftener he seemed to be in silent prayer and meditation. But, at all times, he was quickly attentive to whatever was doing or needed to be done. He gave detailed orders for the adjustment of whatever in his affairs required ;, and superintended and arranged every thing for his own departure from life, as if it had been that of another person, for whom it was his duty to take the minutest care."

When informed that his last hour was approaching, he received the announcement with composure, and expressed a wish to see the female members of his family. In compliance with his request, Mrs. Webster, Mrs. Fletcher Webster, Mrs. J. W. Paige, and Miss Downs, of New York, entered the room. He called each of them by name, and addressed to them individually a brief farewell, accompanied with a few words of religious consolation. It was a deeply-affecting scene. Whilst these beloved members of his family were around his couch bathed in tears, he over whose departure they were weeping was calm, and by the utterance of religious truth was endeavoring to impart relief — the dying administering comfort to the living.

He next had the male members of his family, and the personal friends who were there, called in, viz., " Fletcher Webster, (his only surviving son,) Samuel A. Appleton, (his son-in-law,) J. W.. Paige, George T. Curtis, Edward Curtis, of New York, Peter Harvey and Charles Henry Thomas, of Marshfield, and Messrs. George J. Abbott, and W. C. Zantzinger, both of the state department at Washington. Addressing each by name, he referred to his past relations with them respectively, and, one by one, bade them an affectionate farewell. This was about half past six.

" He now had Mr. Peter Harvey called in again, and said to him, ' Harvey, I am not so sick but that I know you — I am well enough to know you. I am well enough to love you, and well enough to call down the richest of Heaven's blessings upon you and yours. Harvey, don't leave me till I am dead

— don't leave Marshfield till I am a dead man.' Then, as if speaking to himself, he said, 'On the 24th of October, all that is mortal of Daniel Webster will be no more.'

"He now prayed in his natural usual voice — strong, full, and clear, ending with, 'Heavenly Father, forgive my sins, and receive me to thyself, through Christ Jesus.'

"Between ten and eleven o'clock, he repeated somewhat indistinctly the words, 'Poet, poetry, Gray, Gray.' Mr. Fletcher Webster repeated the first line of the elegy, —

> 'The curfew tolls the knell of parting day.'

'That's it, that's it,' said Mr. Webster; and the book was brought, and some stanzas read to him, which seemed to give him pleasure."

At another time he was heard to say, "This day I shall be in life, in glory, in blessedness."

He did not deem it beneath him to remember his servants, most of whom had been for many years in his service, "and had become to him as affectionate and faithful friends." These also were called into his chamber, to each of whom he addressed a few kind words, and left with them his dying blessing.

From the time that he had announced to his physician that "he should die that night," he seemed to be solicitous to recognize his advance towards the

dark valley, and especially to know when he was
actually entering it.

"Once, being faint, he asked if he were not *then*
dying? and on being answered that he was not,
but that he was near to death, he replied simply,
'Well;' as if the frank and exact reply were what
he had desired to receive. A little later, when his
kind physician repeated to him that striking text of
Scripture, 'Yea, though I walk through the valley
of the shadow of death, I will fear no evil, for thou
art with me; thy rod and thy staff, they comfort me,'
he seemed less satisfied, and said, 'Yes; but the
fact, the *fact* I want;' desiring to know if he were
to regard these words as an intimation that he was
already within that dark valley. On another occasion, he inquired whether it were likely that he
should again eject blood from his stomach before
death, and, being told that it was improbable, he
asked, 'Then *what* shall you do?' Being answered
that he would be supported by stimulants, and rendered as easy as possible by the opiates that had
suited him so well, he inquired, at once, if the stim-
ulant should not be given *immediately*; anxious again
to know if the hand of death were not *already* upon
him. And on being told that it would not be *then*
given, he replied, '*When* you give it to me, I shall
know that I may drop off at once.'

"Being satisfied on this point, and that he should,

therefore, have a final warning, he said a moment afterwards, 'I will, then, put myself in a position to obtain a little repose.' In this he was successful. He had intervals of rest to the last; but on rousing from them, he showed that he was still intensely anxious to preserve his consciousness, and to watch for the moment and act of his departure, so as to comprehend it. Awaking from one of these slumbers late in the night, he asked distinctly if he were alive; and on being assured that he was, and that his family was collected around his bed, he said, in a perfectly natural tone, as if assenting to what had been told him, because he himself perceived that it was true, ' I still live.' These were his last coherent and intelligible words. At twenty-three minutes before three o'clock, without a struggle or a groan, all signs of life ceased to be visible; his vital organs giving way at last so slowly and gradually as to indicate — what every thing during his illness had already shown — that his intellectual and moral faculties still maintained an extraordinary mastery amidst the failing resources of his physical constitution."

> "' *Still I Live.*' — The flesh was failing;
>   All in vain the healer's skill;
> Light in that deep eye was paling,
>   And the mighty heart grew still;
> Yet the soul, its God adoring,
>   Clad in armor firm and bright,
> O'er the body's ruin soaring,
>   Mingled with the Infinite.

Where he sleeps, that man of glory,
  Marshfield's mournful shades can say,
And his weeping country's story
  Darkened on that funeral day;
But the love that deepest listened
  Caught such balm as heaven can give;
For an angel's pinion glistened
  At the echo, ' *Still I Live.*' "   L. H. S.

CHAPTER XVIII.

THE funeral of Mr. Webster took place at Marshfield, on Friday, October 29, 1852. Large numbers of persons, of all sects and parties, from various parts of the commonwealth, were gathered there to testify their respect for the honored dead. According to his own request, every thing was arranged with the greatest simplicity possible for so public an occasion.

His remains were attired in the dress which he usually wore, embalmed in an elegant coffin, and then, that all might have the opportunity of beholding once more his noble form and manly brow, the coffin was brought from the library, and "placed in front of the house, beneath the open heavens, and under a tree which, in its summer foliage, was a conspicuous ornament of the spot. The majestic form reposed in the familiar garb of life, with more

329

than the dignity of life in its most imposing moments. Suffering had changed without impairing
those noble features. , The grandeur of the brow was
untouched, and the attitude full of strength and
peace. For more than three hours a constant stream
of men and women, of all ages, passed on both
sides, pausing for a moment to look upon that loved
and honored form. Parents held their children by
the hand, bade them contemplate the face of their
benefactor, and charged them never to lose the
memory of that spectacle and that hour. Many
dissolved into tears as they turned aside; and one
— a man of plain garb and appearance — was heard
to make, in a subdued voice, the striking remark,
'Daniel Webster, the world will seem lonesome
without you.' "

The funeral services were performed by Rev.
Ebenezer Alden, pastor of the Orthodox Congregational Church of the town, after which the embalmed
remains were borne to the tomb by six of Mr. Webster's Marshfield neighbors, and deposited in the
place of his own selection, where the voices of
the wind, blending with the subdued notes of the
rolling surf, furnish unceasingly a mournful re-
quiem.

The day of Mr. Webster's funeral at Marshfield
was a day of sorrow throughout the land. In Boston, especially, it was observed with every indication

of sorrow. At no time since the death of General Washington has the city presented so universally the habiliments of woe. Business was suspended; schools were discontinued; banks, courts, markets, offices, and public institutions of all kinds were closed. A large proportion of the city was arrayed in the drapery of mourning. Hotels, stores, public buildings, and private edifices were clothed in materials whose colors of black and white, mingling to gether, imparted to them a sombre and funereal aspect. Flags of all kinds, tied with crape, appropriately ornamented, and containing inscriptions, were hung over doorways, on the fronts of the houses or festooned across the streets. The impressiveness of these arrangements was increased by the fact that in the city there were no public exercises on that day; no procession, no address, no religious service. As all business was suspended, the people were at leisure, and consequently large numbers spent the day in slowly perambulating the streets, gazing upon the drapery, reading the various mottoes and inscriptions, and indulging in their own mournful reflections.

Amongst the sentiments which were suspended in conspicuous places on that sad occasion were many beautifully significant and impressive. We give the following specimens: —

THE GLORY OF THY LIFE, LIKE THE DAY OF THY DEATH,
SHALL NOT FAIL FROM THE REMEMBRANCE OF MAN.

———

HIS WORDS OF WISDOM, WITH RESISTLESS POWER,
HAVE GRACED OUR BRIGHTEST, CHEERED OUR DARKEST HOUR.

———

WHEREVER AMONG MEN A HEART SHALL BE FOUND THAT BEATS
TO THE TRANSPORTS OF PATRIOTISM AND LIBERTY,
ITS ASPIRATIONS SHALL BE TO CLAIM
KINDRED WITH HIS SPIRIT.

———

KNOW THOU, O STRANGER TO THE FAME
OF THIS MUCH-LOVED, MUCH-HONORED NAME,
(FOR NONE THAT KNEW HIM NEED BE TOLD,)
A WARMER HEART DEATH NE'ER MADE COLD.

———

THOU ART MIGHTY YET. THY SPIRIT WALKS ABROAD.

———

THE GREAT HEART OF THE NATION THROBS HEAVILY AT THE
PORTALS OF HIS GRAVE.

———

LIVE LIKE PATRIOTS! LIVE LIKE AMERICANS! UNITED ALL,
UNITED NOW, AND UNITED FOREVER.

———

THOU HAST INSTRUCTED MANY, AND THOU HAST STRENGTHENED
THE WEAK HANDS.

———

WE'VE SCANNED THE ACTIONS OF HIS DAILY LIFE, AND NOTHING
MEETS OUR EYES BUT DEEDS OF HONOR.

———

SOME, WHEN THEY DIE, DIE ALL. THEIR MOULDERING CLAY IS
BUT AN EMBLEM OF THEIR MEMORIES. BUT HE HAS LIVED.
HE LEAVES A WORK BEHIND WHICH WILL PLUCK
THE SHINING AGE FROM VULGAR TIME,
AND GIVE IT WHOLE TO LATE
POSTERITY.

Similar scenes were presented, when, on the 30th of November, the city of Boston gave another public expression of the high respect entertained for the memory of Mr. Webster. A long and imposing civic and military procession, with craped arms, shrouded flags, and muffled drums, passed through the streets to Faneuil Hall, where a chaste, eloquent, and highly appropriate eulogy was pronounced by Hon. George S. Hillard, the close of which will furnish an appropriate termination to this volume.

"There, among the scenes that he loved in life, he sleeps well. He has left his name and memory to dwell forever upon those hills and valleys, to breathe a more spiritual tone into the winds that blow over his grave, to touch with finer light the line of the breaking wave, to throw a more solemn beauty upon the hues of autumn and the shadows of twilight.

"But though his mortal form is there, his spirit is here. His words are written in living light along these walls. May that spirit rest upon us, and our children. May those words live in our hearts, and the hearts of those who come after us! May we honor his memory, and show our gratitude for his life, by taking heed to his counsels, and walking in the way on which the light of his wisdom shines!"

WE here give a picture of the Family Tomb at Marshfield, in which now repose the mortal remains of the "great American Statesman,"

DANIEL WEBSTER

For a particular description of the Tomb, its location, the various inscriptions, etc., we refer the reader to page 214.

The $1000 Prize Series.

*Pronounced by the Examining Committee, Rev. Drs.
Lincoln, Rankin and Day, superior to
any similar series.*

STRIKING FOR THE RIGHT,	$1.75
SILENT TOM,	1.75
EVENING REST,	1.50
THE OLD STONE HOUSE,	1.50
INTO THE LIGHT,	1.50
WALTER McDONALD,	1.50
STORY OF THE BLOUNT FAMILY,	1.50
MARGARET WORTHINGTON,	1.50
THE WADSWORTH BOYS,	1.50
GRACE AVERY'S INFLUENCE,	1.50
GLIMPSES THROUGH,	1.50
RALPH'S POSSESSION,	1.50
LUCK OF ALDEN FARM,	1.50
CHRONICLES OF SUNSET MOUNTAIN,	1.50
THE MARBLE PREACHER,	1.50
GOLDEN LINES,	1.50

*Sold by Booksellers generally, and sent by Mail, postpaid,
on receipt of price.*

BOSTON:
D. LOTHROP & CO., PUBLISHERS.

CURRENT RELIGIOUS BOOKS.

CONCESSIONS OF "LIBERALISTS" TO ORTHODOXY.
By *Daniel Dorchester*, D. D. 16mo. 1 25

AT EVENTIDE. By *Nehemiah Adams*, D. D. 12mo. 1 25

THE SEVEN WORDS FROM THE CROSS. By *Rev. Wm. H. Adams*, Pastor of the Circular Church, Charleston, S. C. 12mo... 1.00
> Meditations on the Last Sayings of Christ abounding in "beautiful fancies, sweet sentiments and pathetic touches."

CONFESSIONS OF AUGUSTINE (The). Edited with an Introduction by Prof. *Wm. T. Shedd*. 12mo.............. 1 50

UNERRING GUIDE (The). By *Rev. H. V. Dexter, D. D.,*
Extra Cloth.................................... 1 50
Morocco, gilt 2 50
> This book is composed of selections from the Bible arranged according to subjects. It may be used for reference, for private or family devotions, for Bible Readings and Prayer Meetings, and is particularly useful for Ministers in furnishing ready material for Sermons, Lectures, &c.

NINETY AND NINE (The). By *Elizabeth C. Clephane*.
Quarto. Gilt edges 2 00

MIND AND WORDS OF JESUS AND FAITHFUL PROMISER. By *Rev. J. R. MacDuff*. Complete in one volume, good type, in neat cloth binding.................. 50
Red-line edition.................................. 1 50

MORNING AND NIGHT WATCHES. By *Rev. J. R. Mc-Duff*. Uniform with the above, at same prices.

ROCK OF AGES. By *S. F. Smith, D.D.* New Edition; Reduced price 1 00
Red-line edition, reduced price.................... 1 50

GRACE AND TRUTH. By *W. P. MacKay, A. M.* 12mo.
Paper 50
Cloth...................................... 1 00

TO ALL PEOPLE. ⎫ Sermons by *D. L. Moody*. Each, Paper 1 00
GREAT JOY. ⎬
GLAD TIDINGS. ⎭ Each, Cloth................ 1 50

DAILY MANNA, for Christian Pilgrims. By *Rev. Baron Stow, D.D.* 24mo, plain..... 25
Full gilt 40
16mo, red line.............................. 1 00

MEMORIAL HOUR (The); or, The Lord's Supper in its Relation to Doctrine and Life. By *Jeremiah Chaplin, D. D.,* author of "Evening of Life," &c. Large 16mo. 1 25

STILL HOUR; or, Communion with God. By Prof. *Austin Phelps, D. D.* New Edition. Plain.................... 60
Tinted paper, gilt edged 1 00
> More than 100,000 copies have been sold, and we know of no other work of the kind having so constant a sale, or receiving such high commendations.

www.ingramcontent.com/pod-product-compliance
Lightning Source LLC
Chambersburg PA
CBHW021801110726

47902CB00006B/1610